MURDER MOST TREASONABLE

Also by Paul Doherty

The Margaret Beaufort mysteries

DARK QUEEN RISING *
DARK QUEEN WAITING *
DARK QUEEN WATCHING *
DARK QUEEN WARY *

The Brother Athelstan mysteries

THE ANGER OF GOD
BY MURDER'S BRIGHT LIGHT
THE HOUSE OF CROWS
THE ASSASSIN'S RIDDLE
THE DEVIL'S DOMAIN
THE FIELD OF BLOOD
THE HOUSE OF SHADOWS
BLOODSTONE *
THE STRAW MEN *
CANDLE FLAME *
THE BOOK OF FIRES *
THE HERALD OF HELL *
THE GREAT REVOLT *
A PILGRIMAGE TO MURDER *
THE MANSIONS OF MURDER *
THE GODLESS *
THE STONE OF DESTINY *
THE HANGING TREE *

The Canterbury Tales mysteries

AN ANCIENT EVIL
A TAPESTRY OF MURDERS
A TOURNAMENT OF MURDERS
GHOSTLY MURDERS
THE HANGMAN'S HYMN
A HAUNT OF MURDER
THE MIDNIGHT MAN *

* *available from Severn House*

MURDER MOST TREASONABLE

Paul Doherty

SEVERN HOUSE

First world edition published in Great Britain and the USA in 2023
by Severn House, an imprint of Canongate Books Ltd,
14 High Street, Edinburgh EH1 1TE.

Trade paperback edition first published in Great Britain and the USA in 2024
by Severn House, an imprint of Canongate Books Ltd.

severnhouse.com

British Library Cataloguing-in-Publication Data
A CIP catalogue record for this title is available from the British Library.

ISBN-13: 978-1-4483-0865-1 (cased)
ISBN-13: 978-1-4483-1374-7 (trade paper)
ISBN-13: 978-1-4483-1073-9 (e-book)

All Severn House titles are printed on acid-free paper.

Typeset by Palimpsest Book Production Ltd.,
Falkirk, Stirlingshire, Scotland.
Printed and bound in Great Britain by
TJ Books, Padstow, Cornwall.

Praise for the Brother Athelstan medieval mysteries

"As always, Doherty makes a past century come alive"
Publishers Weekly on *The Hanging Tree*

"Hair-raising descriptions of life in the Middle Ages enhance a challenging puzzle"
Kirkus Reviews on *The Hanging Tree*

"A tortuous, fascinating historical mystery"
Kirkus Reviews on *The Stone of Destiny*

"With consummate skill and pacing, Doherty answers the plot's mysteries in a series of startling revelations"
Publishers Weekly on *The Stone of Destiny*

"Outstanding . . . Doherty keeps the action brisk, the crimes baffling, and the deductions and solutions fair"
Publishers Weekly Starred Review of *The Godless*

"Doherty displays exceptional narrative flair as he brings the often-squalid sights, sounds, and smells of medieval London to life"
Booklist on *The Godless*

"Conjuring up medieval London in all its grime and glory, Doherty keeps readers guessing and the pages turning with another intricately plotted whodunit"
Booklist on *The Mansions of Murder*

About the author

The author of more than eighty highly acclaimed historical mysteries, **Paul Doherty** studied History at Liverpool and Oxford Universities, and is now headmaster of a school in Essex. He lives with his family in north-east London.

www.paulcdoherty.com

To the Arshad family, Imran, Saika, Danny, Deen and Zaki.
In grateful thanks for their hospitality and kindness over the years.

HISTORICAL NOTE

The savage battles of the Hundred Years War had subsided into an uneasy peace. England had won then lost in Northern France. The deaths of the warrior, Edward III, and his son, the Black Prince, brought an end to a string of victories which, at one time, threatened even Paris. Nevertheless, in the 1380s, both the French and English courts circled each other like swordsmen on a tournament field. War cogs might not clash in the Narrow Seas, Chevauchees might not advance with fire and sword across the green fields of Normandy, but the war continued in another way. A hidden struggle where one court desperately tried to learn the secrets of the other. A filthy, sordid campaign of violence along the streets of Westminster and in the shadow-filled runnels of Paris. Men and women fought, died and betrayed on behalf of the princes they served. French and English circled each other, sword and dagger drawn, each looking for an opening, desperate to inflict a deadly wound. This war of secrets was carried on relentlessly. Indeed, as it always had . . .

The quotations at the beginning of each section are Old English words taken from a narrative poem, written circa 1380, describing a meeting between St Erconwald, Bishop of London, and the revived corpse of a pagan nobleman.

The Prologues

Cloyster: an enclosed space

Vincent Edmonton, clerk in the office of the Secret Seal, a retainer who had formally sworn fealty to the English Crown, was returning home. Edmonton carefully made his way down Snakes Lane towards his very comfortable lodgings, a vestibule and two chambers with a small scullery, situated above a prosperous draper's shop. Edmonton was a mailed clerk who had seen service aboard the royal cogs which patrolled the Narrow Seas and protected the approaches to the prosperous Cinque ports along the south coast. Edmonton was certainly a man ready to defend himself. If the Narrow Seas were perilous, the streets of London were even more so. Edmonton strode along one side of the runnel, wary of the sewer running down the middle, nothing but a cleft in the ground crammed with all kinds of ordure, both animal and human. The stench was stomach-churning, the reek so sickening, that Edmonton pulled up his visor to protect his nose and mouth.

Edmonton paused as he glimpsed a shadow, swift as a hunting cat, flit from one alleyway across to another. Sensing danger, Edmonton drew his sword and dagger so the light peeping through shutters or from beneath doors glinted on the polished steel: this would warn off those hunters in the shadows, the naps, foists and sewer squires. These creatures of the dark were so desperate they ignored the warning signs so clearly proclaimed at either end of the street: moveable gallows where four housebreakers, caught in the act, had been immediately strangled on the end of a gibbet rope. Edmonton startled as a bat, fleeing the light, flickered like a devil, a darting shadow around his head. This was, Edmonton ruefully reflected, the hour of the bat. As if to confirm Edmonton's gloomy thoughts, an owl hooted deep in the trees of a nearby cemetery.

Edmonton walked on, then abruptly stopped as a procession

emerged from a side street: a group of magicians, garishly dressed, faces daubed white, hair a fiery red. They moved slowly, only stopping to clap their hands and leap in the air. They were followed by a Friar of the Sack reciting the vespers of the dead over the corpses of felons hanged outside Newgate and destined for some desolate burial ground. Edmonton paused and stared up at the slit of night sky between the houses either side, which leaned over like ancient lovers desperate to embrace. The glimpse of the executed housebreaker provoked Edmonton's memory, something which had occurred today, mentioned in the Secret Chancery and also later at La Delicieuse.

'Ah, that's it!' Edmonton whispered. 'The Radix Malorum!'

Edmonton walked on, recalling what he had learned: how the Radix Malorum, that king of housebreakers, was back in London. He even had the impudence to proclaim his arrival, as well as taunt Sir John Cranston, Lord High Coroner of London, who had been pursuing the Radix for many a year without any success, much to the delight of London's underworld. 'Ah well,' Edmonton whispered to himself.

He passed a midden heap; the stench was so revolting that he pulled the visor further up his face, welcoming the fragrance from the small silk perfume pouches. The Lady Heloise, or one of her household, had stitched these little silk pockets into his visor as well as those of his comrades in the House of Secrets. Edmonton had been ever so pleased. These little silk pouches of perfume were not only fragrant but stirred tender memories of La Delicieuse and the happenings there.

Edmonton reached the draper's shop and went up the outside stairs. He unlocked the door to the vestibule then that to his chamber. He went in and, as usual, immediately lighted the candles on their spigots as well as the two lanternhorns on a dresser against the far wall. As he did so, he froze at a sound from a shadow-filled corner to his right.

'Good evening, Master Edmonton.' The clerk turned slowly. The voice was soft and sibilant. 'It's been some time, Vincent. Now you know the order of our service, of our meetings. So come, draw close.'

Edmonton did so. He could just make out the outline of his unexpected guest. He also knew that the man's face would be completely masked, whilst the small crossbow he carried would be primed and ready to loose.

'Sit down, Vincent.'

The clerk did so, drawing up a cushioned stool, as he always did, when this mysterious figure appeared. Sometimes, Edmonton wished that he had not entertained such a guest but now he was committed. Edmonton loved silver and gold. He was as enmeshed into collecting it as he was to his profound love of gambling; the game of hazard, the rattle of a dice in its cup, the air of expectancy as he cast his numbers against those of his opponent.

'Master Edmonton, you are well?'

'Yes, yes, I am. I wish you would give me your name.'

'I have told you that. I am the Key-Master. No door, be it physical or metaphysical, poses a problem for me, which is why I can enter this chamber so easily, unlocking whatever doors I need to.'

'You are from the Chambre Noir in Paris,' Edmonton exclaimed. 'This really should stop. I could be accused of treason.'

'Nonsense, my friend. What secrets have you sold to me? None! So, what treason? I am very careful, Master Vincent, about what I receive from you. Oh yes, I could ask you for the odd juicy titbit. But is it worth it? Such a morsel might be traced back to you, which would endanger you and, of course, myself. No, no, our arrangement is much safer. You, Vincent my friend, love the roll of the dice. Now that could be costly but, there again . . .' The shadow leaned forward and tossed the small purse, which clinked as it fell near Edmonton's booted foot. 'Pick it up, Vincent.' He did so. 'Good English silver and gold, eh? To supplement the fees you already earn as a high-ranking clerk in the Secret Chancery, the House of Secrets or the Secret Cloisters, whatever Master Thibault wishes to call them. I, on the other hand, as you well know, am a custos in the Chambre Noir in Paris.'

'So what are you here for?'

'Listen, Vincent, and listen well. Only forty years ago the Goddams, you English, invaded my country, the Kingdom of France. They smashed the armies of the Valois in ferocious battles at Crécy and Poitiers. They seized Normandy and adjoining provinces.'

'Only to be driven out by the likes of du Guescelin.'

'True, true, Vincent, but the cost was great. Towns burned to cinder. Harvest fields blighted. Orchard and vineyards ruined. Trade disrupted, not to mention the collapse of good order and the King's own peace. The English plundered Northern France as robbers would a treasury. We fear they might return. Your young King Richard dreams the same imperial dreams as his father and grandfather. Of course, he is guarded and guided by his uncle, John of Gaunt, who may well invoke the dream of English kings who also want to wear the Crown of France. Vincent, we must ensure this does not happen. Can you understand the devastation that would cause? Can you imagine the bloodshed? In a way, my friend, you and I are allies in the cause of peace, maintaining things as they are now. So, what wrong are you doing? You tell me nothing of importance. You do not offer secrets. You simply pass on the chatter and gossip of your fellow clerks.'

'Yes,' Edmonton agreed. He now felt more comfortable, except for a slight sense of unease that, somehow or other, he might be telling his mysterious visitor more than he should.

'So, Vincent, all is well with your companions? They frequent La Delicieuse, that brothel masquerading as a tavern.'

'Yes they do, and that harms no one.'

'And tell me. Madam Heloise and her ladies, are they still obdurate in their dislike for all they left behind in Paris?'

'Sir, I cannot answer that.' Edmonton decided to be as tactful as he could. 'All I know is that Heloise and her ladies are most settled in London. Why should they leave? Heloise is deeply smitten with our principal clerk, Hugh Norwic, and he with her.'

'That must, if your previous reports were correct, cause bad blood between Norwic and his fellow clerk Master Nigel Hyams. According to you, Hyams is also eager to win Madam Heloise's favour.'

'True.' Edmonton half laughed. 'But that is the way of the world.'

'So,' the shadow moved in his chair, 'what other gossip have you? Come, Vincent.'

The clerk wetted his lips. He had determined not to raise such a matter with his visitor but now he felt he had no choice.

'Yes, Vincent what is it?'

'There is, sir,' he retorted, 'a growing chorus of rumour about treason and betrayal.'

'What!' The Key-Master's voice turned brittle and harsh.

'That English affairs in Paris are not what they should be,' Edmonton replied.

'Such as?'

'According to rumour, our spies have fallen eerily silent and Thibault, Gaunt's Master of Secrets, seems deeply perturbed.'

'Yes, yes, he may well be.'

'Which means?'

'Quiet Edmonton. I pay you for gossip. I do not trade it with you.'

'My apologies.'

'Accepted. Anything else I need to know about at the House of Secrets? Any visitors? Any disturbance in the horarium? The daily routine along the Secret Cloisters?'

'Oh yes,' Edmonton stammered slowly, 'we have few visitors. The only people who join us are the scavengers who clean the place. We call them the Dies Domini, each one after a day in the week. They are led and managed by their custos Dimanche, who has been given the French name for Sunday.'

'Oh yes,' the Key-Master replied. 'You have mentioned them before. Creatures of the dark as stupid as a coop of chickens under their leader. They are earthworms, they live and feed in the mud, as they should do. Never mind them. Anything else?'

'The Ghostman.' Edmonton half smiled.

'Who is he?'

'An anchorite who wanders the precincts of Westminster. He claims to talk to ghosts. There must be a veritable horde down there. The Blackrobes have been burying their dead for centuries in their cemetery. Then we have the people of Westminster, as well as those hanged outside Westminster gate. So, I wish him well.'

'What of him?'

'Well, the Ghostman is as frenetic as a frog in a box. We tend to tolerate him as he leaves us alone. However, recently he asked to see Norwic, something about the "Lords of the Air"?'

'Who are they?'

'God knows.'

'Anything else, Master Edmonton?'

'No, not that I can recall.'

'Then, my friend, I shall bid you adieu.'

The shadow rose. Edmonton could only make out the thick black robe, undoubtedly expensive, as was the perfume Edmonton caught as his visitor brushed by him. The clerk heard the door to his chamber open and close, then silence. For a while Edmonton sat, clammy with fear. He had first met the Key-Master after a particularly costly evening at hazard. Edmonton had wagered heavily and lost. He had staggered out and returned here to find the mysterious stranger waiting for him; apparently no lock was a problem to this stranger.

Edmonton reflected further on his visitor. 'What he wanted seemed harmless enough,' he whispered to himself. 'Just the gossip and chatter between the clerks at the chancery, and what happened during their visits to La Delicieuse and any other items of interest. The mysterious stranger had kept his word. No secrets were demanded, no information injurious to the English Crown was handed over and yet . . .' Edmonton got up and locked the door. He crossed to the dresser and poured a generous goblet of wine. 'And yet,' he repeated in a whisper, 'there was a change.'

He sat silently, reflecting. Messages from Nightingale, Thibault's principal clerk in Paris, were beginning to dry up. Merchants, pilgrims and other travellers were leaving scraps of information in the secret cache fixed to the inside of the gate leading to the Secret Chancery. The documents, mere jottings, the writing scrawled, had referred to rumours of English spies being taken up and disappearing into the cells and dungeons of the Valois. Surely this could not be connected to Edmonton's secret visitor? He quietly cursed both his gambling and his sinister visitor. What would happen if he was taken up? Edmonton had seen traitors executed at Smithfield, half hanged, their bodies slashed open, hearts plucked out, heads severed. Surely, he did not deserve that. However, that would not be a matter for him to decide, would it? Edmonton fell to his knees, praying for help against the horrors lurking in the dark.

'*Timor mortis conturbat me!*' Hugh Norwic, principal clerk in the Secret Chancery of His Grace King Richard, second of that name since the Conquest, mouthed the words scrawled beneath a triptych delineating Death as a skeleton garbed in a white sheet. This gaping, grinning monster from the dark stood armed with the longest scythe, overlooking an open death pit in which hosts of people of every kind were tumbling like leaves driven by the wind. On either side of this grotesque painting stood another skeleton figure, each given its title 'Lord of Disease' and 'Master of Violence'. Norwic studied the painting. He fully accepted that Death was always very close, not realizing that his own demise was fast approaching, an unseen shadow blending with the darkness, waiting for the chance to pounce and strike one blow. Norwic, however, was intent on his surroundings. He was principal clerk of the Secret Chancery. Norwic always walked through this Cloisters of Secrets before the Compline bell pealed out its summons. By that hour all doors and shutters were to be closed and barred.

The Secret Chancery building was small and stark. It was easy to inspect and built for simplicity, so its real business could be clearly seen by those who worked there. The Chancery comprised six clerks in all. They sat in the long hall, each given a chancery chamber with its horn-filled window and a candelabra above a table with its thickly cushioned, high-backed chair. The floor of each carrel or chancery chapel was covered with the finest blue turkey rugs; these, together with judiciously positioned capped braziers, kept all six clerks warm and comfortable. Each chancery table was well stocked with rolls of parchment, wax, quill pens and ink horns holding blue, green and red ink.

Norwic walked slowly down the passageway, stopping to study each carrel until he reached the heavily studded, iron-bound door that sealed off the sharp, steep staircase spiralling down to the arca beneath. This was where the secret archives were stored in coffers, chests and caskets containing the King's secrets. The King's secrets! But were they the King's secrets, Norwic wondered? Or those matters controlled by the self-styled Regent, the young King's uncle, John of Gaunt, and Thibault, the Regent's sinister Master of Secrets? Did this precious pair have all their nefarious affairs stored away here under lock and key? Norwic turned and leaned against the door, staring back down the murky long hall. He glanced to his right at the shady enclave which housed a spacious jakes closet. Norwic smiled to himself. Since they had hired the scavengers, such places no longer stank – indeed the opposite.

'Oh well, the day is done.' Norwic whispered to himself. 'And we are for the dark.' The clerk smiled thinly. 'And no matter,' he added, 'how the day is long, at last the bell will peal out Compline song.'

Norwic reflected on the words of the poem. It was true, the day was finished, but the work of the Secret Chancery never really rested. Master Thibault, seething with anger, had disrupted Norwic's peace of mind. He had come here and, in a private interview, had hinted that this hallowed place, the heart of all his intrigue, actually housed a traitor. This Judas was selling secrets to the French, to the Luciferi, the Light Carriers, that cabal of spies and assassins who worked for King Charles of France. The Luciferi also had their own house or home, the Chambre Noir, the Black Chamber, deep in the bowels of Charles's principal palace, the Louvre. Thibault, over the last few days, had revisited his own Secret Chancery. Now it was no longer a matter of whispers and murmurs. Thibault had urged Norwic and his companions to do a careful search. The Master of Secrets had no definite proof that treason was being committed here in the royal precincts of Westminster. Nevertheless, what he had whispered to Norwic, as principal clerk of the Secret Chancery, was most worrying. Nightingale, their principal spy in Paris, had fallen silent. He no longer sent news or chatter collected from those elusive shadow people who provided information to the English Crown. Nightingale was well named. A constant singer of news, but now both he and his flock had fallen eerily silent. Worse, the only news which had trickled through was most worrying, even though it was only gossip along the streets. Rumours about English spies being taken up, imprisoned and tortured, before being summarily hanged at Montfaucon, the great gallows near the Porte St-Denis in Paris. So who, Thibault had whispered heatedly, could have provided the Chambre Noir with the names, titles and dwelling places of those men and women who worked the length and breadth of Paris on behalf of the English Crown? Information about these shadow people was only held here, deep in the secret cloisters of Westminster, but this was a most fortified place. Once again,

Norwic reflected on how well defended the chancery actually was. This Hall of Secrets had only one door leading into the buttery at one end, whilst all its windows were barred. At the other end of the Hall of Secrets was the arca, where the coffers and caskets were stowed deep in the crypt of this sombre building. This underground chamber was protected by an iron-bound door with two locks which, when opened, led on to the steepest, sharpest spiral staircase, snaking down into the darkness.

'What else?' Norwic murmured to himself. Outside, the House of Secrets was defended by a soaring curtain wall. Tower bowmen patrolled the parapet walk under the strict eye of a Captain of Archers. The wall was truly unassailable, its heavy steel-studded gate could not be forced, whilst the small postern door built into it was always closely guarded. The gate also had a narrow leper squint with a locked casket on the inside, an ideal place for those who wished to give information collected both at home and abroad. News about what was happening across the Narrow Seas, especially in Paris, Normandy and the wine-rich province of Gascony. In the yard or bailey, contained by the curtain wall, there was nothing of note except shabby lean-tos, stables and bothies, where the archers could eat, drink and rest. The yard was kept warm by a firepit dug deep into its cobbled centre, and protected by a heavy iron cap or lid. It was here where the rubbish of the day, scraps of parchments, discarded memoranda, letters, writs and other missives used to draft final documents could be safely destroyed. Norwic paused in his pacing.

'So,' he whispered into the darkness, 'how had such a formidable mansion of secrets been so easily penetrated by the enemy?'

According to Thibault, the situation in Paris was growing worse by the day. In his last letter, Nightingale had talked of how a coven of spies, a '*cohors damnosa*', a deadly battle group of French spies, had arrived in London. A company of the Luciferi, who called themselves 'Les Mysterieux', and were determined on sending vital information back to their masters in Paris. But who these were, where they were lurking, and how they hoped to be so successful truly was a mystery.

Norwic walked back to stare at the triptych. He thought he heard a sound and whirled around, but there was nothing except faint trails of river mist seeping under the door. Norwic returned to his reflections. Who could be responsible for such chaos, he wondered? The Dies Domini – the Days of the Lord? The nickname Norwic and his companions had given the scavengers who had been hired to cleanse the House of Secrets, to keep it free of all kinds of vermin. But these poor men had only been employed because they were simple illiterates, scavengers who were used to working in the stinking alleys and runnels of Westminster. Indeed, they could not even write their own names or read a simple line. Moreover, apart from their leader Dimanche, who had been given the French name for Sunday, each of these scavengers only came one day a week, whilst they would be scrutinised carefully before leaving the Secret Cloisters. Norwic rubbed his face. It was time to make one final check on the arca and join Heloise and his comrades at La Delicieuse, an expensive but well-furnished tavern with delightful ladies and . . . Norwic caught his breath. 'Heloise!' he whispered to himself. Her ladies, his comrades, his friends made Norwic's world. Could the Judas be one or more of these? Had a member of the Secret Chancery been seduced, bought body and soul, for whatever reward? Is that why Thibault had warned him to keep a secret watch and listen for anything suspicious?

Norwic decided he best join his comrades. He tried to control his breathing as panic surged within him. He had not even considered the possibility of a traitor within, yet this was a logical conclusion. Norwic breathed in slowly as he realized he had made a hideous mistake, though he drew comfort that it was one he could hide and later rectify. He had been too absorbed with the fair Heloise, owner of La Delicieuse; indeed, he was as infatuated with her as she was with him. Such dalliance, Norwic conceded to himself, had distracted him from his duties. After all, he was the principal clerk in the Secret Chancery. It was his duty to keep all matters under sharp scrutiny, to be as vigilant as any guard dog, yet he had failed.

Norwic chewed the corner of his lip. If there was a traitor within, then surely it must be one or more of his fellow clerks. Was there a coven of spies? Did it include anyone else? What about the fair ladies at La Delicieuse? What about Heloise herself? She and all the other courtesans had loudly proclaimed that they hated Paris and had found peace in London. Was that really true? Certainly, he should have been more watchful and followed Master Thibault's advice. Trust no one! But of course, how could he keep a sharp eye if nothing was going wrong? These present troubles were . . . what? Only a month old, according to Thibault. Nevertheless, there were matters Norwic had overlooked. Such as that strange creature the Ghostman, with his enigmatic remark about how the Lords of the Air had their secrets. What did he mean? Norwic felt that he really should summon the Ghostman back here for questioning, part of Norwic's vow to be more vigilant.

Norwic, hands slightly shaking, unhooked the ring of keys from his warbelt. Lost in thought, he unlocked the crypt door. He opened it and flinched at the cold, musty air which billowed out as the crypt yawned its sombre welcome. Grasping the guide rope, Norwic went down the first steps. The clerk felt he was entering the domain of the deepest darkness, an eerie, blood-chilling sensation which he always experienced when he came here. Norwic crossed himself, murmuring a prayer. Once again he recalled how a soothsayer, an old crone with a garishly painted face, had warned Norwic to be careful of a place he was responsible for, since that's where his death might be waiting, poised like a viper ready to strike.

'The snares of death surround me,' Norwic murmured. 'The coils of the grave strive to hold me fast.' Norwic shook himself free of the dread. Heloise would be waiting for him in the warm, opulent comfort of her chamber at La Delicieuse.

Norwic went down a step, then he turned to face the enclave carved in the wall which housed a lanternhorn already primed and ready to be lit. Norwic opened the small lantern door. He rubbed the candle wick between his fingers, then picked up the sharp tinder, struck a spark and lit the pure beeswax candle within. The flame flared, shedding a widening pool of light. Norwic sealed the lantern, picked it up and turned. He was ready to go down when a sudden blow to his back sent him staggering forward. Norwick tried to regain his balance, only to slip, and he tumbled, crashing down the sharp-edged steps which cut savagely at both body and head. The further he fell, the faster he rolled, his body mauled from head to toe. By the time he reached the bottom, Norwic was dead.

* * *

The English spy Nightingale was full of fears as he joined the crowds streaming along the narrow winding paths which cut through the quarter of St-Denis down to the great gallows at Montfaucon. Dawn had broken. The countless bells of the city were ringing out their summons and the people of Paris responded, glad to be free of the unseen terrors of the night. It seemed as if everyone was out. Huntsmen with their fierce dogs straining on leather leashes. Ladies in their gold and silver brocade, costly clothes and ornate headdresses. Beggars were on the hunt, crawling like spiders with their clacking dishes. Priests, their shoulders shrouded in colourful copes, carried the viaticum to the sick. Altar boys in dirty white surplices ran beside them, carrying swinging censers. Gangs of pilgrims chanted their hymns. Monks and friars elbowed their way through to pray before the different shrines erected at corners along the street. Baker boys, hot-pot girls and sweet squires shouted for custom. Mongrels barked and howled. Carts heaped with produce clattered noisily by. Smells and odours, fragrant and foul, swirled through the air. The noise was a constant clamour, the streets a stage for all kinds of behaviour: lewd, crude, pious or pathetic.

One factor united many of the players, be it the wandering minstrel or pattering priests: they were all going to Montfaucon! They would stand beneath the great gallows which soared above the foul, fetid pits. Here, the decomposing corpses of those hanged weeks ago slipped in gruesome slime to make room for fresh victims of the merciless mill of the city courts which despatched, whatever the season, more gibbet fodder. Today was no different. There were to be at least twenty hangings, certainly enough to glut the macabre appetite of the death watchers who clustered close to the gallows mound.

Nightingale, one hand on his dagger, the other on his purse, forced his way through, past the lower gibbets, their clanking chains covered in the slop of human decay. The English spy at last reached the tall wooden barrier, beyond which the death carts would congregate to unload the condemned. Nightingale breathed a sigh of relief at securing a place, then gagged as a stinking gust of air swept his face. He immediately bought a pine-soaked pomander and pressed this against nose and mouth as he stared around. All the grotesques of Paris, those who constantly lived the dusk of life, had gathered to celebrate the execution of men and women they had rubbed shoulders with along the nightmare tunnels and runnels of the city. They sang or shuffled in their dances. Horns brayed. Trumpets shrieked, whilst a host of tambour boys kept up their insistent hollow banging. The light strengthened, turning the countless spires and towers of the city black against the freshening sky. A great roar went up, followed by the deafening blare of trumpets. The death carts were approaching!

Nightingale pressed himself against the palisade, peering through a wide crack. Garbed in dirty leathers, stained jerkin and hood, with battered, mud-encrusted boots, the English spy looked what he pretended to be, a wandering labourer who had decided to watch the day's executions. Nightingale moved slightly so that he had a good view of the sinister gallows. Another blast of trumpet rent the air as the death carts rolled in to stop in a queue leading up to the execution platforms. City guards garbed in jerkins of blue and faded mustard, conical helmets on their heads, the broad nose-guards almost hiding their faces, unlocked the tailgates and began to pull the condemned out of the carts. The prisoners looked pathetic; men and women battered and tattered, hands tied tightly before them. A line of white scabrous faces, hair caked with mud, garbed in ragged and rent clothing. The line of the damned, as a clerk bellowed, would be despatched in batches of six.

A cohort was assembled. Nightingale, straining his neck, quietly moaned. He glimpsed what he had been searching for: the bruised, chalk-white face of his friend and comrade known as Starling. Starling had mysteriously disappeared from his lodgings and he had not attended their usual meetings deep in the shadows of some shabby winehouse. Nightingale now knew why. Starling had been arrested. Judging by the bruises on his face and the way Starling staggered, the prisoner had also been cruelly tortured in the dungeons at the Louvre Palace. Nightingale had seen enough. He could not stay and watch his comrade strangle in the air. He now had real proof, but what could he do?

Nightingale turned and forced his way through the crowd, knocking aside the bread boys who offered waffles and freshly baked cake. He did not need a battered cup of wine, water or a stoup of ale. Nor did he want his fortune told, or to buy some powder which would turn him into a stallion in bed. Nightingale shoved all these street traders away as he hurried through the crowd to where it thinned. Once there, he abruptly stopped and turned, as if he was lost. He stared around but could detect nothing suspicious. Nightingale hurried on into the warren of cul-de-sacs, the maze of needle-thin streets of St-Denis. He knew his way. He was also alert and vigilant about anything and everyone: be it the dung collector with his barrels crammed with steaming offal, or the housewife at a window above him emptying the chamber pots so that a veritable rain of human waste splashed the streets below and drenched any unfortunate passing by. The light was dim, the shadows shifting, whilst the air was riven with a low, incessant hymn of noise.

Pushing the pomander against his nose and mouth, Nightingale hurried on until he reached the Street of the Lanterns. Nightingale hugged the shadows as he crept towards the corner. He edged around and stared at the dingy auberge which rejoiced in the title of The Sunburst. The door to this tavern had been flung open by the drunk who sprawled in the entrance, bellowing insults at his companion, who had slipped and tripped into the broad, ancient horse trough. The drunk spluttered about, loudly cursing, as he tried to get out. Nightingale half smiled, the usual frenetic nonsense of The Sunburst. He was about to creep out of the shadows, but promptly froze as he glimpsed the glint of steel from the alleyway which ran down the right side of the auberge. Nightingale crouched and stared. The more he did, the more convinced he became that armed men clustered very close to the mouth of the alleyway.

Nightingale withdrew, turned and fled, hurrying down to the Petit Pont where the twilight people camped for the night. He entered that village of perpetual dusk. He paid the Keeper of the Gates and was shown to a dirty but thick palliasse, deep in the cellar of a dilapidated wine shop. The keeper also suppled a threadbare blanket and the wooden token which gave Nightingale the right to take some of the onion stew that hung bubbling above a leaping fire. Once he had settled and gulped the deep bowl of soup, Nightingale sheathed his horn spoon as he watched the shadows dancing around him. He crossed himself and murmured a prayer of thanksgiving for his escape, even as he vowed never to return to any of the places he frequented. In fact, Nightingale concluded, it was time to leave Paris. He would head as swiftly as he could to Boulogne, in English-held Ponthieu, and get speedy passage on some cog bound for Dover. He must reach Westminster. He had to inform Master Thibault that the Secret Chamber nursed a traitor deep in its heart. How else could these slippery shadows of the Chambre Noir know which taverns he frequented? Spies like Starling had some information about him, but Nightingale had never informed any of his comrades, not even his lover Jean-Luc, about where he lived or what places he frequented. Nightingale drew a deep breath. He had already informed Thibault how many of 'Nightingale's flock', as he called them, had either simply disappeared or been taken up. Starling's capture, and those armed men lurking in the shadows outside The Sunburst, were proof enough of how dangerous life now was.

Nightingale leaned back against the wall of the cellar, wrinkling his nose at the stench, as he reflected on Les Mysterieux, that *cohors damnosa* of French spies which had been despatched into England. It was all part of the continuous secret war waged between France and England, along the streets and across the squares of both kingdoms' principal cities. However, this was different, more serious. Information about the whereabouts of himself and others was only known to Master Thibault and his cabal of Secret Chancery clerks. Consequently, one of these, or more, must be in the pay of the Chambre Noir, but who?

Nightingale went through the possible names. Surely not the likes of Norwic and Hyams? They were highly paid, well-trusted clerks, who had studied in the halls of Oxford and Cambridge. Men patronized by the Crown and fully embraced by the love of the King. These were Master Thibault's men, as was he – body and soul, in peace and in war. Nevertheless . . . Nightingale chewed the corner of his dry, split lips. He made a decision. Tonight, he would sleep here and, on the morrow, flee for his life.

PART ONE

Molde: clumps of earth

Brother Athelstan, Dominican Parish Priest of St Erconwald's in Southwark, truly wished he were back in his little house overlooking God's Acre. He would love to be sitting before the hearth with Bonaventure, the great one-eyed tomcat who'd adopted him. Philomel the old warhorse would be slumbering in his solitary stable, whilst Hubert the Hedgehog, rolled up in a ball, would be nestling deep in the little hutch that Crispin the Carpenter had so skilfully fashioned. Yet Athelstan was not there. He was here in the dead of night, a mere stone's throw from the lofty curtain wall of the Church of St Martin Le Grand Church in London.

Athelstan turned and peered over the narrow bank which kept him and others well hidden. He glimpsed the forbidding towers and spindle-shaped turrets of the ancient Norman church. Somewhere, carried on the breeze, echoed the fluted voice of some drunken minstrel staggering through the streets of the Shambles, the great fleshing yard which stretched out not far from the church. Athelstan strained his hearing and caught the words of a famous love song, '*Ma Dolce Amour*'. The words evoked memories from Athelstan's past. Indeed, what seemed an eternity away. Memories of a beach close to the port of Civitavecchia only a few miles from Rome. Athelstan had been there as a student, a scholar. He also became the fervent lover of the fair Claudia long before he took vows as a Dominican priest. The memory was bitter-sweet, a truly beautiful evening rich with fragrant smells. The full moon had washed the sandy beach to a light gold. Claudia had come to meet him, swift, flitting like the angel she was.

'No, no,' Athelstan whispered to himself. 'I must close that door and keep it locked.'

'What's the matter, little monk?'

'Friar, Sir John, and there is nothing the matter.'

'Not yet, Brother.'

Sir John Cranston, Lord High Coroner of the City of London, eased his great bulk so he could stare down at his bosom friend, counsellor, secretary and chronicler.

'You know why we are here, my little friend. Soon,' Cranston pointed up at the sky, 'it will be time. The best time,' he added. 'Just before dawn, when the horde of outlaws beyond that curtain wall will still be sleeping like hogs in their filthy pens. Now, Brother, to pass the time, I am busy listing the most suitable ingredients for the best cup of hippocras. They must include cinnamon, mace, cloves, more than a pinch of fine sugar . . .'

Athelstan closed his eyes again. At least those memories, those deep echoes of the past, did not return. He must accept where he was, close to St Martin Le Grand, with the great fleshing yards nearby. These had closed just before the Compline bell, but trickles and rivulets of blood still shimmered in the moonlight, whilst the air continuously reeked of the slaughter sheds.

We live in a blood-drenched world, Athelstan reflected, a great deal of it innocent so appealing to God for justice. Dark thoughts, he concluded, so the friar forced himself to reflect on his parish and the congregation of souls entrusted to his care. In fact, St Erconwald's was proving to be particularly difficult at the moment. Lent had begun. Easter was fast approaching, and the parish was beginning to stir, to prepare for the great feast. To celebrate this correctly, Athelstan's parishioners were passionately committed to staging their great miracle play celebrating the crucifixion, death and resurrection of Christ. The parish artist and painter, Giles of Sempringham, otherwise known as the Hangman of Rochester, had already bought his canvas sheets, which he would cover in eye-catching paintings. Once completed, these would be set around the makeshift stage, set up just before the entrance to the rood screen. Judith the mummer was writing, in a clerkly hand, the different lines to be delivered by a wide range of characters. Athelstan's task was much more difficult. He would be the final arbiter. He would decide which parishioner would play what role. At the same time, he must try to correct some of the bizarre perceptions of his parishioners, such as those of Pike the Ditcher, who mistakenly believed Pontius Pilate and Herod were man and wife. Crispin the Carpenter, on the other hand, argued that the Good Thief also rose from the dead to join Jesus in Jerusalem.

Matters were not helped by the arrival in the parish of Radulf and his henchman Malak. 'Radulf the Relic Seller', as he styled himself, was the charming but very irresponsible father of Cecily the Courtesan and her sister Clarissa. Two young ladies of the night who, Athelstan secretly believed, knew every inch of St Erconwald's sprawling cemetery, God's Acre. It was the favourite trysting place for both young ladies to meet their 'customers', 'clients' or 'guests', whatever word they liked to use when Athelstan confronted them.

Radulf, their father, was just as enterprising, being a self-proclaimed relic merchant. According to Radulf and his henchman, the shaggy-haired, sour-faced Malak, both men had journeyed across to kingdoms beyond the Narrow Seas, visiting all the great shrines of Christendom. Radulf and his minion had returned to St Erconwald's in exuberant and expansive mood. Apparently, they had become the proud owners of a real, yet miraculous copy of the Holy Face of Lucca. Athelstan knew a great deal about this relic, supposedly an accurate representation of the face of the suffering Christ. According to legend, a true image of the divine face had been captured on a veil used by the holy woman Veronica to cleanse Jesus as he carried his cross to Calvary. Athelstan had seen the version brought by Radulf, and he openly conceded that the relic looked most impressive. It stood in the centre of an oaken triptych, its two side leaves decorated with sacred texts. The leaves could be closed over to seal the face itself, only to be reopened for the faithful to venerate and make their supplication. If their offering was generous enough, tiny spots of blood would appear on the divine brow. The relic was kept in an elm-wood box lined with the costliest taffeta and sealed with copper hooks and clasps. Naturally, along with the preparations for the great mystery play, Radulf's relic provoked deep interest amongst Athelstan's parishioners.

The friar had not yet decided what to say publicly about the relic. He intended to do so that morning after he had celebrated the Jesus Mass, but the portly, white-whiskered giant of a coroner had intervened. In a word, Cranston needed Athelstan not so much as his clerk but as a priest to anoint the dying and shrive the wounded once they'd attacked the ruffians in St Martin Le Grand's cemetery.

'You see, little brother,' the coroner had declared, sitting in his favourite chair at his most favoured tavern, The Lamb of God on Cheapside, only a short walk away from the Guildhall. 'You see, Athelstan,' the coroner repeated, as he gently poked Athelstan's shoulder with a porky finger, 'there will be fighting and there will be deaths. You, my little friend, may well have to prepare souls for judgement.'

'Including our own, Sir John?'

'Yes, Brother, as always Death strides close to my shoulder and its shadow often crosses my path. However,' Cranston picked up a piece of crisp pork and popped it into his mouth, followed by the most generous gulp of the finest Bordeaux from his miraculous wineskin.

'However, what?' the friar demanded.

'There is little to be done about threats, and we both know that.'

Athelstan closed his eyes. What a contrast! A few hours ago, he and Cranston had luxuriated and relaxed in the comfortable, warm, perfumed solar of The Lamb of God. Now they were lying on a frost-covered mud bank preparing for battle. Sir John, who had eventually finished listing the ingredients for an excellent goblet of hippocras, now eased himself up to peer through the thinning mist.

'Sir John,' Athelstan demanded, 'could you please tell me why we are here at this unearthly hour. I know all about St Martin's being a sanctuary, but why now? Why not a month ago, or in a month's time?'

'Ah well, Brother . . . London, as I have discovered whilst writing my great history of the city, has over one hundred churches, never mind the chapels, chantries and shrines. Indeed, some of these have stood for centuries. Holy places.'

'With the right of sanctuary?'

'Precisely, Brother. St Martin's is the most popular. It houses almost an army because any felon, nighthawk or dark walker, who in truth should be decorating Tyburn gibbet, can shelter there. Believe me, Brother, the rabble camped in the cemetery are dangerous and impudent: their latest escapade was to climb the wall at night and sneak into the city to rob signs . . .'

'Signs?'

'Signs, Brother, for this tavern or that shop. Now, as you may know, such signs are often the work of skilled craftsmen. They proclaim to the world what a particular shop or tavern offers and they hang from chains . . .'

'So they can be easily unhooked.'

'True, Brother. Those thieves beyond the wall plucked down sign after sign and carted them back to God's Acre where, if they wish, their former owners can come and redeem them for a hefty price, but not so hefty as if they had to commission a new sign.'

'Impudent indeed,' Athelstan breathed.

'The Guild Masters, the lords of the city, have had enough. That's why we are here: to clear God's Acre, arrest notorious malefactors, and seize back stolen property.'

'The Church will be furious. Archdeacon Tuddenham will thunder warnings.'

'The Church can go hang,' Cranston whispered hoarsely. He paused as a cock crowed, a raucous, strident call which was answered by others.

Athelstan glanced up. The sky was lightening. On a morning such as this he should be standing on the top of his church tower, watching the moon wane and the stars disappear, leaving Athelstan to wonder yet again at the gorgeous mystery of it all. How did daybreak happen? So methodically, so harmoniously? But not here, not on this part of God's earth.

Cranston had now stirred himself. Clambering to his feet, the coroner gripped Athelstan's shoulder.

'Stay here,' he warned. 'Rhys,' he bellowed at the Captain of Archers standing further down the long ridge of earth. 'Rhys, the signal!'

Athelstan watched as dark shapes milled about. A pot of fire abruptly flared then, one after the other, flaming shafts were loosed high into the brightening sky. Others followed. Trumpets shrilled. Horns brayed. Archers and men-at-arms seemed to spring out of the darkness, racing towards the curtain wall of St Martin's cemetery. The church had been surrounded on all sides and the attack was intense. Scaling ladders crashed against the walls, whilst a war cart carrying a sharpened battering ram forced open the sturdy lychgate, smashing it aside. Fire arrows were then loosed, hitting the sacks of oil fastened to the battering ram. More fire erupted, flames leaping against the thinning darkness.

The clamour of battle turned more strident. Shrieks, screams and war cries echoed. Abruptly the bells of St Martin's began to toll. A mournful dirge, as if the church itself was protesting at the abrupt violation of its sacred precincts. Athelstan decided to move. He rose and, opening his chancery satchel, took out his stole and put it around his neck. Then, holding a crude, hand-sized crucifix, he left his place of concealment. Athelstan, walking at a half-crouch, followed the soldiers now sweeping into the cemetery, a broad stretch of rough grass, gorse and bramble, which sprouted vigorously amongst the gravestones, crosses and other funereal memorials. Those who had taken shelter there, the outlaws and the felons, had turned God's Acre into a camp with tents, bothies and lean-to sheds; these too were now torched and pulled down.

The fighting had been savage, but any resistance was swiftly collapsing. Some of the sanctuary men had fled, scaling the walls and fleeing into the protective darkness of the city. Others had fought back and been ruthlessly cut down, their blood-drenched corpses littering the unpruned vegetation. A few had even been hanged out of hand, their corpses twisting on the noose ropes thrown over the branches of the trees which peppered the graveyard. The fury of battle, the lust to cut and kill was ebbing. Cranston's officers, and those of the sheriff, were now forcing those they had taken captive to kneel with their hands lashed behind their backs. A group of mailed clerks, despatched by the lords of the Guildhall, moved along the rows of prisoners. Tattered cowls, hoods, capuchons and face masks were dragged off so the clerks could clearly see the prisoners' faces. Some of these whimpered for mercy, but most of them just knelt, faces impassive.

The clerks worked swiftly. Crouching beside each of them was a servant carrying a spluttering torch. Certain prisoners were immediately recognized by scars, wounds and other distinguishing marks. These were wanted men, 'utlegati', who had been put to the horn as outlaws and their descriptions proclaimed for all to hear. A few were truly notorious, and the sheriff's men could scarcely conceal their glee. Many of these now fully realized what had happened and offered, for a pardon, to turn King's approver, so they could point out former comrades and name the crimes they had committed. The mailed clerks brazenly proclaimed this truly was a rich harvest of lost souls. A good number of them turncoats, Judas men, were dragged to their feet and used as guides, as the law officers moved through their horde of prisoners. The turnkeys of Newgate eventually arrived to fasten iron chains and manacles on those captured. Once done, these unfortunates were pushed to the prison carts now assembling outside the ruined lychgate. Athelstan felt a hand on his shoulder and whirled round to face a grinning Cranston.

'Brother.' He leaned down, his breath richly layered with the fragrance of Bordeaux. 'You probably have customers begging for your help.' Cranston re-sheathed his sword and bellowed across to Flaxwith, his master bailiff who, accompanied by his mastiff Sampson, probably the ugliest dog in London, swept across the cemetery to give the friar a comradely hug. Flaxwith then pointed back to where his cohort of bailiffs stood guarding a long line of wounded and dying.

'Brother,' the master bailiff breathed, his broad face and bushy beard and moustache still flecked with blood, 'we have men begging for your help. They want the consolamentum!'

Athelstan nodded and followed Flaxwith across to the pathetic-looking bundles which had been laid out in an orderly row. Many of these had hideous wounds, gashes and cuts to their face, chest and stomach. Athelstan realized he could only give a little ghostly help, but he would do what he could. He moved from one stricken man to the next, murmuring the words of a general absolution. He would then recite a requiem, sketch a blessing, and walk on. He had almost reached the last of the fallen when the bells of St Martin's, which had fallen strangely silent, now began to toll again. A long and mournful clanging, which ended as the great doors to the church crashed back and a priest garbed in a blood-red and silver cope swept out to stand on the top step of the main entrance. The priest pushed back his hood as he moved into a pool of light. Athelstan quietly groaned as he recognized the harsh, severe face of Archdeacon Tuddenham, the Bishop of London's man in all things ecclesiastic. A stickler for procedures and a most skilled peritus in canon law, Tuddenham was, in the words of Sir John, a veritable pain in the nether regions.

The archdeacon now stood on the steps, hands dramatically

extended, as a trumpeter, waiting in the shadows behind him, brayed a brazen call for silence. A mailed knight had now joined the archdeacon: armoured for war, a flaming torch in one hand, his drawn sword in the other.

'Sir Gervaise Brocken,' Cranston murmured, coming up beside Athelstan. 'Believe me, Brother, Brocken is a greater pain than our noble archdeacon.'

Athelstan repressed a slight shiver of apprehension. He had heard Cranston talk of Brocken before and it was never in amicable terms. Indeed, the coroner nursed a profound dislike of the man. On occasion, Cranston had betrayed this when he and Athelstan discussed the politics of both court and city.

'The Church's champion,' Cranston murmured. 'Always ready to defend any priest or cleric . . .'

'As well as the right of sanctuary,' Athelstan added, warningly. Both coroner and friar watched as Brocken whispered words to the archdeacon. The eerie stillness that had descended now deepened. Dawn had already broken, though the light remained grey. Torches spluttered and danced, their flames leaping like demons wanting to break free. Cries and groans of the fallen echoed but, for the rest, all eyes were on Brocken, now striding towards Cranston. He stopped before the coroner and jabbed a finger in Cranston's face.

'You shouldn't be here, Fat Jack,' he taunted. 'This is Church land.'

'I hold the King's Writ, as well as those of His Grace John of Gaunt and Master Thibault. Brocken, I am not interested in your homilies on canon law and the rights of the Church. This cemetery houses felons guilty of the most heinous and hideous crimes. So, take your finger from my face, turn round and piss off.'

'The Church is all,' Brocken chimed back sonorously. 'You, as always, are in the wrong. Remember Saint Thomas Becket who died defending the rights of the Church.'

'His cathedral didn't house a nest of outlaws.'

'No, no, Fat Jack, you are in the wrong as always. Do you understand me?'

Brocken came closer, his finger not very far from Cranston's face. Athelstan moved to intervene. He grabbed Sir John's arm, but then Brocken lunged forward, lashing out with his spurred boot a vicious kick which brought the friar to his knees.

'What now, Brocken?' Cranston shouted. 'You have just harmed a priest, a friar, but more importantly, my friend.'

'For heaven's sake,' Athelstan gasped, 'this is not necessary. It's not necessary.' But it was too late. Cranston had stepped back, drawing his sword. Brocken had now dropped the torch, holding his own war sword in two hands. Both knights shifted, then closed in a circling arc of glittering steel, sword scraping sword as they darted and feinted. Athelstan, nursing his bruised leg, watched helplessly. He had every faith in Sir John. Despite his bulk, the coroner was a master swordsman, surprisingly swift on his feet.

At first Brocken countered Cranston's cuts. The fight continued. No one dared intervene. This was, so it seemed, '*Une lutte à outrance*' – 'a fight to the death'. Athelstan watched, skin clammy with fear. He wondered about Cranston's deep dislike and then recalled something he had been told years ago which explained the intense hostility between the two knights. The Lady Maude, a great beauty in the city, had many would-be suitors, Brocken being the most dedicated. Lady Maude, however, had spurned him and others, for she had fallen deeply in love with Cranston, who was now fighting to defend her choice. Apparently, Cranston and Brocken had many times come to harsh words. However, as the years passed, they had both simply honoured an agreement to stay well away from each other. Athelstan watched as the fighters broke, stepped back, then closed again. Sword against sword, so sharp and violent that sparks of fire drifted from the clashing steel. Archdeacon Tuddenham, along with Cranston's officials, tried to intervene, but it was futile. Like Athelstan, they had no choice but to stand and watch, ignoring the groans and cries of the prisoners.

Cranston, now taken by the full flush of battle, was wearing Brocken down. Athelstan sensed the end was near. The coroner abruptly retreated, lowering his sword as if tired. Brocken edged closer, but then Cranston darted forward, sword blade flickering like a lunging viper. He caught Brocken off guard. Cranston twisted his blade. Brocken lost his grip and dropped his sword. He then tried to retrieve it, only to slip and crash to the ground. He made to rise, but stumbled again on the mud-drenched grass. He fell back, staring up at Cranston who, sword half raised, now bestrode his prostrate opponent. Athelstan hurriedly prayed. Cranston had fought like a true warrior. He'd attacked with speed and skill. Despite his bulk, Cranston was a dancer skilled in the deadly rhythms of the street fight as well as those of the formal tournament. So, what would happen now? Brocken was the guilty party with his violent words and physical attack. Cranston had simply defended himself and a friar. Moreover, the coroner was here in St Martin's on the authority of the Crown. Sir John would certainly be supported by the young King, who admired him deeply, not to mention Gaunt and his Master of Secrets. In addition, Athelstan was a priest who enjoyed the full protection of Holy Mother Church.

'Sir John,' Athelstan shouted, but his voice came out in a croak.

Cranston whirled his sword, sheathed it, then stretching out his hand, pulled his opponent shakily to his feet.

'God save us all, Gervaise,' he trumpeted, 'but we are finished here. You fought well but you haven't improved your skill. You fell for that trick like any young squire. Here.' He extended his hand. Brocken grasped it, murmuring his thanks.

'We are finished here,' Cranston repeated. 'Flaxwith,' he bawled, 'and all officers of the Crown. Let us get this canting crew into the carts so we can safely lodge them at Newgate.' He then patted Brocken on the shoulder and walked towards the ruined lychgate, beckoning to Athelstan to join him.

St Martin's cemetery now rang with shouts, cries, groans and curses. Weapons and prisoners were gathered into the clattering, noisome carts. Clerks shouted orders. Horses neighed and shook the morning dew from their manes. The light strengthened. Officers hurried about, shouting orders, urging everyone to leave. Cranston and Athelstan had passed through the lychgate when the coroner paused as a voice shouted his name. Brocken, now recovered, strode forward, clutching a bedraggled prisoner by the nape of his neck.

'Well I never!' Cranston chortled. 'No less a person than No-Breeches, one of London's most skilled housebreakers. Well, Gervaise, a fine fish netted. A felon with a veritable litany of offences. But why have you brought him to me?'

'Sir John.' Brocken, still grasping the unfortunate felon, stepped closer. 'I thank you for your charity. I apologize unreservedly for what I said and what I did. Brother Athelstan, I shall do penance.

It was most unacceptable, a cowardly blow. I simply lost my temper. So, to both of you, my deepest apologies for who I am and what I did—'

'And?' Cranston intervened.

'Sir John,' Brocken's face creased into a smile, 'there are so many echoes from the past.' Brocken gave No-Breeches a shake. 'This is one. Tell him,' he shouted. 'Tell him what you know.'

'Oh Sir John,' No-Breeches wailed. 'Mercy!'

'Mercy indeed,' Cranston retorted.

'A pardon, Sir John?'

'For what, you cunning little bastard?'

'The Radix Malorum has returned to London. He has come back to haunt you, Sir John.'

'Has he now?' Cranston stepped closer. 'How do you know all this?'

'Chatter, my Lord Coroner, gossip along the runnels.'

'So, in fact, empty rumour?'

'No, Sir John, more than that. First, do you remember Split-Nose?'

'How could I forget a face like that?'

'Well, on one occasion Split-Nose was breaking into a goldsmith's shop near the Standard. He is, or he was, one of the very few people who saw the Radix up close.'

'And?' Cranston bent down, staring into the battered, bloodied face of this notorious felon, with his sunken cheeks and deep-set eyes, his scrawny, grease-drenched hair all spiked and glittering.

'Split-Nose was the one who told me that only a few days ago he'd glimpsed Radix near London Bridge. That's how he knew he had returned.'

'And where is Split-Nose now?'

'He was here, Sir John. He had a metal pot on his head and carried a cleaver. Little good it did him. One of your archers ran him through and Split-Nose is no more. More than that, Sir John, I cannot say, except late this evening, so I was informed, the Radix posted proclamations saying he is back to settle scores with you.'

'So,' Cranston straightened up, 'we have this notorious felon Radix Malorum who plagued us some years ago. He has reappeared in London and is brazen about it. He not only scrawled his crude proclamations saying he is back, but dares to taunt me, the Lord High Coroner.' He grasped No-Breeches by the shoulder and pulled him close. 'And how, my good friend, do I know that you are speaking the truth? Is this a lie? A ruse to save your scrawny neck?'

'Sir John,' Gervaise intervened. 'I can vouch for what No-Breeches said. Split-Nose's revelation was shared with others but, in the main, with No-Breeches here. Moreover, if those proclamations were posted, we will know soon enough.'

'What else did Split-Nose say?' Cranston demanded. 'What information did he give you about what he saw or who the Radix might be?'

'Dressed like a flesher, he was, according to Split-Nose, an apron tied around him and a bright feather in his hair.'

'Did Split-Nose give a physical description?'

'Split-Nose said that he'd glimpsed him but the fellow was wearing a hood which he swiftly pulled up.'

'Anything else?' Cranston demanded.

'No, Sir John, except can I go now?'

Cranston nodded at Brocken.

'Cut him loose on one condition. No-Breeches, you will do careful search and come back to me either at the Guildhall or my chambers in The Lamb of God. You must bring me any fresh information you garner on Radix. Now, you might think I will forget you. However, you know what will happen then, don't you? I'll come hunting you.'

'Yes, Sir John.'

'Then go in peace.'

Athelstan watched as the prisoner's bonds were cut. No-Breeches, despite his age and the rough treatment he had received, raced off like a greyhound from the slips. Cranston watched him go, then turned to Gervaise and once again clasped his rival's hand.

'It was a small favour,' Brocken declared. 'Sir John, I wish you well.' Brocken then nodded at Athelstan and walked off to join Archdeacon Tuddenham still standing on the top step of the church, glaring across God's Acre.

'A strange turn of events, Sir John.'

'Yes.' Cranston peered down at Athelstan, 'And before you ask, Brother, the Radix Malorum and I have a story that stretches back years. However that, I'm afraid, is for another time and another place.'

Two days later, Athelstan recalled these words as he stood on the broad, blood-soaked execution platform, staring across the crowds massing into Smithfield to witness the King's justice being done. News about the attack on the sanctuary at St Martin's had swept the city. The rumour flames had been fanned by special commissions of Oyer et Terminer held in the Great Judgement Hall at Newgate. Royal justiciars, together with the sheriff's men and lords of the Guildhall, had quickly sifted the prisoners captured at St Martin's. They issued death sentences as well as 'petty sanctions' to be carried out immediately. The law described them as minor punishments, but in fact they were bloody and, in some cases, fatal.

Athelstan gazed across the platform where the Hangman of Rochester, a member of the friar's parish, was preparing the nooses on the five lofty gibbets, each with their four jutting branches. Scaling ladders had been placed against these for speedy ascent, followed by the even swifter deadly fall. The city bailiffs and the sheriff's men were now busy marshalling their prisoners, a motley mob of ragged, bruised men and women. They were being pushed towards the scaffold platform to wait near the steps leading up to it. In the meantime, the so-called minor sentences were being carried out on the edge of the gibbet platform. Here large braziers, packed with flaring charcoal, warmed the air with their darting tongues of flame. Two city executioners stoked the blaze to heat their knives, cleavers and branding weapons. Cranston stood watching these for a while before lifting a hand for the condemned to be hauled up on to the platform.

Athelstan sat down on a stool the coroner had provided on the far corner of the scaffold. Athelstan crossed himself and put his face in his hands. He tried to pray. He truly hated these gruesome, macabre, bloody rituals. He had not wanted to come here. However, the coroner had begged him to attend, living proof that Sir John was observing the ordinances that a priest be present at all executions, in case one of the condemned wanted to be shrived. Cranston had tried to find a priest, but what had happened at St Martin's had certainly not favoured relationships between the coroner and the city clergy. True, he could have called on the Franciscans or the Friars of the Sack, a number of whom had already flocked to Smithfield to sing hymns of mourning and psalms for the soon-to-be-departed. However, as Athelstan knew full well, the Friars of the Sack viewed themselves as champions of the downtrodden, the earthworms, the dispossessed, be it the peasants of the shires or the petty tradesmen and tinkers of the towns. The Friars of the Sack never lost an opportunity to condemn the rich and powerful, especially here in London. Some of this fraternity had already pushed themselves to the front of the crowd, eager to harangue the people. Athelstan strained his ears and caught the words chanted by the 'Choir of the Hanged', as the friars liked to call themselves.

'The new Jerusalem will come,' a powerfully voiced friar sang out. 'For the Lord is restoring the vineyard of Israel. The plunderers have broken off their branches but now is the time of judgement. Woe to this city soaked in blood. London is crammed with lies and stuffed with booty, the property of the poor. The plundering by the rich knows no end. But the time of judgement will come! You will hear the crack of the whip. The rumble of wheels. The pounding of galloping horses. The flash of swords, the gleam of spears. So, what will be left, will be a mass of wounded, hosts of dead, countless corpses.'

The chant, taken up by other friars, was brought to an abrupt end by heart-rending screams. Athelstan closed his eyes and murmured a prayer. The mutilations had begun! A notorious foist, skilled in the nap, had been captured at St Martin's. He was now fastened to a huge, upturned log, set close to the scaffold steps. A cleaver from the Shambles had severed the felon's right hand; the wound was immediately and brutally cauterized. Once finished, the severed hand would be fastened to the remaining one. The felon could then stagger through the crowds and the city, demonstrating the punishment for such a crime as his. Other punishments followed. The shrieks and cries continued to the thud of the cleaver. Blood sprayed up to tinge the breeze and so leave its deadly mark all over. Athelstan just stared down, trying to recall the words of the *De Profundis*: 'Out of the depths have I cried to thee, O Lord . . .'

At last it ended, the screams and cries fading. A drum began to beat as a sign that the hangings would begin. The first of the condemned was dragged to the gibbet ladder, but the proceedings were roughly interfered with by a discordant blast from both trumpet and war horn, followed by the screeching of bagpipes. Cranston roared at the Hangman of Rochester to wait until he could find out what was happening. The coroner clambered off the platform only to return, shaking his head. He thrust a tattered page of parchment at Athelstan.

'Nailed to a death cart along with other copies. Of course the earthworms and their musicians are only too pleased to proclaim it louder.'

Athelstan, feeling slightly sick and giddy, read the crudely scrawled proclamation.

'A letter from the Radix Malorum.'

Athelstan mouthed the words.

'I have returned to this city as I swore I would. I am here to find more wealth and show that Fat Jack is still a fool despite his years.'

Athelstan passed the proclamation back to the coroner. From what he could hear and understand, Cranston was right. More copies of this proclamation had been found nailed to carts or pinned to trees. The street swallows, sewer squires along with all the other heralds of the alleyways, were sharing the same message which mocked the city and Cranston in particular. Athelstan however, felt weak. A darkness was gathering around him which chilled his blood. He really must go. He felt Cranston grip his arm.

'*Pax et bonum*, little brother,' the coroner whispered. 'This is not for you. It's time you were gone. You are no longer needed. Master Flaxwith will take you to the comforts of The Lamb of God.'

Athelstan stretched in the cushioned chair placed before the roaring fire in the small solar in The Lamb of God, the Lord High Coroner's special chamber in what he called 'his private chantry chapel'. Athelstan felt much better. He had taken a goblet of wine and slept like a babe, only wakened by Cranston's arrival. The coroner assured Athelstan that the day's business was finished: those intended to join the 'choir invisible' had been despatched on their way long before sunset. The King's justice had been done and, more importantly, had been seen to be done. Now it was time to feast.

They both washed their hands and faces in the perfumed water of the solar's lavarium, before dining on highly spiced venison pie, a large dish of vegetables, accompanied by goblets of the best Bordeaux.

'Oh yes.' Cranston had doffed his warbelt, beaver hat, cloak and high-heeled riding boots. 'Oh yes,' he repeated, 'the Hangman of Rochester is as swift as he is deadly.'

'Giles of Sempringham,' Athelstan murmured. 'That's his real name, Sir John. He became a hangman only after he hunted down and executed those responsible for the murder of his wife and children. He feels he must still continue his war against the sons and daughters of Cain. I do pray that one day soon he will declare he is satisfied. He can then dedicate himself fully to painting, for which he has a God-given talent.'

Athelstan paused and crossed himself as he heard the Crier of the Dead, just outside the tavern door, proclaim the names of those who had died that day: 'So all good citizens could pray for the repose of the souls of these faithful departed.' No sooner had the crier finished his litany when the door to the solar burst open, with a wailing Mine Hostess protesting at the intrusion. Leif, the one-legged beggarman, and Rawbum his constant companion, burst into the chamber after her. Rawbum, who had earned his name by drunkenly sitting on a pan of scalding oil, helped his one-legged friend hop across the solar to confront Sir John with a litany of salutations. Mine Hostess, her fair cheeks fully flushed, tried to drag them back. Cranston, however, simply flicked two coins, which were expertly caught, and the noisome two fled. Once they had gone, hotly pursued by Mine Hostess, Cranston filled their goblets and sat back in his chair.

'The Hangman of Rochester?'

'Never mind him,' Athelstan retorted. 'The Radix Malorum. Who is he?' Athelstan peered at the coroner. 'And I suspect you have something else to tell me, yes?'

'The Radix Malorum,' Cranston hastily replied, eager not to be too closely questioned as yet on other business he intended. 'Oh yes, yes.' The coroner gulped from his goblet. 'About sixteen years ago I was an undersheriff here in the city.'

'About to begin your elevation to high office.'

'Quite. Anyway, a sneak thief, a housebreaker, skilled and cunning, perpetrated a number of thefts in the mansions and stately homes along Cheapside and the area around.'

'The homes of the powerful and rich!'

'Of course. Now this thief was different. Not only did he break in and steal but he taunted his victims too, leaving crudely written insults posted all over the city. He'd proclaim the famous axiom, "*Avaricia Radix Malorum*" – "love of money is the root of all evil". He would also taunt the Guildhall, and in particular me, that with his cunning he would always escape our clutches. Eventually this thief became known as the Radix Malorum. Rewards were offered to any who might help capture him. I mean good bulging purses . . . However, it all proved futile. Of course, the lords of the Guildhall wanted a resolution to the matter but there was none to be had. Scapegoats were sought, myself included. But I tell you this, little brother, the Radix Malorum remained as elusive as a sunbeam. Months passed, then the Radix perpetrated a truly audacious robbery. He broke into John of Gaunt's palace at the Savoy and stole a pendant carrying the Redstone, one of the world's most magnificent rubies.'

'And then?'

'Silence, little brother, nothing! The Radix disappeared and so did the ruby. And before you ask, we know nothing of any significance. As I said, a great silence descended on this issue and remained so until tonight. As we learned at St Martin's, news has trickled in that the Radix is back in the city, intent on mischief.'

Athelstan held up his hand.

'Sir John, one matter does intrigue me. Split-Nose is now dead, but he claims to have seen the Radix whilst carrying out his own robbery in Cheapside. Why didn't he inform the authorities, claim the reward, give the description to you or some other law officer?'

Cranston patted Athelstan gently on the head.

'In many ways, Brother, you are a true innocent. First, Split-Nose would have had to confess to being a thief himself, which makes any allegation rather weak. Secondly, people might well think that Split-Nose himself was the Radix and simply trying to pass the blame on someone else. Thirdly, as you saw today, the Radix is seen as a hero of the people. I do not think any felon turning King's evidence and handing the Radix over to the Crown, would survive for long in the halls of the underworld.'

'I see, I see,' Athelstan murmured. 'A tangled mess. Split-Nose glimpsed him during a robbery and thought it best to keep his mouth shut.'

'In a word, little friar, yes.'

'So,' Athelstan demanded, 'the Radix has returned, but why is he proclaiming himself the length and breadth of the city?'

'Little brother, I really don't know the truth, except that the Radix is a true mummer, a lover of the masque, the play. He likes to proclaim and extol himself and win the approval and approbation of the poor earthworms. However, I do concede that what he is doing is highly dangerous. He's a villain. I would dearly love to trap him and, in doing so, settle a score which is well over a decade and a half old.'

Cranston picked up his goblet and sat as if listening to the sounds drifting in from the street. The clop of hooves, the creak of carts, the crack of whips and the different cries, be they those of the itinerant hucksters or the instructions of the market beadles. Athelstan crossed himself as the bells of the city churches began to toll, a sign to all good citizens that the day was ending and thanks should be offered to God. The Church was also reassuring the faithful that the peals would drive away the demons. As dusk fell these always clustered close around church spires, ready and eager for malicious mischief.

'There's more to this, isn't there, Sir John?'

'Yes, Brother, and it involves your beloved parish.'

'Oh, Lord save us,' Athelstan breathed. 'Sir John?'

'The burglary at the Savoy, totally devastated during the Great Revolt, took place on the evening before the feast of St Matthew, twentieth of September, the year of Our Lord 1369, some thirteen years ago. The Radix broke into a chamber on the second gallery of the palace, a small, jewel-like chapel which housed the Redstone in a silver filigreed coffer. The door to this small tabernacle, dedicated to the angels, remained locked and bolted. The Radix must have entered through a narrow window overlooking the street, the shutters both within and without were forced, whilst the violation of the casket needed tools such as a hammer and chisel . . .'

'And they must have had a ladder,' Athelstan murmured, 'to get to that window.'

'Yes, Brother, remember that. Now, I think it would be very difficult to wander London at night with a barrow containing a ladder, hammer, chisel and so on. It's very suspicious and would certainly provoke the attention of the watch. Anyway, the robbery was soon discovered by a vigilant guard. The alarm was raised and the tocsin sounded, whilst the streets and alleyways around the Savoy were chained and guarded, as indeed happened after every such robbery. Anyone caught wandering was stopped and searched, but nothing was ever found.'

'There wouldn't be many abroad.'

'No, Brother, no one really, apart from the occasional beggar or a whore desperate to earn a coin, not to forget a few revellers drinking well after the chimes of midnight. Anyway, Gaunt deployed his Spanish mercenaries and they were ruthless in their searches. The Guildhall received a number of complaints. I dealt with them. I also went through the list of those stopped and noticed two from St Erconwald's in Southwark. Members of the dung collector's guild, no less than those two worthies who now sit high on your parish council, Watkin and Pike.'

'Why do you remember this?' Athelstan asked.

Cranston chuckled and tapped the side of his head.

'I know, I know,' Athelstan sighed. 'Your memory is a wonder of God.'

'No, Brother.' Cranston gripped the friar's shoulder. 'Watkin and Pike were official dung collectors, but what was most memorable about them was that they also had a horse and cart, so they were obvious suspects. A cart would be needed to transport the ladder and all the tools necessary for such a burglary.'

'Of course,' Athelstan shrugged.

'But,' the coroner shook his head, 'that cart was searched, and I mean thoroughly searched. No hidden bottom or secret shelf, no ladder, no tools nothing. I later crossed to Southwark to question them. Brother, they hardly had the wit to wander, never mind participate in such an audacious crime.'

'I am not too sure about that precious pair, Sir John. Sometimes I think they are sharp, too sharp for their own good. But yes, I agree, I doubt very much whether Watkin and Pike would be strolling through Cheapside with a stolen ruby.'

'I dismissed them, as I did the rest of the night-walkers, dark-dwellers and twilight people. Eventually we had to give up the search, so the Guildhall hired bounty hunters. The best of these was Boniface.'

'Boniface, the bounty hunter,' Athelstan murmured. 'I met him years ago. He visited St Erconwald's. He always believed my parish housed wolfmen; outlaws who had been put to the horn. Now and again, he would seize such a villain.'

'A strange fellow,' Cranston mused. 'Boniface served on the galleys across the Middle Seas. He loved poetry and was always ready to extol this poet or that. He was babbling about Chaucer when I visited him at the hospital in St Bartholomew's.'

'You are correct,' Athelstan declared. 'I remember Boniface once wandering into St Erconwald's, talking of a poet he had met in a city tavern, a minor incident. Continue, Sir John. So, you visited Boniface at St Bartholomew's?'

'Yes, the poor bastard was dying, sweat-soaked and delirious. The good brothers did their best but he was past all care. Boniface would float in and out of his delirium, then talk quite sensibly. During one of these intervals, he begged Father Prior to send for me as he wished to talk about the Radix. I hastened to St Bartholomew's. Boniface had turned delirious. He gabbled about the Redstone and how the bishop and the corpse knew all about it.'

'What on earth did he mean by that?'

'Brother, I haven't the slightest notion.'

'It was then that he also talked, or rather ranted, about the Radix Malorum. He declared how the first three letters of each held the truth.' Cranston clinked his goblet against Athelstan's. 'God only knows what the poor bastard meant by that. I still don't know.' Cranston gave a deep sigh. 'Boniface died soon afterwards. He left no heirs, no will – nothing. Now, he had received fees from the Guildhall and still owed money, so the Lords of the Dunghill seized all of Boniface's paltry possessions to be stored in the great debtors' chamber at the Guildhall.' Cranston fell silent, swirling the dregs around his goblet. Athelstan studied him closely.

'There's other business, isn't there, Sir John?'

* * *

Stygal, chamberlain and chief porter of La Delicieuse tavern, which stood only a short walk away from the soaring walls, turrets, spires and cornices of the royal precincts of Westminster, knocked on the door to the chamber of the tavern's owner, the Lady Heloise.

'Come in.' The voice was soft, mellow yet carrying.

Stygal opened the door. Heloise sat swathed in a robe behind her ornately carved chancery desk. She glanced up and smiled. Stygal swallowed hard and tried to remain composed. Heloise, as Stygal had often declared, was truly beautiful, with her lustrous black hair, flawless skin, deep-set blue eyes and full red lips. Lady Heloise, in Styal's estimation, was beautiful enough to seduce an angel. In truth, she dazzled him, and he always felt slightly uncomfortable in this exquisitely furnished chamber which housed such beauty.

'Stygal?' Heloise smiled at her chamberlain. 'You stand and stare?' Even her voice, with its tinge of Norman French was most alluring. 'Stygal?' Heloise's smile faded as she showed that hardness which would brook no opposition.

'Mistress.' Stygal closed the door behind him. 'It's Master Hyams, the chancery clerk.'

'What about him?' Heloise, who Stygal knew had hidden her deep grief at the death of Norwic, now crumpled into sadness.

'Hyams,' she murmured, 'my beloved Hugh's comrade. Oh, Lord save us.' She sat staring down at the ledger open on the desk before her. She glanced up, eyes blinking with tears. 'Tell me, Stygal.'

'Hyams is in the Venus Chamber. He must be waiting for you or one of your ladies!'

'Not me,' she snapped. 'No.'

'I sent a maid to check on him, mistress.' Stygal spoke more swiftly. 'The door to the chamber is locked and bolted from within. As you know, the window is narrow and heavily shuttered. In brief, Master Hyams does not respond to our knocks or shouts. We must force the door.'

Heloise shuddered. Stygal could see she was lost in her grief.

'Daylight dies at the window,' she murmured. 'The silver thread is broken; the golden vase is shattered.'

Stygal just stood and listened. He knew his mistress deeply mourned the sudden death of another clerk, Hugh Norwic, found dead at the foot of the steps leading down to the arca of the Secret Chancery at Westminster. 'Nothing lasts,' Heloise murmured. 'And there's nothing new under the sun. Ah well.' She glanced at Stygal and forced a smile. 'Break the door down,' she ordered, getting to her feet. 'I shall be with you.'

Stygal hurried off down to the tavern's common taproom, where he hired four men, ordering them to bring up a heavy log from the fire stack. He then led them out of the taproom and into the luxurious interior of the house. Heloise was waiting outside the Venus Chamber. She instructed the labourers to begin; to ignore any damage done but simply pound the door until it wrenched off its leather hinges. The hired men did so, and the door snapped free, slamming down on to the floor like a drawbridge. Heloise allowed Stygal to grasp her hand and lead her through the shattered entrance into the dimly lit, sweet-smelling chamber. Heloise withdrew her hand and walked over to the broad bed, where Hyams the clerk sprawled. The dead man's face was a grotesque parody with his popping eyes, liverish skin and swollen, froth-lined lips. Heloise moaned softly and turned to Stygal.

'Lord protect us,' she whispered softly. 'He's been poisoned, by the look of it.'

Stygal murmured his agreement and turned to the people gathering in the doorway. He shouted at them to disperse, except for the scullion, Roncal, chief spit-boy from the kitchens.

'Mistress.' Stygal turned back to Heloise, who sat slumped in a chair, her face in her hands. 'Mistress,' he repeated. 'It is Monday evening; the physician Argentine has visited us as he always does. He's busy with one of our ladies.'

'Call him.' Heloise took her hands from her face. 'Find him and tell him it is most urgent.'

Stygal despatched Roncal, then walked over to the dead man. Hyams must have died in agony, his face was evidence enough for that, but how? Stygal glanced at his mistress, now threading her ave beads, then stared around the chamber. Nothing was out of place; everything was neat and orderly. No sign of any food or drink, except for the jug and half-empty goblet. The chamberlain picked both up and sniffed but could detect no malignant odour.

'Leave them be,' a voice ordered.

Stygal turned.

Argentine, the physician, stood in the doorway, red hair dishevelled, his cotehardie and hosts untied. The physician's round plump face was wine-flushed, his speech slightly slurred. Nevertheless, Stygal knew Argentine to be a most skilled and observant physician. Mistress Heloise only hired the best, and Argentine was famous throughout Westminster and across the city.

'Let me see.' Argentine clambered over the fallen door. He first went to Heloise, kissed her on the top of her head and gently rubbed her arm, murmuring comfort to her before he crossed to the bed. He examined the corpse, pulling up the jerkin and the chemise beneath, closely scrutinizing belly, chest, neck and face, before turning the corpse over to inspect the dead man's back as well as his hands and fingernails. He then moved the corpse to a more dignified position and crossed to sniff at the jug and goblet.

'Nothing,' he declared. 'I cannot detect even the faintest tinge of any foulness. However, be that as it may.' Argentine turned back to Heloise. 'Hyams was royal clerk, yes?'

'He worked in the Secret Chancery.'

'Oh, heaven save us,' Argentine exclaimed. 'Master Thibault must be informed. Well, at least about the death. As for its cause?' He pulled a face. 'Or the possible perpetrator? That's not for me to decide but a matter for Master Thibault.'

PART TWO

Kyrke: church

Brother Athelstan had risen early to kneel on his prie-dieu to pray before the crucifix nailed to the side of the door of his priest's house. Once finished, he rose, washed at the lavarium and hastily dressed. He was grateful for the thick woollen black-and-white robes, his legs warmed by knee-high stockings, his feet firmly encased in a pair of the stoutest sandals. Athelstan crouched and stroked his constant companion, Bonaventure, who sat purring over a bowl of milk that Athelstan had placed on the hearth after he had banked the fire earlier. He got to his feet and looked around at what he called his 'Parvum Paradisium', his 'Little Paradise'. Satisfied all was well, Athelstan left the house. He locked the door, shivering at the misty cold. He then hurried down to the church to celebrate his Jesus Mass. Once finished, he helped Crim the altar boy, his dirty face heavy with sleep, to stow away the vestments, as well as lock the chalice, paten and other sacred items in the sacristy area. Only then did he re-enter the sanctuary, going down and out through the rood screen to meet his parish council.

Mauger, the bell clerk, dry and black as maulkin, his fingers stiff with the cold, had prepared everything. The throne-like sanctuary chair had been moved and set up before the rood screen. Athelstan took his seat and stared across at Mauger, who sat organizing his small chancery desk. The ink horn was now opened, to be warmed by a candle placed close by. Next to this a row of sharpened quill pens, strips of wax and, most importantly, the parish ledger. The bell clerk caught Athelstan's eye and gestured at the parishioners still thronging about, gossiping and joking, as they made themselves comfortable on the simple long benches Mauger had arranged. The bell clerk wished to begin, but Athelstan just shook his head, raising a finger to his lips for silence. The rows were quickly filling. Most of the parish had turned out on this cold morning. Athelstan was determined not to begin until everyone was present. The friar fully realized why so many had assembled today. The great parish mystery play!

Athelstan's congregation was split into factions over this, each plotting to push matters the way they wanted. At the root of all this intrigue were those two mischievous imps, Watkin, the dung collector, and Pike, the ditcher. They had already taken over the first bench and would only allow members of their coven to sit with them. Athelstan watched them even as he reflected on what Cranston had told him the previous evening about the theft of the Redstone and how both these parishioners had been taken up for questioning. Athelstan smiled to himself. Both men must have been terrified.

He studied the other benches. Oh yes, the entire motley crew had assembled for this important meeting: Moleskin, the barge master; Ranulf the Ratcatcher with his two ferrets, thankfully boxed in; Joscelyn the one-armed former river pirate, now the proud owner of The Piebald tavern, only a short walk away. Next to him was Merrylegs, master of the cook shop close to The Piebald. On a separate bench, Crispin the Carpenter and Thomas the Toad, with his box of leaping frogs, or whatever he called them. Thomas lived in the House of Abode, the parish death house, the mortuary which Athelstan had recently paid to be built. Thomas was as mad and as frenetic as what he carried in his box. Nevertheless, he had been given the House of Abode to act as guardian of God's Acre. Athelstan had instructed Thomas to set up close watch over the great, sprawling cemetery of St Erconwald's. He was to keep a sharp eye for fires or torches glowing in the dead of night. Warning signs that warlocks and wizards were gathering for their filthy midnight festivities.

For all his madness, Thomas was an ideal choice. He hardly slept at night and loved to wander the cemetery looking for fresh recruits for the cohort of toads he so carefully kept in his lodgings. Thomas used these in the crowded houses of parishioners so that they would eat the flies, moths and other such vermin that crowded in crevices and cracks. Thomas had also been given a bell, so as to raise the alarm. Athelstan often glimpsed him staggering around God's Acre, a lantern in one hand, in the other a box of toads with the bell on a cord slung around his neck.

Athelstan startled as the church door was flung open and Cecily the Courtesan, along with her sister Clarissa, swaggered into the church. They were followed by their errant father, Radulf the Relic Seller and the latter's henchman, Malak. Small, hairy and squat, Malak could almost be taken as Thomas the Toad's twin brother. Radulf raised his hand in greeting to Athelstan before walking over to the baptismal font with its closed wooden lid. The self-proclaimed 'Herald of God', as Radulf liked to call himself, opened the leather sack he carried and placed the heavy triptych on the lid of the baptismal font. He then opened the side leaves to display the dark, wounded face within. Athelstan, deeply intrigued by the artefact, got up and walked across to the font. He stood staring at the sacred face of the Saviour, the large deep-set eyes, the regular features, the reddish-brown hair parted to fall down to the shoulders, the brow stained by the crown of thorns embedded deep in the skull.

'A face of sorrowful beauty.' Athelstan turned round. The Hangman of Rochester stood, eyes narrowed, as he peered at the painting. Beside him stood Benedicta the widow woman, garbed in a Lincoln-green gown, its fur-lined hood pulled close against the cold.

'Sorrowful beauty.' Benedicta repeated the hangman's description. 'Do you agree, Father?'

'I certainly do, Benedicta.' Athelstan stepped closer to exchange the kiss of peace with the woman he secretly loved. 'As I do,' he whispered, 'that you look as magnificent as an army in battle array, which is one of the reasons you are so welcome to this cauldron of bubbling intrigue.'

Benedicta stood back, hand over her face to hide her smile, her beautiful eyes dancing with mischief.

'What do you think, Father?' The hangman was still deeply immersed in the object of his attention. 'I mean, do you believe the forehead truly bleeds?'

'I think,' Athelstan whispered, 'and keep this to yourselves, that the painting is a very accurate replica of the Holy Face of Lucca. It is, in truth, a costly piece of art. However, as for the blood miraculously appearing, I suspect that the deep frame which holds the picture also contains a small sponge, soaked in blood, as well as a secret button or lever which causes the so-called miracle to occur. I have seen the likes before when I visited shrines in Italy, though I must admit,' Athelstan pointed at the painting, 'this is one of the best I have ever seen.'

'But, Father, if it's a forgery . . .'

'No, Benedicta, to prove trickery would mean the destruction of this precious and quite beautiful artefact. Secondly, if this painting deepens the fervour and piety of God's children, and I am sure it does, then perhaps the coins the petitioners pay are fair enough. Now . . .'

'Father, it is time,' Mauger sang out.

Athelstan sighed, nodded and returned to his chair. Mauger tolled the hand bell until he had silence. Once an expectant stillness had descended, Athelstan intoned the '*Veni Creator Spiritus*'. He invoked the Holy Spirit, humbly asking for his help which, Athelstan believed, he so desperately needed. The friar then blessed his parishioners, murmured a swift prayer for patience and turned to the bell clerk.

'My friend, our first business.'

'The play,' Judith the mummer, a tall, bossy woman sang out.

'Shut up!' Mauger bawled back.

'You shut up,' Watkin roared.

Athelstan just sat and let the ranting sweep backwards and forwards until weariness set in.

'Good,' Athelstan murmured. 'Now we have peace, God's peace in God's House. So Judith, we have our Easter play.' He pointed at her. 'Yes or no?'

'Yes, Father.'

'And it's what we agreed?'

'Yes, Father.'

'In which case, let us now decide who does what and who takes what part. I will act as the Saviour.'

Athelstan felt like adding that sometimes the parish felt like a crucifixion. Nevertheless, he held his peace, as his wayward congregation murmured amongst themselves then took a vote agreeing with Athelstan's proposal.

'Very well,' Athelstan murmured. 'Now the rest.'

The council moved with relish to reach conclusions and so make decisions. They had almost finished the business for the day when the corpse door creaked open and Tiptoft, Cranston's messenger, clad in the colours of a royal verderer, his bright red hair spiky and greased, slipped like a shadow into the church: his arrival silenced all sound. Tiptoft beckoned at Athelstan and the friar nodded acknowledgement. Cranston wanted him. The coroner had intimated the previous evening, before they had parted, that some nasty business at Westminster required his attention. Athelstan immediately prepared to leave. He collected his chancery satchel, walking cane and robe. Once garbed, the deep capuchon pulled close over his head, Athelstan sketched his parishioners a blessing. Raising a hand at their acknowledgments, the friar followed Tiptoft out on to the enclosure which stretched before the church.

The weather had improved, the sun was strengthening. All the dark-dwellers were crawling out from their underground dens to mingle with and plunder the unsuspecting. Athelstan kept a firm grip on his chancery satchel as he followed Tiptoft. The courier strode fast ahead of Athelstan, carrying a white splintered wand to knock away any attempt to impede or to harm either himself or his companion. They went down the alleyway, past The Piebald, before turning left on to the approaches to London Bridge. Here the noise and the surge of the crowd was breath-taking. The money-lenders were out behind their stalls, all protected by club-wielding rifflers. Very few people, in fact, would dare challenge this horde of skin-flinted usurers as they touted their rates. Criers, chosen for their brazen lungs, also bellowed messages, be it the joys of a nearby tavern or a freshly replenished bathhouse. The raucous noise, the devilish din, was like the constant beat of a mallet hammering its anvil. The flow of noise had so many sources: gangs of men-at-arms gathering in a tavern doorway; the drumming and bawling of cheap-jacks and mountebanks; the rattle of carts and horses; the constant chiming of bells, be they those of the street heralds or the constant pealing which accompanied a funeral cortege or wedding procession. Everyone seemed to shout raucously, whether a group of scholars challenging a bevy of foul-mouthed fishwives, or the wealthy burgesses cursing the mud as they shielded their nose and mouths against the reeking sulphur recently thrown over the filthy streets to stifle the horrid smells. Beggars wailed and clacked their dishes. Fiddlers, minstrels and storytellers touted for an audience, whilst the strumpets and whores stridently described the pleasures they might provide. Ruby-nosed topers lurched from the different alehouses thronging either side of the trackway, be it The Striped Ass, The Harp, The Swallow, The Spinning Sun and the rest. Tiptoft led Athelstan past these, the air ringing with the clink of goblets, cups and tankards, the noise blending with the clash of steel and the cries of the Daughters of Joy being taken roughly by their customers deep along some dark alleyway.

At last, they reached the outer bailey of the bridge, which also served as an execution ground and punishment yard. Corpses swung in the breeze, an ominous creaking as the sun-dried and wind-whipped cadavers performed their own macabre dance. Their gruesome black, sticklike figures, hanging by their necks, served as a perch for the river birds which stabbed at the dead, hollow eyes of the hanged. Fetid smells swirled, so offensive that Tiptoft turned and thrust a pomander into Athelstan's hand, the only protection against the stench of the lay stalls, manure heaps and offal buckets. Despite the filth and dirt, wandering cooks, their moveable stoves fixed on wheelbarrows, offered strips of burnt meat and fish of questionable origin. Bailiffs milled around, fixing petty felons in the stocks and pillories. Athelstan recognized a few of the perennial offenders, including Mistress Overdone and Mistress Not-So-Quickly, both of whom kept whores in a nearby stable. This truly is a place, Athelstan reflected, where the seven sins merrily clashed their symbols. The haunt and home of so many of the night-dwellers, brigands, dice-coggers, footpads, locksmiths, and the rest of the legion of the damned.

Tiptoft abruptly turned a corner, going down to the quayside close to the church of St Mary Overy, where fishing smacks, herring-boats and wherries clustered close on the water. All of them had moved to make space for the massive war barge displaying the red, blue and gold of the royal household on its canopied stern: a stiffened pennant embroidered with the same colours adorned the poop. Tiptoft and Athelstan climbed aboard and sat in the protected stern, whilst the six oarsmen, under the command of their captain, lowered their oars. The poop boy blew a long blast on his hunting horn and the war barge pulled away, aiming like an arrow across the Thames.

The day was fair and bright, the river fast-flowing under a stiff breeze. The Thames was certainly busy with cogs and galleys making their way to the different wharfs and quaysides. Athelstan sat back in the stern, threading a set of ave beads through his fingers as he prayed to the Virgin. The river, however, with its colour and frenetic business distracted him. Athelstan glimpsed the colours of different craft: the blue and silver of Venice, the dark green of the Hanse and the scarlet and gold-fringed banners of Genoa and other Italian cities. They passed a mud bank where a gallows had been erected for the summary punishment of river pirates. Three corpses, black and pecked beyond recognition, twirled like tops in the breeze. Athelstan now felt the pitch of the barge as the swell of the river pushed and swirled. The air was bitterly fresh with the smell of salt, brine, fish and tar. The poop boy abruptly brayed on his horn. Athelstan leaned forward to get a better glimpse of a second war barge, the *Thanatos*. This magnificent craft was the newly refurbished and recently renamed barge of the Fisher of Men, that macabre, black-garbed lord of the river who combed the Thames for corpses. The Fisher harvested the waters as a farmer would his fields. He would bring back the gruesome fruits of his work to be exposed and, sometimes, collected from the Chapel of the Drowned Man on a deserted quayside just past La Reole. The *Thanatos* was magnificent yet macabre as it broke through the mist, with its captain standing like the figure of death on the high stern. At the other end of the barge stood the Fisher's henchman, Ichthus, who sat crouched, perched in the poop, ready to slip into the water to haul aboard some river-soaked corpse. A strange being, Ichthus! He had no hair, so he looked most fishlike, with his webbed feet, hands, and scaly white skin. Apparently impervious to the cold, Ichthus would slide from his linen tunic into the water, to swim as swift and as sure as any porpoise. Athelstan watched the *Thanatos* disappear into the mist, then readied himself as the captain shouted orders to turn the royal barge alongside King's Steps under the grey soaring mass of Westminster.

Two hours later, Athelstan sat in the buttery which flanked the cloisters of the House of Secrets. This special chancery stood in its own ground, surrounded by a curtain wall of sharp grey ragstone like the buildings it housed within. Athelstan had visited this place before and he certainly wasn't pleased to return. The cloisters of the Secret Chancery exuded a watchful silence, as if something malevolent lurked deep in its shifting shadows. Athelstan knew all about the House of Secrets' impressive fortifications: the leper squint in the gateway and the iron coffer hanging beneath it to receive all kinds of information, some of it spurious, petty, malicious but, now and again, the odd item of valuable news. Athelstan, shortly after he arrived that morning, had also visited the long Hall of Secrets with its six carrels stretching down to the doorway which sealed the steps leading to the arca. Athelstan had also visited the fire pit nicknamed 'Gehenna', under its iron cap in the centre of the bailey. The only place Athelstan had yet to visit was that underground arca. He also needed to view the corpse of the dead clerk Norwic, which had already been moved to the abbey death house.

Athelstan warmed his fingers over a chafing dish as he tried to curb his impatience. Cranston, muffled in a thick blue robe, had been waiting for him at King's Steps. The coroner had provided his companion with a few details, but Thibault had declared that he would fully inform both the coroner and Athelstan once they had arrived. Athelstan squinted at the red-striped hour candle. He had been here for just over two hours and his patience was thinning.

'I know . . .' He leaned across towards Cranston, who was nursing his miraculous wineskin.

'You know what, Brother?'

'That this is important, yes? It's not just murder, wicked though that be . . .'

'Treason,' Cranston hissed. 'Treason and therefore highly dangerous. We are about to join a game of hazard where the loser could end up being torn apart at Tyburn. Ah yes, this game of kings is most perilous.'

Cranston fell silent as the door to the buttery was flung open. Thibault, dressed in his hunting garb, a black cloak slung over his shoulder, swept into the room.

'Sit down, sit down,' he ordered, kicking the door shut behind him. 'You need refreshment? No? Good! I've gulped a cup of Alsace, washed my hands, and now I feel much better. Nothing like a good hunt, is there, to refresh yourself? And the hunt I have summoned you to is much more important.' He gestured at Athelstan and Cranston. 'You are ready?'

'We certainly are,' Cranston replied

'Well, well, well.' Thibault sat down in the chair at the top of the table. 'Let me tell you, and I do so under the Secret Seal. What I say here is *sub rosa*, as confidential as any secret of the confessional.'

'You need not worry about that,' Cranston grated. 'Our loyalty is to the King.'

'And to his noble uncle, Lord John of Gaunt,' Athelstan added, desperate to prevent Sir John replying in a more malicious manner. 'Not to forget your good self.'

'Quite, quite.' Thibault pointed to Athelstan's chancery satchel. 'By all means list the items. I understand you write in a cipher known only to you.'

Athelstan nodded.

'Good.' Thibault waited until Athelstan was ready.

'The root of these present troubles is, in short, that the Crown of England believes that it also has a right to the Crown of France.'

'And my Lord of Gaunt,' Cranston interrupted, 'believes those rights include claims to the Crown of Castile, Aragon and Leon.'

'I agree,' Thibault murmured. 'My Lord of Gaunt is an ambitious man.'

'That truly is an understatement . . .' Cranston fell silent as Athelstan's sandal pressed against his foot.

'Whatever my Lord of Gaunt believes,' Thibault continued, 'our young King also insists on his rights to the French Crown. Naturally, the self-proclaimed Charles VI, together with his great Lords, Orléans, Burgundy and the rest, think differently. Cause enough for war but, at the moment, an uneasy peace holds. However, that peace only masks a secret war being waged along the streets of London and Paris. We need information, so do the French. Now we have a spy, a very good one, Nightingale, who, together with his henchman Starling, and a multitude of others, provide, or used to, detailed information about the French court, be it the movement of troops or the rivalries amongst the great lords.'

Thibault waved a hand. 'Nightingale's principal opponent, of course, is the French Secret Chancery, known as the Chambre Noir, deep in the Louvre Palace. The clerks who work there are known as the Luciferi. We have crossed swords with them on many occasions. The Luciferi, or Light Bearers, work in small cohorts or covens, almost a battle group, each under a leader or custos known as the Magister. They adopt different names and titles.' Thibault paused, eyes blinking, lips moving wordlessly, as if he was carefully preparing what he was going to say next. 'Quite recently,' he continued, 'Nightingale sent warning that the Chambre Noir was organizing a "*cohors damnosa*", a deadly cohort of spies known as Les Mysterieux, under their Magister known as the Key-Master.'

'Who, what, where?' Cranston intervened.

'Sir John, we know nothing about them, except that a very dangerous cohort of French spies has probably been despatched to England. Don't forget, we hunt in a maze where lies are commonplace, falsehoods are portrayed as truths and loyalty conceals the basest betrayal.'

'Which means what?' Athelstan demanded.

'This could all be a fiction, a fable. We don't even know if such a cohort exists. The important thing is that webs are spun and people caught.'

'And your spies, your legion of informants, have discovered nothing here in London or elsewhere?'

'Nothing, Brother.'

'Lord save us,' Cranston breathed.

'And now,' Thibault sighed, 'we make our descent into Hell. Nightingale has become extremely alarmed. Over the last few weeks, many of his informants, his spies, have fallen silent. Nightingale began to feel both haunted and hunted. Haunted by the memory of those he had worked with, men and women whom he viewed as comrades.'

'And hunted?' Athelstan asked.

'Oh, that Nightingale and members of his company were being closely watched. The situation worsened as a number of important informants simply disappeared. The Luciferi seemed to know where they lived and what they did. Just as importantly, information about any war-like preparations of the French along the Narrow Seas and beyond simply dried up.'

'And?'

'And, Brother, we now approach the eye of the storm. Nightingale controlled a net which he spread across Paris. He'd organized that net to inform his colleagues here in the cloisters of the Secret Chancery. In other words, Nightingale dealt with the collection of information, but he always passed everything on to Westminster and the Secret Chancery. Nightingale is most skilled. The net he'd fashioned, the web he wove, provided us with a rich harvest of information about the French.'

'And the net began to break?'

'It certainly did, Brother. But the cause was not in Paris. Nightingale believed his net was being cut, sliced and damaged by someone here in Westminster.'

'How?'

'Someone, Brother, is feeding vital information to the Chambre Noir. Whoever it might be is betraying all our twilight people, with hideous results. As I have said, some of our spies have just disappeared. Others we now know have been taken up, tortured and hanged.'

Thibault rose and crossed to the dresser. He offered to pour morning ale, but Cranston was content with his miraculous wine-skin. Athelstan simply shook his head. 'Now,' Thibault retook his seat, 'we have six clerks cloistered here. They work solely for me. They are in fact the Secret Chancery. They work in the carrels you have visited. They dine here on food and drink prepared by the royal kitchens. They begin work when the bells peal for Prime, they finish at Vespers. By the time the Compline bell sounds, the Secret Cloisters are closed.'

'And you have no reason to distrust any of them?'

'No, Brother, those clerks are my liege men. In peace and war, body and soul.' Thibault's voice trailed away and Athelstan caught the slight doubt in his words.

'And the murder here?'

'We do not know whether Norwic's fall was an accident or murder. All I can say is that last night my principal clerk, Hugh Norwic, came into the House of Secrets. He wandered the cloisters to ensure all was well. He then opened the door to the steps leading down to the dungeon containing our arca. This consists of locked chests and coffers where the Secret Chancery records are stored. God only knows what truly happened. Norwic would, as everyone did, pause on the fifth step down, where there is a wall enclave carrying a lanternhorn which could be quickly fired and used to continue down the steep spiral staircase. Now, everyone knows how dangerous such steps are, each with a razor-sharp edge. Be that as it may, all I can tell you is that the following morning, when the other clerks assembled here, they found the door to the cloisters open, on the latch but unlocked. They found the same when they came to the door leading down to the arca. The door hung open. One of the clerks went down and discovered Norwic's corpse at the foot of the steps, his body wounded in many ways.'

'And anything else? Any other sign of violence?'

'No, nothing disturbed, Brother, nothing amiss.'

'And you think all this might be connected to the troubles faced by Nightingale in Paris?'

'Possibly, Brother. But of course, Norwic's death was not the only one. Last night, the clerks of the Secret Chancery gathered at their usual trysting place, La Delicieuse, only a short walk from here. A most prosperous tavern, which provides all forms of comfort: its principal customers are usually the high-ranking clerks of Westminster, including this place.' Thibault's words held a sharp note of disapproval. 'Last night they assembled there, waiting for Norwic, whom they thought would join them. Of course he failed to do so. We know what happened this morning and their discovery. Later this day, Norwic's henchman, Master Nigel Hyams, visited the tavern. He was in a chamber, locked and bolted from the inside. The door had to be forced; Hyams was found poisoned.'

'Just to clarify matters,' Athelstan intervened. 'This morning Norwic was found dead at the foot of the steps leading down to the arca?'

'Yes.'

'His comrades spent the night before at La Delicieuse? They were all there?'

'No, Hyams was delayed, some business in the city. Late this afternoon, the same Hyams was found poisoned in a chamber at La Delicieuse. Well.' Thibault rubbed his face. 'I cannot make any sense of what is happening. Has the Chambre Noir declared total war against our Secret Chancery? Is it determined to wipe out all that we do here and in Paris? Nightingale's net has been truly split and rent. Two of my most trusted clerks killed within a matter of hours of each other.' Thibault closed his eyes. 'Soon,' he whispered, 'all this will become common knowledge. The Commons will learn of our men being taken; of our ignorance about what is happening along the Narrow Seas or in France. Questions will be asked.'

'Then let us try and answer them,' Athelstan interrupted. 'Let us take these mysteries like beads on a string, examine each before moving on to the next.'

'Which means?'

'The only people who work here are?'

'My six clerks.'

'Anyone else?'

'The Dies Domini.'

'The Days of the Lord,' Athelstan replied. 'And who are these?'

'We hire scavengers, refuse collectors, dung farmers, street cleaners, the lowest of the low. These men are hired to keep these cloisters free of the vermin which can wreak terrible damage in a chancery, gnawing at the wax, vellum, or whatever else they feast on. Our scavengers also empty sacks of waste, discarded and overused parchment – not to mention the many drafts before the final document is written. All this rubbish is taken out to Gehenna, the fire pit in the centre of the bailey.'

'And their names? Why are they called the Dies Domini?'

Thibault smirked and glanced away. 'The lowest of the low.' He murmured. 'We choose men who can neither read nor write, and that includes their own name.'

'Of course,' Athelstan whispered.

'They pose no threat,' Thibault declared. 'We have a cohort of five under their custos or keeper whom we nicknamed Dimanche, the Norman French for Sunday. Each of the others were given a name of the day in the same tongue, so they know which day they must work here in the Secret Chancery. On a Monday Lundi, on a Tuesday Mardi, on a Wednesday Mercredi, on a Thursday Jeudi and on Friday Vendredi. No work is done on a Saturday or Sunday. Dimanche is the only one here for the full five days. They work under his supervision.'

'So apart from Saturday and Sunday, these scavengers work only in the Secret Chancery on their named day? And even then, under the watchful eye of their custos. Not to mention the clerks themselves?'

'Precisely, Brother. All six men are illiterate. They would never know what truly goes on here.' Thibault shrugged. 'Even so, they are still watched, as well as being scrutinized when they leave.' Thibault grinned. 'The Tower bowmen hate them. They complain that our Dies Domini reek to high heaven. Nevertheless, they perform a useful task and keep the House of Secrets, its latrines, the bailey, the parapets and the steps clear of rubbish and ordure.'

'And their hours of work?'

'Between Prime and Vespers, Sir John.'

'So,' Athelstan declared, 'we have what you call the cloisters, the House of Secrets here in Westminster. The house is very secure behind a high curtain wall. There is only one fortified gate, which has a leper squint, through which messages can be left for the Secret Chancery. There are six clerks in all. They work in the carrels which form the secret cloisters, yes? There is a bailey outside and Tower bowmen patrol the curtain wall. The entire place is kept clean by a group of scavengers. Each works one full day a week, under the guidance of the custos, who rejoices in the name Dimanche.' Athelstan tapped the table top. 'Who actually hired the Dies Domini?' he demanded.

'I did,' Thibault replied. 'The custos Dimanche came with a recommendation from Norwic. Once he was appointed, he recruited the others, but he did so under our strict instruction. We needed expert scavengers who could clean, that was the only skill required.'

'And they are scrutinized when they leave?'

'Yes.'

'Are your clerks also scrutinized when they leave?'

'No, Brother, but they are under strict orders that nothing is ever to be taken out of here.'

'And you have found nothing stolen, broken into, nothing suspicious?'

'Nothing, Brother.'

Athelstan caught the note of desperation in this enigmatic Master of Secret's voice. Thibault was frightened and Athelstan sensed the reason. Both Commons and Lords hated Gaunt and his henchman. Once the chaos caused in Paris became common knowledge, Gaunt's enemies and those of Thibault would swarm like a ravenous pack of wolves. Thibault, in the first instance, would be their quarry.

'The clerks, the scavengers. They are all trustworthy?'

'Yes, Brother.'

'And the Tower archers?'

'All good men, sworn and true.'

'In God's name,' Athelstan retorted, 'we have no evidence of a spy here in Westminster. You maintain that a stream of information filched from here has left Nightingale and all his coven in Paris truly vulnerable. Yes?'

Thibault nodded.

'Are you sure it was sent from here?'

'So it would seem.'

'But could the source be from somewhere else?' Cranston interjected. 'Letters from here could have been intercepted.'

'Possibly,' Thibault replied. 'All I can say is that the leak is relentless not piecemeal. Our work in Paris and elsewhere has been shattered, brought to nothing, by this traitor. Someone has deliberately exposed us, left us naked to our enemies.'

'In which case,' Athelstan replied, 'we do need to speak with those who work here.'

'Certainly, they wait for us, but first,' Thibault pointed at Cranston, 'trouble comes in sheaves. As you know, the night-walker, the felon Radix Malorum, is back in London. You must also know that he has proclaimed his return with crudely written proclamations posted at St Paul's Cross, the Standard in Cheapside and on the approaches to London Bridge. He intends fresh outrage, more robberies, and he mocks the King, my Lord of Gaunt, myself, and of course you, Sir John. He is not only a thief, but one who openly revels in his nefarious deeds. He is fast becoming the darling of London's underworld. My spies inform me of toasts being offered to him in taverns and alehouses. He is depicted as a hero and we, including you, Sir John, cast as fools.'

'He certainly has unfolded his banners and raised his standard.' Cranston shook his head. 'It's as if he has declared war on the city and, in particular, its officers and wealthy burgesses. The lords of the Guildhall are as agitated and flustered as hens with a fox in their coop. They are demanding this and that. They want this felon caught and they want it done immediately. I have posted rewards for any information leading to the trapping of this wolf-shead. All the Judas men, the paid informants and the bounty hunters are as busy as ferrets along the streets and alleyways of Cheapside. Our cohort of city bailiffs have been increased, the night watch especially.' Cranston coughed and cleared his throat. 'Master Thibault, like you, I am puzzled. I just cannot understand why an outlaw, a wolfshead who faces the most horrific punishment if he is caught, is so eager not only to return to this city but also to proclaim his return.'

'Gaunt is deeply interested,' Thibault observed. 'He has not forgiven nor forgotten the theft of the Redstone. If you catch him, Sir John, Gaunt would personally tear him apart.'

'I am doing my best,' Cranston continued. 'I have offered rewards to the riffler chiefs who rule the dark-dwellers and their ilk around Whitefriars and elsewhere. Whores and strumpets have been promised generous rewards for any information about this felon.'

'And?' Thibault demanded.

'Nothing so far.'

'The candle burns,' Athelstan murmured, 'time is passing. We must visit where Norwic died.'

'I have more to tell you,' Thibault interjected. 'There is a tavern, La Delicieuse, a most comfortable place only a short walk from here. This tavern is in parts most luxurious, as it should be, for it houses a brothel, a very expensive one. Its owner and principal courtesan is a Frenchwoman who calls herself Heloise Abelard. Whether that is her true name when she was held over the baptismal font is a matter of conjecture. Heloise is most elegant and personable, as are her coterie of young ladies.'

'And her provenance?'

'According to what I have learned, Brother, she is the widow of an English captain, master of a cog which, with everyone on board, was lost during a violent storm in the Narrow Seas. He left Heloise well endowed. She is most successful, and her business at La Delicieuse is a testimony to her skill and acumen.'

'And the clerks from the Secret Chancery visit this place?'

'Brother, they haunt it. It's where they revel after a hard day's work. In fact, it's their second home.'

'Is such a situation wise, prudent?'

'Sir John, I am sure I can spell out your suspicions as well as those of the good friar here. Clerks of the Crown, high-ranking officials in the Secret Chancery, should they be consorting with French ladies of dubious repute? Let me assure you, the clerks have more than satisfied my suspicions, whilst I have also carried out my own searches. Believe me, Heloise Abelard is no friend of the French. Born and raised in Paris, she hates the place. Some nasty experience or other.' Thibault shook his head. 'As I have said, my clerks have assured me constantly of the loyalty of the woman. However, La Delicieuse is, for other reasons, involved in these mysteries facing us. Earlier this afternoon, as already mentioned, one of my clerks, Nigel Hyams, visited the tavern. Now Hyams, like Norwic, was a high-ranking clerk who worked at the heart of the Secret Chancery. God only knows his reasons for visiting the tavern; we have very little information about what actually happened. He was given the Venus Chamber. I suspect he was waiting for some lady to join him. The door of the chamber was locked and bolted from within. Eventually, people became concerned. When they tried to rouse Hyams, there was no reply. The door was then forced and Hyams was found on the bed, clearly poisoned. A notable physician, Giles Argentine, was also present in the brothel.'

'Yes, yes, I have heard of him,' Cranston declared, 'he enjoys a very good reputation.'

'Too true, Sir John. Argentine often visits La Delicieuse and was in attendance this afternoon. He examined Hyams's corpse and declared poison to be the cause of his death; a swift-acting one, because apparently the clerk had been dead for some time, his cadaver found cold.' Thibault drew a deep breath. 'I am glad Argentine was there. He believes the poison was not given before Hyams entered the chamber. Our noble physician suggested that the poison could have been belladonna also called nightshade; both of these have all the speed of a well-aimed shaft.'

'Was there food and drink in the chamber?'

'Yes, some wine but totally untainted. They soaked a piece of bread with it and fed that to the rats that haunt the tavern's cellars. They suffered no harm.'

'So,' Athelstan put down his quill pen, 'we have a house of secrets where the confidential matters it is supposed to guard are gushing out like water from a cracked cup, the loss of valuable information to the Chambre Noir in Paris. Nevertheless, we have no knowledge of who could be responsible or how they have managed to wreak such destruction.'

'Correct, Brother,' Thibault agreed.

'Then we have the death of two clerks who work in the Secret Chancery. Are their deaths, or perhaps murders, connected? Do those deaths have anything to do with the traitor within? Why did they die? And in such a way?' Athelstan shrugged. 'I cannot say. However, we do need to visit the places mentioned in the account, and the sooner the better.'

Thibault, who now seemed to have lost his usual arrogance, took the hint. He led Cranston and Athelstan out of the buttery and along the gallery past the carrels. Athelstan heard the murmur of voices from one of these. He peered in and glimpsed a group of figures hunched around two glowing braziers. He heard the clink of goblets and realized the clerks of the Secret Chancery were relaxing before Thibault summoned them. They reached the end of the gallery and the heavy fortified door fitted into the wall. Thibault hastily explained how the House of Secrets was built over caverns and pits dug centuries ago by the churchmen of Westminster; these served as hiding places against the marauders whose war barges sailed the river and caused great devastation along either bank. Thibault then took off a ring of keys from his belt. He unlocked the door, both top and bottom, and pulled it back on its oil-soaked leather hinges. The Master of Secrets gestured into the darkness, black as pitch. Cranston offered to go down and investigate, but Athelstan playfully tapped the coroner on the stomach.

'Sir John, I will go down. Master Thibault?'

The Master of Secrets took down a sconce torch and thrust it into the friar's hand. Athelstan walked carefully on to the top step and, grasping the guide rope, started his descent. He stopped on the fifth step and peered into the large enclave containing a lantern-horn, tinder and a stout beeswax candle.

'People prefer the lantern, Brother Athelstan.'

'Do not worry, Master Thibault, the torch will suffice.'

'Little friar,' Cranston warned, 'for the love of God, those steps are highly dangerous.'

'I will be careful and, God willing, safe.'

Athelstan continued down, his footsteps echoing eerily. He had seen the likes before. Steep, spiral staircases, winding down into the darkness, a place which had its own defence in its sharp-edged steps. A fall or a tumble would certainly result in savage wounds or death. Athelstan moved cautiously, one hand clasping the guide rope, the other the torch. He could hear Cranston and Thibault talking, their words echoing through the hollowness of this place. At last, he reached the bottom, a great cavern twice as high as a man, stretching into the darkness. Athelstan lit some of the sconce torches fixed into wall brackets. The flames flickered, the strengthening glow illuminating the caskets, coffers, chests and crates, all iron-bound and locked. On each was posted a parchment sheet, which served as an index to what documents each coffer held.

'All the King's secrets,' Athelstan whispered to himself. And what else, he wondered? Did Thibault also keep his secrets here? Athelstan stared around. Despite the locked chests, the friar could still smell the perfume of the chancery, scrubbed parchment, dried ink and wax. Satisfied, Athelstan doused the torches and made his way carefully back to the top where Cranston and Thibault were waiting.

'Questions, Brother?'

'Oh, I have questions, Master Thibault, but for the moment only one. When Norwic's corpse was discovered, was he wearing a dagger belt?'

'Yes, and the blade was still sheathed.'

'Was it now?' Athelstan clicked his tongue. 'Ah well,' he continued, 'it's best if we now meet with those we have to question. The clerks!'

'They are waiting.'

'Good.' Cranston took a generous swig from his wineskin. 'We will meet them where?'

'They are waiting in one of the carrels. Less haste,' Athelstan murmured, walking over to the enclave built into the wall close to the entrance to the arca.

'A jakes cupboard,' Thibault declared.

Athelstan opened the door and went in. The closet was large and airy, the latrine itself made of polished wood, with a turd hole in the middle. Everything was clean and tidy, even the hinges to the door were well oiled. Athelstan sniffed the air and smiled to himself. Someone had been here for a while and filled the passing time with a generous drink of coarse red wine. He left the jakes cupboard. 'Nothing,' he murmured. 'Nothing at all.'

A short while later Thibault, who seemed distracted, eager to please, ushered his visitors into what had been Norwic's carrel. All the candles and lanterns had been lit to create pools of light around the bench where the four clerks sat facing the three stools Thibault had arranged for himself and his two visitors. Whilst introductions were made, refreshments offered and refused, braziers moved to provide more warmth, Athelstan closely studied the four clerks: Vincent Edmonton, Alexander Davenant, Michael Sheffield and Mark Scot. Youngish men, clean shaven, their short hair neatly coiffed. They wore sleeveless houppelandes down to the knee over costly padded jerkins and cambric shirts, whilst soft cordovan boots protected their legs and feet against the creeping cold of such a place. They all sported rings, bracelets and neck chains, with a medallion displaying the royal colours of blue, red and gold. All four clerks wore warbelts with a sheath dagger, as well as pouches for an ink horn and a sheaf of quill pens. For comfort's sake, they were now taking these off, placing them on the ground between booted feet. Athelstan recognized the type; mailed clerks who had proven their worth both in the schools of Oxford and Cambridge as well as on the battlefield. They exuded a self-confidence, yet there was a watchful wariness; after all, they were more accustomed to asking the questions than being interrogated themselves.

'Sir John?' Thibault stilled the murmurs of conversation.

'Yes indeed.' Cranston got to his feet and walked closer to the clerks. 'I have one question to you. On your allegiance to the Crown, do you know anything which might explain why this House of Secrets is no longer that but a cracked pitcher, which loses everything it collects?'

'You imply treason!' Mark Scot, hard-faced and hot-eyed, sprang to his feet.

'*Pax et bonum*, my friend,' Cranston declared. 'I ask these questions on the authority of the King.'

'And our answer,' Vincent Edmonton, smooth face betraying spots of anger, got to his feet and gestured at his comrades, 'I will go on oath, as will they, the most holy oath a soul can take, one sworn over the body and blood of Christ.' He paused to catch his breath. 'None of us, and this includes our two comrades who now lie in the abbey death house, know anything about the hideous chaos and confusion which has swept over our affairs in Paris. We have been instructed by Master Thibault and by our custos, poor Norwic, on what has emerged.' Edmonton raised his right hand. 'Before God we mourn deeply for what has happened, but the blame cannot be laid at our door.' Edmonton let his hand drop and sat down as his comrades shouted their agreement.

Athelstan watched them carefully and, the more he did, the more certain he became that they were telling the truth. Years of sitting at the mercy seat listening to people confess what they had done had honed Athelstan's skill of sifting who was genuine from who was not. So far, in his estimation, these clerks were innocent. He could sense their deep outrage and their anger was real. It was time to intervene. Athelstan rose and nodded at the coroner, who took his seat next to a taciturn, tight-faced Thibault.

'Gentlemen.' Athelstan spread his hands. 'I believe you, and I am sure so does the Lord High Coroner.' Athelstan's words created a stillness. 'So,' he continued, 'let us turn to the death of your comrades. First Hugh Norwic.'

'God's own clerk,' Sheffield declared.

'Skilled and astute,' Edmonton added.

'And the night he died?' the friar continued.

'Brother, we had finished our work. The Vespers bell had sounded. We left for La Delicieuse; you know about . . .'

'Yes, we know, and we will return to that in a while. So, while you departed the House of Secrets, Norwic remained?'

'Yes,' Edmonton replied. 'He often did that before joining us at La Delicieuse.'

'But he never came.' Davenant, the youngest of the clerks, spoke up, his fair face flushed as he rubbed the medallion hanging on his neck chain. 'He never came,' Davenant repeated. 'We thought he must have gone straight home to the chamber he rents above a jeweller's shop not far from the Great Conduit.'

'My searchers have been there,' Thibault interposed. 'They found nothing untoward, either in his chamber or that of poor Hyams.'

'And this morning?' Athelstan turned back to Edmonton.

'This morning, Brother, we all gathered here as the bells rang out for Prime. The door to the buttery was closed. Well, we thought it was locked. After a while we became restless. Norwic was very punctual and never late. Eventually,' Edmonton spoke up, 'I tried the door. It was on the latch, not locked. We became deeply concerned. I went in and my comrades followed. We found nothing amiss until we reached the door leading down to the arca.'

'Stop!' Athelstan ordered. 'Which one of you went first? Who discovered Norwic's corpse?'

'I did,' Edmonton replied.

'Then tell me, accurately, what you discovered.' Athelstan held up a hand. 'Slowly, carefully.'

'I arrived before the rest. Of course, I sensed something was very wrong. The door to the arca hung open. The sconce torches had burned out. I took a fresh one from an arrow chest nearby, fired it and opened the door as wide as I could. The rest were hurrying to join me. I didn't wait but went down. The lanternhorn stored in the enclave had gone. When I reached the bottom, I found it shattered. I shouted up to my companions to bring a fresh one and put it in the enclave.'

'I did that,' Sheffield declared.

'The torch I'd lit was now burning strongly,' Edmonton continued. 'As I said, I reached the bottom, found the lantern shattered and poor Norwic, a huddled, bloodied corpse. It was more than obvious what had happened; indeed, Norwic must have tumbled so swiftly it seemed as if his body had been thrown into the darkness.' He shook his head. 'There was nothing I could do, Brother. I have told you how it was.'

'Very well.' Athelstan stared at the floor, wondering what line of questioning he should pursue. He let the silence deepen, ignoring the whispering amongst the clerks. 'La Delicieuse?' Athelstan lifted his head. 'You frequent that tavern, which serves more than food and drink?'

'Mistress Heloise and her ladies . . .' Edmonton, who had apparently established himself as leader of the group, replied before glancing sideways at his colleagues.

'Master Edmonton?'

Edmonton gave a crooked smile. 'Yes, Brother, it is as you say, we frequent La Delicieuse. We consort with Heloise and her beauties and the tavern is our second home. And why not?' Edmonton spread his hands. 'We are bachelors, well paid and honoured . . . The ladies are warm and welcoming. We laugh, we talk, we even play hazard with them.'

'And other games,' Sheffield laughingly interjected.

'Are you going to ask us,' Davenant interrupted, 'if it is prudent for clerks of the King's Secret Chancery to consort, to mingle, with French courtesans?'

'It certainly catches our attention,' Athelstan replied.

'We have discussed that issue,' Thibault rasped. 'I too would go on oath that we have not discovered a single jot of suspicion against the ladies. Indeed, they seem very settled, happy and content to be here in Westminster.'

'Are you fond of Heloise?'

'We each have our favourite,' Edmonton replied. 'Heloise, however, nursed a deep love for Norwic, and he for her.'

'Truly?'

'Yes, Sir John, truly. I believe she really loved him. She was deeply distraught at his sudden death.'

'Hyams,' Edmonton declared, 'Hyams was also in love with Heloise. But, as I said, her heart was with Norwic, no one else.' Edmonton's words were greeted by murmurs of agreement from his companions.

'And earlier today Hyams died, mysteriously poisoned in a chamber at La Delicieuse?'

'Following the death of Norwic,' Davenant spoke up, wiping the sweat from his forehead, his light blue eyes blinking so as to control the tears welling there, 'we did little work here,' Davenant blurted out.

'Of course,' Athelstan replied. 'That would be understandable.'

'Hyams said he wanted to visit La Delicieuse to ensure that Heloise and her ladies were coping with the news of Norwic's sudden death. Hyams left.' Edmonton pulled a face. 'And that was it. Until we received the news about what had happened at La Delicieuse.'

'Did anyone else visit La Delicieuse earlier today?' Athelstan's question was answered with a chorus of denials. 'Tell me then,' Athelstan continued, 'has anything suspicious occurred here?' The friar spread his hands. 'Anything, be it ever so insignificant?

Anything at all?' He turned to Master Thibault. 'And with all due respect, Sir John has asked you the same question.'

'And I can repeat what I told him at the time: nothing,' the Master of Secrets replied. 'Nothing, because nothing was reported to me.'

'I can.' Edmonton abruptly paused. 'Just one thing.' He put his finger to his lips. 'Yes, just over a week ago, I was working in my carrel. No, I am wrong, I was actually talking to Dimanche, one of the scavengers. Norwic came in, we chatted about minor matters. He did say, however, that the Ghostman wanted to have words with him, because the Lords of the Air also hold secrets.'

'Satan's tits,' Cranston exclaimed, 'what nonsense. Who is this character?'

'The Ghostman,' Thibault replied, 'is an anchorite, a hermit, a recluse.' He waved a hand. 'Whatever. He has an anker-hold in the abbey grounds, built into one of the enclaves close to the crypt. The abbot and his community see no harm in him. The Ghostman wanders the precincts of both abbey and palace. He can also be found squatting in God's Acre where, according to him, he talks to the ghosts and they talk back!' Thibault forced a smile. 'Mad as a march hare but just as harmless.'

'Be that as it may,' Cranston declared, 'what did the mad bugger mean about the Lords of the Air holding secrets?' Cranston's question was greeted with shrugs and shakes of heads.

'Why should he approach Norwic?' Athelstan asked.

'Hugh was very kind and generous,' Edmonton retorted. 'He humoured the Ghostman, let him drink in the buttery and gave him the occasional coin. The Ghostman would then regale him with stories about the ghosts he'd met. Sometimes he'd bring whatever he found in God's Acre; items dropped by the many who cross between the abbey and the palace.' Thibault spread his hands. 'Apart from that . . .'

Athelstan took his seat. He sensed that, for the moment, they had finished with the clerks. He caught Cranston's eye and nodded. Cranston rose and walked away, busy with the miraculous wineskin. Athelstan had urgent words with Thibault, who assured him that the scavengers, the Dies Domini, would now be waiting for them in the buttery. Athelstan then informed Cranston of the same.

'Good,' the coroner exclaimed, 'but first . . .' He turned back to the clerks and raised a hand. 'Gentlemen,' he declared, 'we are about to interrogate the Dies Domini. What do you know of them? What can you say about them? What do they do?'

'They are good workers,' Edmonton replied. 'On the day the appointed scavenger arrives with the custos, Dimanche, they eat and drink by themselves in the buttery. They collect discarded parchment.'

'Stop there!' Cranston exclaimed. 'What do you mean by discarded parchment?'

'Sir John, we continuously write drafts, and do so until we are satisfied that a certain document, be it a memorandum, letter or indenture, is complete and ready for signature or seal or both. We each do that in our carrel. Norwic would then collect the finished documents and personally hand them over to Master Thibault.'

'Either I would come here,' Thibault declared, 'or Norwic would visit me in the royal palace. And, before you ask, Brother Athelstan, Sir John, nothing amiss ever occurred.'

'We keep all documents safe,' Edmonton declared, 'until they are handed over to Master Thibault.'

'And the rough copies, the drafts?'

'Brother Athelstan, I can see where this is leading.'

'Which is where?'

'The discarded documents pose no danger,' Edmonton replied. 'Sometimes we would cut them before throwing them into the wicker basket close to our desk. The scavenger of the day, one of the Dies Domini, as we have jokingly defined them, comes to us before Vespers. He will empty the basket into a sack, which is then taken out to Gehenna, the fire pit in the bailey outside.'

'And you said you knew where I was leading you?'

'Yes, Brother Athelstan. Do you suspect that one or more of these filthy scavengers is a spy? Brother, we write in a clerkly hand in Norman French. We often use a secret cipher. All of this is totally beyond their comprehension and skill.'

'What else do they do?' Cranston demanded.

'They sweep the gallery and buttery and they do the same outside.' Edmonton paused. 'They keep the archers on the parapet safe and warm; they clear rubbish on the steps and walkways. They also ensure the braziers are regularly fed and fired. See for yourself, Brother Athelstan. The scavengers will tell you the same as we have.'

'In which case,' Athelstan replied, 'we must see them now.' The friar got to his feet.

'Gentlemen,' Cranston declared. 'I thank you for your cooperation. Remember, you must remain in Westminster and its environs. You cannot leave, for we shall return to question you again.'

Cranston and Athelstan took their leave and followed Thibault out of the carrel and down to the buttery where Dimanche had assembled his five comrades. Athelstan was immediately struck by how all of them closely resembled Watkin, the dung collector, with their ragged leather jerkins, hose and battered boots. They were unshaven, their hair, moustaches and beards a tangled, stained mess; their eyes, however, looked bright enough – sharp, inquisitive, eager to discover what was happening. They sat either side of the buttery table. Cranston and Thibault took chairs at the top and bottom. Athelstan moved his stool to be close to the coroner.

Thibault made the introductions, talking very slowly as he described what had happened. The Dies Domini sat like children, eyes blinking, mouths gaping in astonishment. Dimanche was their custos, but even he was hard to understand. The scavengers whispered amongst themselves in the jabbing patois of London's poorest. They continued to act like children in the schoolroom, shouting at each other as well as the custos. Cranston rapped the table for silence and the clamour trailed away.

'They know nothing,' Athelstan whispered. 'Nothing at all, do they? Answer me.' He pointed at Dimanche.

'Sir John, Brother Athelstan, that is the truth.' The man spoke slowly. 'Every working day, hence their name, one of my companions here joins me at Prime. We work until the Vespers bell. We keep all areas free of rubbish, especially here in the House of Secrets. Above all we empty the baskets and burn the rubbish in the fire pit called Gehenna.' Dimanche waved a gauntleted hand. 'We come in, we work, we go. We are clad in rags, though we protect our hands with good, strong gauntlets. Sir John, Brother Athelstan, we know nothing about these matters, the business of bustling, mighty men. We cannot help you, except to repeat what I've already said . . .'

A short while later, Cranston and Athelstan left the secret cloisters. Daylight was fading. A cold frost threatened under a clear, icy sky. Athelstan dutifully followed the coroner as he strode down the narrow runnels and slit streets of Westminster. They passed washerwomen beating their clothes, servants hastening on their errands, sharp-eyed pimps and their mammets touting for business. Joy girls, their breasts half naked, jostled with seedy-looking retainers searching for employment. The crippled and the beggars, genuine or not, lurked in the darkness, one hand holding their clacking dishes, the other a dagger. Old hags, chins on their knees, crouched in doorways, sucking their gums begging for coins. Bonfires were burning the day's rubbish, the flames leaping in bright orange tongues. Street vendors offered food on makeshift platters. Taverners and ale-masters stood in the doorway of their shops, bawling for business.

At last, they reached La Delicieuse, ushered into its perfumed warmth by Stygal, who introduced himself and said he would do everything he could to help. He led them up to the luxurious solar with its beautiful, brilliantly hued wall hangings, soft turkey rugs and heavily perfumed braziers.

Lady Heloise, as she styled herself, was waiting for them wrapped in a thick, ermine-lined robe emblazoned with spangles of gold and silver roses. She sat enthroned in a high-backed chair and gestured at the cushioned stools before her. Cranston ignored her. He turned and nodded at Argentine the physician, sitting on a stool close to Heloise. Cranston, still ignoring the lady of the house, took a generous swig from his miraculous wineskin and bellowed at Stygal, standing in the doorway, that he and Brother Athelstan would need chairs similar to the one his mistress now sat in. Once these had been brought in and arranged, Cranston sat down with Athelstan behind him. The coroner loosened his cloak and pointed at the physician.

'I thank you for coming and waiting for us.'

'Sir John, it is always an honour and a pleasure to meet you.'

'Is it now?' Cranston scoffed. 'Well, never mind that. You madam,' he pointed at the pale-faced, red-eyed Heloise, 'have questions to answer.'

'And I will do so, Sir John, though your manner,' Heloise's voice turned brittle, 'renders me nervous.'

'Mistress,' Athelstan intervened, 'we are sorry for your loss. You and Master Norwic were close, yes?'

Heloise, clutching a piece of red satin which she used to dab her eyes, nodded and forced a smile.

'True, Brother Athelstan, we were close, very close. In fact, we talked about becoming handfast, taking our marriage vows at the church door.'

'Mistress,' Athelstan persisted, 'Hugh Norwic could have slipped and fallen or he could have been deliberately pushed. Such a fall in such a place is usually fatal. So, do you know of anyone who would wish Norwic dead?'

'No, no. He was loved and admired by his comrades and others.'

'And the evening he was killed. Were those same comrades here?'

'Yes of course, apart from Hugh and Nigel Hyams, who was delayed by some errand in the city, though he joined us later.'

'And that same Master Hyams returned here today and was poisoned?'

'So it would appear,' Argentine interrupted, cradling the goblet he'd filled. He now raised this in silent toast to Cranston and Athelstan. 'Poisoned he certainly was.' Argentine seemed eager to press the point.

'And with what potion, physician?'

'Brother Athelstan, something swift-acting and deadly. I would suggest plants to be found in many a herb plot: belladonna, or the juice of the lily. Such potions are highly malignant. The mouth absorbs them and, within a matter of heartbeats, the victim feels sudden pain, leading to an even swifter death. I examined Hyams's corpse, now lying in the abbey death house alongside poor Norwic's. The cadaver bore all the marks of a noxious substance. An ugly discolouration to the chest and belly, filthy froth bubbling to a dryness between swollen lips, protuberant eyes and, of course, there was a discharge from both belly and bowel.'

'I must view it myself,' Cranston replied. 'As well as the possessions found on both dead men.'

'All neatly tabulated and listed by the clerk of the death house,' Argentine replied cheerfully.

'We will go there now, Sir John?'

'We certainly shall, Brother, but first let us examine the chamber that Hyams died in.'

Preparations were made. Heloise, grasping a ring of keys, led them out and up a highly polished staircase to what she described as the 'Venus Chamber' on the first gallery. She opened the door and waved them in. Athelstan was immediately struck by how opulent the room was, with its four-poster bed, its velvet, gold-edged curtains pulled back and tied with silver cord. Paintings decorated the pale green plaster walls whilst thick turkey rugs carpeted the floor. The furniture, including the shutters pulled back from glass-filled windows, were of polished elm-wood. Snow-white candles stood primed, ready to be lit, whilst small-capped braziers emitted trails of fragrant smoke. Athelstan walked the chamber, stopping to sniff at the silver-chased jug and goblets. Argentine, who followed them in, declared that the wine found in the chamber had been untainted, both the jug and the goblet used. Athelstan stared around. He could detect nothing amiss or out of place.

'Sir John,' he murmured, 'we are done here, we should be gone.'

They bade farewell to Heloise and Argentine and, wrapped in their cloaks, left La Delicieuse, making their way along the thin runnels and alleyways. The evening had turned cold as the light faded. The noisy bustle of Westminster was quietening. The streets were emptying as people made their way home or thronged into the many taverns, alehouses and cook shops. Clerks and officials of the great houses of the Exchequer, Chancery and King's Bench, as well as the royal households, bustled about. Candle glow and lantern light glimmered through gaps and shutters and half-open doorways. Dung carts trundled noisily, and the stench both from them and the lay stalls crammed with human filth was so over-bearing they bought two pomanders from a chapman. Athelstan gratefully pressed his against nose and mouth, the bitter smell preferable to the reek of the streets. Songs, chant, and the music of flute and pipe echoed merrily, to mingle with the noisy creak of rope and wood as the strengthening breeze nudged the corpses dangling from makeshift gallows, a warning to the night-dwellers now beginning to cluster at the mouth of alleyways. Dogs howled at the gathering dark, bells pealed and fell silent.

Cranston and Athelstan left the royal precincts and entered those of the abbey. The air grew cleaner, the smoke of candle and incense drifting on the breeze. Black-robed monks, cowled and hooded, pattered across their paths. Cranston knew his way and eventually they reached the death house, a long, grim-looking building, wedged between the abbey's massive crypt and the monastic cemetery, a tangle of bush and gorse stretching into the distance. Cranston rapped on the door. Bolts were drawn. A key turned and the door flung open. The Keeper of the Dead, as he styled himself, was a Benedictine lay brother, keen-eyed, thin-nosed and prim-lipped. He beckoned them in, inspected Cranston's seal of office, and led them down the corpse hall. Despite the flickering torches, glowing candles and lanternhorns, the corpse chamber was truly eerie. A place of flickering light and dancing, shadowy shapes. Braziers, herb pots and candles provided fragrance, yet the stench of death and decay was pervasive.

Athelstan crossed himself as they passed corpses sprawled under coffin sheets. The keeper led them to a table at the far end of the hall and pushed back the coverings. Both clerks lay on their backs, arms by their sides, heads tilted sideways. Athelstan, with the help of the keeper, turned Norwic's muscular cadaver over.

'Satan's tits,' Cranston breathed. 'He's a mass of wounds.'

Athelstan did a quick scrutiny and agreed.

'All of them,' the keeper murmured, 'could have been caused by such a fall. Not an inch of the poor man's body escaped.'

Athelstan agreed, then turned to Hyams's remains. The mottled face was now grotesque, the limbs swollen, the flesh on front and back deeply discoloured with purple-red blotches. Athelstan blessed the two cadavers and asked the keeper to cover them and fetch whatever was found on both men. The keeper hurried away and brought back two small leather sacks, tied and tagged at the neck. Hyams's items were fairly paltry: a dagger belt with its narrow knife still sheathed, medallions, a purse of coins, ave beads and a small red satin pouch about two inches square with a stud fastener. Athelstan examined this; it was the sort of purse used to carry a medal, but it was empty except for what felt like grains of dust. Athelstan put it back and moved to the contents of Norwic's sack. Again, the same few items except for one: a small chancery scroll, twisted and torn, the vellum scrubbed time and again so as to be used for scribbling notes or making a draft. Athelstan took the piece of vellum across to a candle and carefully unrolled it. The writing looked almost illegible; then Athelstan realized it was some form of cipher, a collection of numbers and letters with no apparent order.

'A clerk's scribbling,' Cranston declared, coming up behind Athelstan and looking over his shoulder. 'And why should Norwic be carrying that?'

'Sir John, I truly don't know. But it's not that surprising. Clerks carry scraps of their work. Nonetheless, why this piece? Anyway, although you thought we should return to the House of Secrets I am tired, my parish awaits, so I should be gone.'

They thanked the keeper and were about to leave when there was a thundering knock on the door.

'God save us,' the keeper hissed. 'I know who that is: the Ghostman! He plagues my waking hours. There is no point in turning him away. He must have learned of your visit. He will harass me until he finds out why you are here, even though he might forget it within the hour. Anyway, I will let him in.'

The keeper hurried off and returned with his strange visitor. The Ghostman immediately bustled by him, anxious to meet Cranston and Athelstan. He then abruptly stopped and stared at both of them. A lanky figure with hardly any hair, the Ghostman, with his skeletal face, reminded Athelstan of a painting, by the Hangman of Rochester, of the Figure of Death. The Ghostman was a most accurate reflection of this. He stood staring for a while and pointed a bony finger at his two visitors.

'You are here to see the ghosts, aren't you?' His voice rose to almost a screech.

'Well in truth,' Cranston caustically replied, 'we are more interested in the dead than some wandering spirit.'

'Master Hugh Norwic in particular,' Athelstan declared, walking forward. He wrinkled his nose at the sour smell from the Ghostman's black tattered robe, a gift, no doubt, from his hosts the Benedictines. 'You apparently visited Norwic in the House of Secrets, didn't you?' Athelstan asked. 'You said something very strange, how "the Lords of the Air also have their secrets", or words to that effect. Tell me, sir, what did you mean by that?'

'Oh, I don't know. I had messages for him, but I do forget. I also become confused.' The Ghostman tapped the side of his head. 'My wits are like candle flames; they flare up only to sink down.'

'That's all very interesting,' Cranston declared, 'but why are you here now?'

'I don't like you.' The Ghostman pointed at the coroner. 'I don't want to speak to you but him.' He jabbed his hand towards Athelstan. 'I came to ask if you could pray for the ghosts who haunt God's Acre.'

'Which ghosts?' Athelstan demanded, ignoring the keeper's low, muttered groans.

'Puddlicott, Richard Puddlicott. He broke into the King's Treasury when it was stored in the crypt. Caught, he was, and hanged at Westminster Gate, after being taken there in a wheelbarrow. They left him dangling naked, then they skinned him and, as a warning, nailed his skin to the door of the crypt. Puddlicott was thrust out of life. He now wanders the desert between death and the road to purgatory. He needs to go forward into the light, but he feels he cannot. Puddlicott needs help so he comes to me, moving like mist between the headstones outside. He taps on windows and rattles doors. Sometimes he complains; it sounds like an owl hooting in the dark.'

'The Lords of the Air?' Athelstan asked. 'Who on earth are they and what are their secrets? You remember what you said to Norwic?'

'I can't, I can't, but it might come back to me.'

'In which case, my friend, if it does – and only if it does – then journey to my church, St Erconwald's in Southwark. Tell me what you must. Explain what you said to Norwic. If you do, I will celebrate a requiem for Master Puddlicott, and we shall pray solemnly for the repose of his immortal soul.'

'Will you really, Brother?'

Athelstan held up his right hand. 'I solemnly promise.'

Cranston and Athelstan made their farewells of the exasperated keeper and the witless Ghostman. They left the abbey precincts, crossing to King's Steps, where Flaxwith and his bailiffs were waiting. Cranston would take no argument from Athelstan but insisted that two of Flaxwith's 'lovelies' would escort the friar back to St Erconwald's. Athelstan was too tired to protest. He clambered into the great war barge and immediately fell asleep in the canopied stern. The bailiffs roused him once the barge berthed close to the steps of St Mary Overy, teasing the friar that he had fallen asleep so deeply, even the turbulent journey across had not disturbed him.

Athelstan tried to tell them that he was now home, but they insisted on walking him to his church. Eventually they reached the long alleyway leading down to St Erconwald's. Athelstan paused at the noise and light pouring out through the door of The Piebald tavern. He instinctively knew that something had happened. He peered inside. What Athelstan called the 'second church in his parish' was crammed with the faithful and not so faithful. He groaned at what mischief might be brewing. He crossed himself, thanked the bailiffs, and strode into the cavernous, sweet-smelling taproom. He was correct! Something had occurred. Joscelyn, the taverner, was holding court from behind the beer table, flanked by the usual worthies – Watkin, Pike and Crispin, as well as Radulf and Malak. The rest of the congregation squatted on stools, benches or canvas bolsters. Athelstan glimpsed Benedicta sitting by herself on a wall bench. She caught his glance and raised a hand. Athelstan crossed to meet her. Immediately the tavern fell silent.

'What is it, Benedicta?' Athelstan asked in a strong, carrying voice. 'Why the excitement?'

'Not excitement, Father,' Watkin protested. 'But horrid theft and hideous sacrilege.'

'What?' Athelstan demanded.

'My relic,' Radulf yelled, getting to his feet, 'the Holy Face, Brother! The Holy Relic of Lucca has been stolen from your church!'

PART THREE

Merke: to note, to write

Athelstan sat in the cushioned, throne-like chair in his chantry chapel, built close to the Lady Altar on the left side of the nave. He sighed, crossed himself and gestured at Benedicta. The parish council had nominated the widow-woman as their speaker. Athelstan had arranged to meet her, so he had risen early that morning, celebrated a dawn Mass and broken his fast, before hurrying down to meet his parish council. Virtually every member had turned up, all with their different theories about what had happened. Athelstan had tried to impose order and had asked the council to confirm the election of its speaker, whom he would meet, along with the principal witnesses, which included Radulf, Malak, Watkin, Pike, as well as Mauger the bell clerk. Once the council meeting had ended, they had assembled here in Athelstan's pride and joy, for the chantry chapel was a place of warmth, comfort and deep peace. Turkey rugs deadened sound, whilst the stained-glass window, with its celebration of scenes from the life of St Erconwald, provided rays of gloriously dappled light.

'Father?' Benedicta sang out.

'Oh yes, let us see,' Athelstan replied. 'We had a meeting last night in The Piebald; the councillors met and now I meet their emissaries. So I am here, all attentive. Let us begin. No,' he gestured at Radulf, 'just Benedicta.'

'Yesterday afternoon,' the widow-woman began, 'I closed and locked the church door. Radulf and Malak had placed their precious relic on the altar here in this chapel.'

'Yes, yes,' Athelstan murmured, 'I had agreed to that.'

'Watkin and Pike were cleaning the church,' Benedicta continued.

'Again yes, they were listed for that task.'

'We did a good job.' Watkin blurted out. 'We filled my barrow with dirt, leaves, twigs . . .' Watkin's voice trailed away.

'I locked both the corpse door and the Devil's door,' Benedicta declared. 'The two side entries into the nave. The sacristy doors, both within and without, were also secure. We eventually left by the postern gate in the main door, and we left the church under the guard of Crispin and Mauger. Father, that's all I can say.'

'And when was the theft detected?'

'Oh, I am sorry.' Benedicta's fingers flew to her lips. 'I should have mentioned that. Anyway, Father, I came back into the nave just to check all was well. You asked me to, remember? Before dusk closed in?' Athelstan nodded in agreement. 'I went into the chantry chapel; nothing was disturbed except that the relic was gone.'

'The relic was heavy, yes?'

'It would be difficult to conceal, Father, very heavy and cumbersome to carry,' Radulf declared, clambering to his feet. 'Heavy and cumbersome,' he repeated. 'And that is the mystery. If the thief tried to carry it across the cemetery, they would have stumbled and staggered. Anyone could have seen them – Thomas the Toad, not to forget my two daughters,' Radulf added wryly, 'who often frequent God's Acre.'

'Oh yes they certainly do,' Athelstan quickly intervened, before anyone could make a salacious remark. 'So,' Athelstan declared, 'we have a heavy, cumbersome relic removed from this chantry chapel and somehow taken through locked doors. Even if such a miracle occurred, the thief and his plunder would have crossed God's Acre, and then what?'

'If they crossed the concourse,' Malak spoke up in a growl, his hairy face twisted in concentration, 'surely they would have been seen?'

Athelstan raised his hand in agreement. Radulf and Malak were correct. The thief would have been seen and stopped.

'So,' Athelstan straightened in his chair, 'we have a theft which cannot be explained in any way.'

'There can only be one conclusion, Father.'

'And what is that, Watkin?'

'Father, the thief would have found the relic very heavy.' Watkin rose to his feet and gestured around the church. 'I suspect the thief has hidden the relic somewhere in or around St Erconwald's; in particular the church, with all its recesses and cavities.'

'Watkin, you have a way with words.'

'Remember, Father, I was training to be a guild clerk before I buggered off to war.'

'Of course. Anyway, do continue.'

'As I said, Father, the thief either hid his plunder here or, God forbid, the cemetery outside.'

'Which is a bewildering tangle of trees, gorse and funeral plinths,' Athelstan declared. 'So, what do you suggest? What can we do?'

'We have a solution,' Watkin trumpeted. 'We need your permission, Father, to search both the church and cemetery!'

'Logical enough,' Athelstan replied, sketching a blessing in the air, 'and you may begin now.'

The parishioners needed no second bidding but sprang to their feet. Athelstan called out for Radulf and Malak to remain with him. Once Mauger and Benedicta had shepherded the others out and closed the chantry door, Athelstan indicated the two men should sit down on the wall bench. Athelstan moved his chair closer to them.

'Who are you?' he began. 'Who are you, what are you?' He stared at Radulf, the man's blond hair brushed back to reveal a bold, brazen face. He had narrow blue eyes, his upper lip was sliced, probably a dagger cut which gave a strange twist to his face. He was garbed in a dark brown houppelande over a murrey-coloured jerkin, patched hose on his legs, worn boots, and an even more tattered dagger belt. Malak was dressed no better; he was almost a dwarf, who seemed to live constantly in the long, deep shadow of his comrade.

'Who are we, what are we?' Radulf echoed Athelstan's question. 'We are what we seem, Father. We are your parishioners. True, years ago, I left. I had to. My wife was killed in a street accident along Cheapside. At the time Malak and I were working as tilers.'

'But not on roofs,' Malak intervened. 'Neither of us can tolerate heights.'

'Our reluctance to climb on to a roof,' Radulf declared, 'meant eventually work dried up. My wife was dead, I could find no real work, so Malak and I decided to travel, and so we did.'

'And your two daughters?'

'Brother Athelstan,' Radulf struck his breast in sorrow, 'I confess, I failed them, but that is my nature. God forgive me,

I am feckless, irresponsible and selfish. But what could I do for two little girls? Clarissa and Cecily were entrusted to an ancient aunt then living in the parish.'

'So you and your,' Athelstan gestured at Malak, 'companion went on your travels, leaving those two little girls to fend for themselves?'

'In the best way they could, Father. Better be joyous girls here in St Erconwald's than beggar maids in the city. They now own their own house in Pigsnout Alley.'

'Yes, I blessed the place for them; it's very tidy, fragrant and pleasant. You lodge there?'

'Oh yes, Father, most comfortable.' Radulf smiled, his sliced lip now more pronounced. 'They have created and offered me the most luxurious lodging.'

'And now what brings you back to Southwark?'

'Homesickness, Father,' Malak grated. 'And we are both growing older. Life can be hard.'

'We were in Paris last winter,' Radulf explained. 'Father, it was gruesome. The plague swept away tens of thousands. The Hôtel-Dieu and other hospitals were filled to overflowing. Corpses sprawled in heaps at every crossroads. Cut-throats prowled through the dark. Winter set in. The Seine froze, and ravenous wolves sloped into the city and attacked the living in Montmartre. We soon decided to leave, moving to the coastal ports of Boulogne and Calais. Once there we took passage to Dover.'

'Was it in Paris where you bought that?' Athelstan pointed to the twisted piece of bronze which hung on a chain round Radulf's neck.

'Oh yes.' Radulf looked down, as if studying the pendant for the first time. He glanced up and grinned. 'A gift,' he declared, 'from the Vagabond King who rules the underworld in Paris. Malak and I intervened in a tavern brawl near the Porte St-Antoine and saved one of his henchmen from a dagger thrust.'

'Did you now? And did you become part of the Vagabond King's entourage? His retainers?'

'No.' Radulf shook his head.

Athelstan nodded, staring at both men, shifty as moonbeams. He believed they were born villains, attracted to mischief as Bonaventure to a dish of cream.

'Tell me,' he asked, 'the Radix Malorum, do you know anything about that felon?'

'Of course,' Malak scoffed, 'everyone knows about the Radix Malorum. Many of the poor of London see him as their champion.'

'He's a thief; a housebreaker.'

'True, true.' Radulf shook his head. 'But he emerged when we were long gone. As we must now be, Father. The Great Hunt of the Lord has begun and we must recover our most holy relic.'

Athelstan gave both men his blessing and they left. Once they had, the friar closed his eyes. He was murmuring a prayer to the saintly Erconwald when the Devil's door was flung open and the hangman, garbed in his usual black, strode into the chantry chapel. He carried large sheets of dark stained parchment, tied together with chancery twine.

'Giles, Giles.' Athelstan rose and walked forward to help.

'No, no, Father.' The hangman's chalk-white face was laced with sweat. 'You call me Giles, but I am the hangman.'

'To me you are Christ's brother, held over the font as Giles of Sempringham. But what do you want now? What are you carrying?'

'Drawings, Father.'

'Of what?'

'A fresco for the church. Something really soul-catching to bring our sanctuary to life. A magnum opus, to be placed either side of the sacristy door. You must see them, Father, I need your approval. I am going to call it the *Dance of Death*. Years ago, when I was a scholar, I visited churches along the Rhine. I was always taken by such frescos. We need one here, Father. It would make our church even more attractive. A hallowed place, a sacred spot where souls can come, study our paintings and reflect on eternal truths.'

'Very good.' Athelstan grinned. 'Giles, you would make a good Dominican. But we cannot discuss the matter here so, my friend, come.'

Athelstan grabbed his cloak and led the hangman out of the church, striding along the coffin path to his house. As he did, Athelstan noticed his parishioners now busy in the cemetery. Under Watkin's direction they were concentrating on one part of God's Acre, scouring it completely, before they moved on to another.

'Could take weeks, Father,' the hangman gasped. 'Heaven knows where it could be or what else is buried here.'

'Giles, I agree with you, but first things first.'

They reached the priest's house. Athelstan opened the door and the hangman staggered in and draped the thick vellum sheets over Athelstan's chancery table. The friar followed him in and stared around. All was well. The fire was banked. The small buttery looked clean and tidy, as did the bed loft and the small recess beneath.

'Do you want some morning ale?'

'No thanks, Father.' The hangman patted the vellum sheets. 'Father, I know you are busy but please take a look at these. I cannot tarry, I must join the rest.'

Athelstan agreed; he opened the door and watched the hangman leave, striding down the coffin path to join the rest of the searchers.

'God save us all,' Athelstan prayed. 'The hangman is correct; Heaven knows what they'll find there.'

Athelstan stood in the doorway staring across God's Acre. The cemetery was really a sprawling heathland, a great stretch of common land. The friar was genuinely worried at what they might find. According to what he'd learned from Cranston and others, St Erconwald's had once been the haunt of outlaws, sorcerers, warlocks, and a veritable legion of thieves. Rumours abounded about murder victims being thrust into ready-made graves along with weapons, stolen goods, as well as the remains of infernal midnight sacrifices.

Nightingale, the English spy, had not left Paris. He had changed his mind. He had moved to a crumbling tenement near the Porte St-Denis, a shabby chamber belonging to Jean-Luc, his lover, who worked as a common servant in the Chambre Noir. Jean-Luc had sent him details in a begging letter brought by a street swallow. A short note, written in the agreed cypher. Jean-Luc had also informed his lover how the Chambre Noir was working into the early hours of the morning, burning candles down to the stump. New plots were being fashioned. More traps and lures hidden away.

Nightingale had replied in the usual way, offering to visit Jean-Luc's shabby chamber. He would do so at noon every day for one week. In the meantime, Nightingale had kept moving, never staying too long in any one place. Now he was hastening back along the runnels as the church bells tolled for the Angelus at noon. The streets were crammed and dark. Nightingale hugged the shadows. He kept his eyes sharp as he shoved his way through a huddle of mopsies with their dyed hair and garishly painted faces. These ladies of the night were arguing with a gaggle of market wives, their filthy repartee cutting like arrows through the air. Fur-gowned burgesses gave the warring ladies a wide berth. Nightingale did the same, even as he glimpsed a royal courier armed with his white wand of office. The courier was forcing his way through a knot of truculent men-at-arms, ragged and bearded. Nightingale sensed danger and slipped into a doorway. He let the courier and the men-at-arms pass before moving out to merge with a line of pilgrims making their way to the tomb of St Genevieve.

The narrow streets reeked with different odours, noisy in the extreme. Nightingale just prayed that he'd escape from anyone who might be hunting him. At last, he reached Rue Corbeil. He shoved his way through a group of noisy scholars celebrating the Feast of Fools, then slipped down an alleyway before turning right, up shabby stairs to his meeting place. The door hung half open. Nightingale drew his dagger. He pushed the door further back. Jean-Luc lay sprawled against the filthy bed, one hand covering the wound in his side, which was soggy with blood.

'Sweet Lord.'

Nightingale crouched beside Jean-Luc, who opened his eyes and smiled wanly at him. 'Good to see the Nightingale,' he slurred.

'What happened, who did this?'

'I have been watched,' Jean-Luc replied, 'and I made a mistake. I was coming here. At the crossroads a fiddler approached me to ask me what tune he should play. I let my guard slip and him too close. He lunged at me with his dagger. I closed with him, a deadly stab, then I staggered here. I don't think I was followed. The fiddler sorely wounded me and I did the same for him. Ah well, listen. Use this, my friend, as best you can. I am not a clerk but a common servant, a retainer in the Chambre Noir. I keep my eyes sharp, my ears attentive.'

'What is it?' Nightingale demanded.

'Let those,' Jean-Luc gasped, 'for whom you work know that a decree has been issued.'

'What?'

'Cranston, yes, that's what he's called. The Lord High Coroner in London.' Jean-Luc closed his eyes. Nightingale looked pityingly at his comrade. Small bubbles of blood stained his lips. Nightingale, a mailed clerk, knew enough about wounds to realize his friend would soon be beyond all earthly help.

'No, no don't pity me,' Jean-Luc whispered. 'Listen, Cranston has a friar friend, a Dominican. The Luciferi know all about these two. They regard both the coroner and friar as highly dangerous to the Chambre's enterprise at Westminster.'

'And, my friend, what else?'

'As I said, the Chambre has issued a decree to be carried out immediately. I overheard this as I served refreshments in the refectory at the Louvre, where the Luciferi gather to eat and drink and gossip amongst themselves.' Jean-Luc paused, coughing and gagging on the blood gathering at the back of his throat. 'They didn't see me. I was in an enclave behind a curtain. Cranston and his friar are to be killed. But how, when, where, or by whom, I do not know. Somebody must have glimpsed me either hiding there or leaving the enclave. I am a mere servant. They would not know where I lived. So,' Jean-Luc gasped, 'they despatched an assassin to follow me. Anyway, warn them.'

Nightingale closed his eyes. He also knew about Cranston and Athelstan. Master Thibault often referred to them. The Secret Chancery at Westminster had to be alerted. Nightingale fought the urge to flee as he sat and watched his comrade slip into death.

'There's nothing to be done for you, my friend. Nothing at all.'

Nightingale stayed for an hour, crouching before Jean-Luc, reciting the prayers for the dying. The grievously wounded man eventually gave a loud sigh as his head sagged to one side. Nightingale pressed his fingers against Jean-Luc's throat but could detect no blood beat. He closed the dead man's eyes and threw a cloth over his face. It was time to leave. He gathered a few possessions, including the purse of precious coins that he and Jean-Luc had hidden in a gap in the poorly plastered chamber wall. Nightingale stroked and kissed Jean-Luc's cold, dead brow. He then slipped down, out into the streets, determined to flee Paris and reach Westminster as swiftly as possible.

* * *

Athelstan sat before the fire in his priest's house and tried not to listen to the shouts and clatter echoing across God's Acre. Three days had passed since his return from Westminster and he had been compelled to act as a silent witness to the chaos which now engulfed his parish, both the church and God's Acre. The disappearance of the Holy Face of Lucca had swept the parish. Urged on by Watkin, Pike and Radulf, the devout and not so devout of St Erconwald's had been drawn into the 'Great Hunt of the Lord', as Radulf constantly described the search being carried out. Both the church and God's Acre were now under constant guard, day and night. Watkin and his henchmen had even set watches on the approach to London Bridge, as well as on the roads going south.

'So far,' Athelstan murmured, 'nothing.'

He stretched out and stroked the sleeping Bonaventure. The tomcat stirred, meowing to itself.

'I know, I know, my brother,' Athelstan comforted. 'You have been sorely disturbed, but all things pass and we must make use of another day in paradise here at St Erconwald's. Time to work.'

Athelstan rose. He let Bonaventure out. They crossed to his chancery table where he had laid out pieces of parchment under small weights. He sharpened two quills then sat down, staring into the fire.

'The Radix Malorum,' he murmured, and began to write down all he had learned. The Radix was certainly arrogant, cocksure of himself; a most skilled burglar and housebreaker. The Radix had plundered the wealthy residences along Cheapside then, about sixteen years ago, he had disappeared after stealing the precious ruby, the Redstone, from John of Gaunt's treasury in the Savoy Palace. This truly audacious robbery had embroiled two of St Erconwald's parishioners, Watkin and Pike, who, at the time, had been carrying out their nocturnal task of cleaning streets and emptying lay stalls. Both men and their cart had been most rigorously searched. The two hapless dung collectors had been closely interrogated but not one shred of evidence had been found against them. Indeed, Athelstan considered this very amusing. He couldn't, even in a flight of fantasy, imagine Watkin and Pike as skilled burglars.

'What else do I know?' Athelstan thought. The Radix Malorum, he continued to write, had disappeared after the theft of the

Redstone. Why? The sale of the ruby, difficult though it might be, would have provided the felon with enough wealth for the rest of his life. In which case, why had he returned now? And why publish his arrival for the world to see and marvel at? He seemed intent on proclaiming himself. Parishioners, returning from the city, had informed Athelstan about how the Radix was still posting proclamations across London. But why and why now?

Athelstan was intrigued by it all, even though it was not really his business. He had been drawn into this mystery out of his deep sympathy for Cranston, whom the Radix was so brazenly mocking. The Lord High Coroner should not be so publicly shamed.

'So,' Athelstan whispered, 'I am hunting you, Master Thief, but I need to know more about you.'

Athelstan continued making notes. The only pointers he had discovered to anything about the Radix was the work of that tireless bounty hunter, Boniface, a man used to hunting wolfsheads both in Southwark and beyond. He was the only one who seemed to know anything about what the felon did. He had told Cranston what he knew when he was dying in the hospice at St Bartholomew's. And what was this? That the Radix was the first three letters of each word and how the bishop and the corpse knew the whereabouts of the Redstone. What could all this mean? The mumbled rantings of a feverish, dying man? Who was the bishop? Who was the corpse? Athelstan sighed in exasperation. He rose and opened the door at Bonaventure's entreaties and insistent scratching.

'Come in, brother cat,' Athelstan declared. 'How is it in the noisy cemetery?' The cat just slumped down before the fire.

Athelstan closed and locked the door and returned to his studies. He wrote a new title on the piece of parchment: 'The Secret Cloisters'. Athelstan reflected for a while then began to write, his sharp quill pen racing across the parchment in his own unique cipher. No doubt, he wrote, there was a traitor in or around the Secret Chancery. How he, she or they managed such treason was truly baffling. The Dies Domini, that gaggle of illiterate scavengers posed no threat whatsoever. Moreover, Athelstan was more than convinced about the loyalty of the clerks and believed their relationship with the ladies at La Delicieuse was innocent and harmless enough. So how did the traitor flourish so vigorously?

'Perhaps I am looking in the wrong place,' Athelstan

murmured. Is the traitor someone beyond the walls; a courier, a messenger? 'I must return to Westminster and soon.'

He needed Sir John's advice, but the coroner was busy hunting the Radix. The only message Athelstan had received from the coroner was that they should meet in The Lamb of God on Sunday evening just after Vespers. Athelstan had replied that he would, and wearily concluded that all he could do was to continue to speculate on what truly did happen in the House of Secrets on that fateful evening.

Once again, Athelstan reviewed what he had learned. Norwic, the principal clerk, had stayed late, probably a common enough occurrence, to check all was well before doors were locked and the place made fully secure. He must have strolled past all the carrels, inspected them, then reached the reinforced door leading down to the arca. Norwic must have opened this and walked down the first few steps so as to light the lantern. And what then? If someone stole up behind him, why didn't Norwic turn around, draw his dagger and close with his opponent? Or was the killer as stealthy and silent as Bonaventure on the hunt? Whatever did happen, one thing was certain, Norwic fell and tumbled violently down those hard, sharp-edged steps, his head and body suffering deadly wounds. And the assassin, if there was one? He must have, silent as a shadow, followed Norwic on to those steps, but how did he escape notice? How did he get into the cloisters in the first place? Did he follow Norwic in, or was he waiting for him inside? And finally, how did he leave?

'He acts as if he is invisible,' Athelstan murmured to himself. 'He enters and leaves, yet no one sees or notices him either within or without, including his victim. He murders a mailed clerk then disappears like dew under the sun. True, both the door to the carrels and that leading down to the arca were found open, but that was all.' Athelstan tapped the table. Was there anything to add? Athelstan returned to his writing. Norwic himself? Athelstan didn't have a shred of evidence to support his theory, but he truly believed Norwic was deeply distracted. Why? Because of the lovely Heloise? Or was it Thibault's anger at a possible traitor lurking in the House of Secrets? Then there was that piece of parchment found amongst Norwic's belongings at the abbey death house. What was that? What did it mean? Athelstan wrote on then glanced up. He really must return to Westminster but, until then . . . Athelstan continued writing. Why was Norwic carrying that piece of parchment? Did it have any real significance? And that eerie creature, the Ghostman. What did he mean when he told Norwic that the Lords of the Air also had their secrets? Was that just a farrago of nonsense from a demented man?

Athelstan rose, stretched and began to pace up and down. And Heloise and all her lovely ladies at La Delicieuse? Were they as innocent as they appeared? There was certainly a paradox here. Heloise and her companions were French, yet Thibault's scrutiny of them had not unearthed anything injurious. Indeed, the ladies, Heloise in particular, had no love for Paris. 'And that,' Athelstan exclaimed to himself, 'brings us to Master Hyams.'

This clerk had been absent for a while on the evening that Norwic had been killed. Where had he been? In the city? Or was it Westminster? Athelstan lifted his head. 'Well,' he informed the darkness, 'we shall never know now.' And on the afternoon he was poisoned, why had Hyams visited La Delicieuse? Who was he really waiting for? And his death? Argentine was a leading physician. He had assured the coroner that the poison Hyams must have swallowed was swift in its effect. Nevertheless, the source of that poison could not be traced to anyone or anything. The jug of wine and goblet found in the chamber had not been tainted in any way. So how did Hyams die? Athelstan crossed himself. At the moment he could make no sense of it.

The friar decided he had reflected enough. He glanced around and noticed the sheets of vellum which the hangman had brought across. Athelstan laid these out on the floor, knelt down and began to study them. The more he did, the more he marvelled. The hangman was proposing a tableau about death, and the different drawings showed that no one escaped from it! The figure of Death stood grinning behind the Pope and the Emperor on their thrones. He grabbed the abbess by the arm as she left her choir stall. He tapped the canon on the shoulder before the end of his sermon. Athelstan turned the parchment over, noticing how the hangman had introduced death into every aspect of life. Be it the priest giving a sermon or the doctor at his books. The astrologer amongst his instruments, the money-lender counting his gold, the drunkard swigging in the port house, the knight fighting at a tournament suddenly realizing his antagonist was Death. A blind man tapping with his stick was led away by a bony hand. A judge looked up from delivering sentence to sit in terror at Death's awful grin. The priest carrying the viaticum through the streets suddenly learnt it was Death, that bony, skeletal figure, ringing the warning bell before him. Even the fool, laughing to himself and sticking straws in his hair, realized he had a grisly, gruesome companion in his games.

Athelstan continued to sift through each of the drawings. They were precise and detailed. He wondered about the cost but, there again, the parish purse could well afford it, thanks to the generosity of Sir John and even Master Thibault and John of Gaunt. Athelstan put the vellum sheets in the small recess beneath the bed loft, then went and sat on a stool, staring into the fire. Studying the hangman's paintings had been a diversion. Yet the deaths he had to investigate were shrouded in a fog of mystery. Why?

Athelstan posed the same question to Cranston when they met in The Lamb of God the following Sunday evening. Athelstan had only been too pleased to escape from his parish and its absorption with the 'Great Hunt of the Lord'! Watkin and all his motley crew were as busy as ferrets, scrambling around both church and cemetery. Matters were not helped by the hangman beginning what he called his magnum opus. He had been truly delighted by Athelstan's praise of the drawings he had submitted, as well as his unstinting support for the venture. The hangman acted as swiftly as he could in case Athelstan changed his mind. The fresco was set to appear in the sanctuary either side of the sacristy door, so furniture, and anything in the way, had been cleared away and neatly stacked behind the high altar. Athelstan had become a bemused observer of all this frenetic activity, even though his mind was still probing the mysteries confronting himself and Cranston. At last, on Sunday evening, he had left the keys with Benedicta, asking her to keep a sharp eye on what was happening, then left to join Cranston.

He found the coroner in a sombre mood. The Radix had posted fresh mocking declarations around the city. These were pinned where the Radix knew there would be no watch by the legion of would-be informants. These now swarmed through the city, hungry for the generous rewards for 'information leading to the capture and successful prosecution of the notorious felon calling himself the Radix Malorum'.

The coroner sat silent as Athelstan listed the questions to which he could find no answer. The friar described in detail his reflections on the murderous events at Westminster. Now and again, Cranston would interrupt with the occasional question. Once Athelstan had finished, Cranston sat back whistling under his breath. He glanced sharply at the friar and sensed his companion's tension.

'What is it, little friar?'

'Nothing as yet, Sir John. Just sharing my thoughts with you and, as I do, I suddenly realized I glimpsed something strange this afternoon but I cannot sift the gold from the dross. Sometimes, Sir John, my wits become befuddled and my mind cloudy. I feel as if I am in a room from which there is no escape, and all I can do is walk round and round. Anyway . . .' Athelstan paused at a knock on the door and the buxom, blonde-haired hostess bustled into the room, fanning her red, flustered face with her hand.

'Sir John, Brother Athelstan, my apologies. You have a visitor. A strange-looking creature who calls himself Dimanche.' She paused. 'Isn't that French for Sunday?'

'It certainly is, my pretty,' Cranston explained. 'Show our visitor in but first ask him what he would like to eat and drink.'

'I heard that, Sir John,' Dimanche replied, standing in the doorway behind Mine Hostess. 'A jug of ale would suffice.'

'Come in, man,' Cranston shouted.

Dimanche shuffled into the room, clutching a cudgel. He leaned this against a wall bench and took the seat that Cranston indicated. He mouthed his thanks, exclaiming how he was so sorry to disturb them.

'Why are you here?' Cranston demanded, once the visitor's ale had been served by the coy, pretty maid.

'I come as a representative, Sir John, for the Dies Domini.' Dimanche spoke slowly, trying to keep his speech clear.

'Oh yes, but why?'

'They are frightened, Sir John. They know something dreadful has happened but they, we, can only protest our innocence. We are poor men. I come in every day but the other five only once a week. We are scavengers, the poorest of the earthworms. Sir John, we are terrified at whispers about treason being committed. Of you being on the hunt. Of whoever is arrested being torn apart, hanged, drawn and quartered at Tyburn or Smithfield. We are just scared.'

'Don't be,' Athelstan soothed. 'But now you're here, can I repeat a question I asked time and again on this matter. Did they or you see anything suspicious?'

'No, Brother, we can report nothing.'

'And the clerks?' Athelstan turned and glanced swiftly at the door, disturbed by a clatter from the taproom.

'There are only four customers,' Dimanche declared. 'It's Sunday evening and they are all sottish.'

'And the clerks?' Athelstan repeated.

'They are good men, Brother, faithful and loyal. They give us alms and do speak kindly to us.'

'And Norwic, the dead clerk?'

'A keen clerk, Brother Athelstan. I know little about him, except what we have learned from the gossip; that he and Hyams were deeply smitten with one of the ladies at a nearby tavern.'

'Heloise at La Delicieuse?'

'Yes, that's it. Norwic seemed most distracted by her.'

'Yes, yes, of course.' Athelstan smiled to himself. At least one hypothesis was correct. Norwic's mind must have been elsewhere, and Heloise was the cause of this.

'By the way, who appointed you?' Cranston demanded.

'Norwic did. He wanted a scavenger to act as custos, as well as five others. I heard about his notice posted at St Paul's. I have been a scavenger in this city and elsewhere. I was appointed by Norwic and my first task was to select five others, and that was hard. Brother Athelstan, we look for lasting work – one day a week is not . . .' Dimanche stumbled over the words that his raucous voice could not pronounce. 'One day a week,' he repeated, 'is not attractive to the likes of us. Ask the dung collector in your parish, he would agree with what I say. That's how I got my job. I promised Norwic that I would recruit five men who would each work one day a week. I promised I could do that. Norwic was pleased and that's the way things . . .' He stuttered to a close at the sound of a door banging open and shut followed by a muted scream.

Athelstan held his hand up for silence as he felt the sweat on his back trickle cold. Something was wrong. Some evil mischief was drawing close. He gestured at Sir John and Dimanche to remain seated, rose and opened the door leading into the taproom. He glimpsed a corpse lying in a widening pool of blood, quickly closed the door and leaned against it.

'What is it, Brother?'

'Sir John, we are under attack. There's a corpse sprawled in the taproom.'

Cranston sprang to his feet, drawing both sword and dagger from his belt that had been slung across the wall bench. Athelstan grasped a wooden hammer used to loosen shutters, Dimanche grabbed his cudgelled walking stick.

'There's no need for either of you . . .' Cranston murmured.

'Nonsense,' Dimanche rasped.

'We are committed!' Athelstan exclaimed.

They both followed Cranston silently into the taproom. Three corpses sprawled there, another simply hung back in his chair, mouth gaping, a crossbow bolt embedded deep in his chest. A nightmare scene. Everything looked normal except for those gruesome corpses. Candles and lanterns still glowed. The fire burned merrily. Tables, chairs and stools stood undisturbed whilst the slayings had not yet soured the air.

Cranston, despite his bulk, was as light on his feet as any dancer. He edged forwards towards the kitchen door which hung slightly open. Candlelight and the smoke from the ovens still seeped out. Cranston reached the door, peered through the gap then beckoned Athelstan to do the same. The friar did so and fought back the urge to scream. The spit-boy lay gasping on the floor. The two women, Mine Hostess and her maid, were now hanging from ropes loose over the roof beams. They had been gagged and bound, their attackers, six in number, were now stripping the women of their clothes whilst wolfing the food they'd found. The eyes of both women betrayed their terror as they twirled on the ropes which held them just above the floor.

'Now,' Cranston whispered. Then his voice rose to a shout. 'For the King, the Crown, England and St George.' The coroner kicked the door open and burst into the kitchen. Cranston raced forwards, sword and dagger twisting, flashes of razor steel which bit into one outlaw and then another. Both men collapsed, screaming, as their wounds bubbled blood like broth in a bowl. Athelstan swung his mallet as another attacker slithered forward, dagger raised. The assailant, however, lost his footing on the greasy floor. He crashed to the ground and fell prostrate as Athelstan brought the mallet down on to the man's exposed head.

The friar swiftly gazed around. The spit-boy was stirring; the two women, still bound, groaned and moaned. Cranston had cornered two more assailants whilst Dimanche was beating another senseless. Athelstan grabbed a stool and swiftly cut the women's bonds. He helped each of them down to sit close to the spit-boy so they could comfort one another.

The struggle was now over. Three of the assailants lay dead; two more had deep, grievous wounds. Only one had survived and now knelt on the floor, hands behind his head. Cranston seemed enlivened by the clash. He loudly thanked Dimanche and despatched the scavenger to the Guildhall to summon Flaxwith and his bailiffs to The Lamb of God. The coroner pressed one of his seals into Dimanche's hand and told him it was urgent. Cranston, with Athelstan's help, moved everyone, including the corpses, into the taproom. Once there, Sir John went through the dead men's possessions, but only found a few paltry items. Flaxwith and his comitatus soon arrived, a host of armed men filling the taproom. Cranston ordered four of these to take Mine Hostess and her two companions up to a chamber, promising them that the tavern would now be placed under constant guard. Once Mine Hostess and her two companions had left the taproom, Cranston pointed to Flaxwith.

'Henry, give each of the wounded the mercy cut. They are beyond all help.'

'Sir John,' Athelstan intervened, 'is that really necessary?'

Cranston, however, was no longer the jovial coroner. He seemed cold and distant, a warrior on the battlefield surveying the dead and wounded.

'They came here,' he rasped, 'to perpetrate hideous crimes; now they are wounded grievously. If you wish, Brother, bless them, but do it swiftly.'

Athelstan hastened to obey, moving from one attacker to the other, providing a final blessing and absolution. Once he had finished, Flaxwith dealt each of the wounded the mercy cut. Once done, he had their corpses dragged out into the tavern yard along with the others. Athelstan, fearful of Cranston's change of mood, watched as the coroner pulled their one remaining prisoner to his feet, dragging him back and forwards across the taproom, its floor now soaked in blood.

'Look what you've done,' Cranston bellowed. 'You've turned my paradise into a slaughter house.' Cranston's voice rang like a trumpet. 'It's no better than a flesher's yard. So, who sent you?' Cranston shoved the wolfshead against the wall, pulling back his hood and dragging down the visor across the outlaw's face. Athelstan watched. The man looked what he was, one of the denizens of London's nightmare-ridden underworld. He was garbed in cloth and battered leather, shabby boots on his feet, whilst his face was almost hidden by his uncombed hair, moustache and beard. He was understandably terrified at Cranston, and fell to his knees moaning, hands outstretched as he begged for mercy.

'Tell us,' Cranston retorted, 'what you are doing here?' He crouched down to confront the outlaw. 'Your companions are dead, soon you will be. All you have to decide is whether you die swiftly or will you be hacked, sliced and gutted on a public scaffold? Do you understand that?'

The man, eyes all fearful, mumbled that he did.

'So, what is your name?' Cranston pulled the man up and made him sit on a stool whilst he stood over him. 'Your name?' Cranston repeated.

'Roughneck.'

'Well-named. For whom do you work?'

'No one.'

'Fine.' Cranston pointed at Flaxwith. 'String him up by his hands, bring a dish of burning charcoal.'

Flaxwith hastened to obey. Roughneck was strung up just above the floor, his battered boots pulled off. Cranston, using a cook's glove, filled a bowl of flaming charcoal from one of the ovens and pushed it beneath Roughneck's bare feet. The man screamed, desperate to escape the flames. The air turned foul, reeking of scorching flesh.

'Now you know what it's like,' Cranston bellowed. 'And we

will continue this until you have no feet left to walk on. Now, who sent you?'

'Foxglove.'

'Ah yes, the riffler chief. To do what?'

Athelstan watched the man struggle against his bonds, desperate to move his feet.

'Why did he send you?' Cranston bellowed.

'To kill you, Cranston, and your friar friend.'

'Ah, I suspected as much.'

'Sir John,' Athelstan pleaded, 'cut him down.'

'I certainly shall.' Cranston snapped his fingers and Flaxwith, who had removed the burning dish, cut the prisoner's bonds. Roughneck collapsed to the floor. 'You were sent to kill me and Brother Athelstan, why?'

'I don't know. Sir John, I truly don't know. Foxglove gave the order to organize a comitatus. He said there would be no danger. On a Sunday evening, The Lamb of God would not be busy. We were to wait for his signal.'

'I see. So, Foxglove kept The Lamb of God under scrutiny. He would see me arrive, followed by Athelstan and our good friend here.' Cranston gestured at Dimanche. 'You entered armed with crossbows. The four poor buggers drinking there died within heartbeats, and then you went to the kitchen. You were tempted, weren't you? Diverted by two plump pretty ladies, as well as the fine food heaped on platters.'

'Our leader Wormwood was a fool,' Roughneck gasped. 'He said you could wait. He was hungry, thirsty, and wanted his pleasures first.'

'Stupid bastard. Right, put his boots back on, and when the rest of the comitatus arrive, we will pay Master Foxglove an unexpected visit.'

Within the hour, Cranston and Athelstan were leading an armed cohort out of The Lamb of God, now securely guarded, marching along deserted streets and runnels. The dark-dwellers and night-hawks, the sewer squires and the rest fled at the harsh sound of boots and the clatter and clash of steel. The torches carried by some of Cranston's comitatus sparked and spluttered in the night breeze, the smoke floating out to merge with the usual stench and stink. They reached Whitefriars, the haunt and home of London's underworld, the prowling ground of the daggermen and a host of other felons. They moved like wolfpacks keen for the hunt, sloping through the darkness, searching for their prey. These all scattered at Cranston's approach. The coroner remained tight-lipped, sword and dagger drawn. They turned into Purgatory Alley. Cranston quickened his pace, marching up to the entrance of a narrow, two-storey tavern, standing in its own grounds, with a huge battered sign advertising The Roaring Pig.

'And soon it will,' Cranston exclaimed as he approached the double doors: he gave them a violent kick and both flew open. Cranston, Athelstan and the comitatus burst into the bitter-smelling taproom. The shadowy figures, grouped around the table of the taproom's one and only window seat, sprang to their feet. Athelstan heard the scrape of steel and glimpsed the flash of blade as these shadow men drew sword and dagger. They came around the table, crouched at the ready, edging towards Cranston and his cohort. However, once they realized who they were facing, the shadow men receded.

'Jack Cranston here,' the coroner bellowed. 'I have come for you, Foxglove, and your henchmen. In fact, I have brought one of your familiars with me.' Cranston raised his hand and snapped his fingers. Flaxwith dragged forward the hapless Roughneck, who had moaned continuously as he was force-marched on his wounded feet through the streets. Roughneck was thrown down before Cranston, two bailiffs standing either side of him with flaring torches. 'Recognize him?' Cranston bellowed. 'The only survivor of that murderous coven you despatched to The Lamb of God to kill me. They apparently did not, but they murdered four of our King's subjects and abused two of my favourite ladies. Foxglove, they are all dead except for Roughneck here, and he has made a full and frank confession.'

A crossbow whirled through the darkness and caught Roughneck full in the face, blood and bones splattered out. Cranston roared his battle cry and swept forward with his men. Athelstan retreated to the safety of a wall bench behind the buttery table. He watched the fight. It was soon over. Foxglove's resistance was futile. The riffler chief was totally outnumbered and his dagger boys no match for Cranston's comitatus of former men-at-arms. Foxglove was wounded and disarmed. The rest of his coven were shown no mercy. They were hacked down, whilst those wounded were given a swift mercy cut. The riffler chief was bound to a chair and dragged into the centre of the taproom. Cranston leaned over and squeezed the man's wounded shoulder until he yelled in torment.

'Good,' Cranston shouted at the balding, frog-faced riffler chief. 'Foxglove, you are responsible for four murders and two rapes. Just as importantly, even more so, you have attacked me, the King's Lord High Coroner in this city, and that is treason. You also attacked Brother Athelstan, protected and patronized by the Lords Spiritual. You will be excommunicated, but that is only the beginning of your sorrows. You will face swift arraignment before the justices of King's Bench and be sentenced to suffer the full rigour of the penalty for treason. Or, there again,' Cranston's voice turned merry, 'you could be hastily despatched here and now, hanged from the sign which advertises this benighted place. So, who paid you to carry out that dastardly attack?'

'Have you caught the Radix Malorum, Fat Jack?'

Cranston leaned forward and grasped the man's shoulder again until Foxglove screamed in agony. 'Don't worry about the Radix Malorum; every fool has his day and you've had yours. So, who paid you and why?'

'He was French.'

'He?' Cranston demanded. 'How could you tell?'

'I don't know, it could have been a woman. My visitor came here, a swordsman flanked either side. He offered me eight freshly minted gold coins. Four now, and four when the task was completed to their satisfaction.'

'The task?'

'Your death and that of the Dominican.'

'I see. So, you chose a Sunday evening when I and the good Friar would be ensconced in my small solar at The Lamb of God?'

'Yes.'

'And you despatched Wormwood to carry this out?'

'I made a mistake; I should have chosen better.'

'Well, you can discuss that with Wormwood when you meet him in Hell sometime in the next hour. So, this visitor, male or female, but definitely French yes? They placed a bounty on my head and that of the good friar here. Why?'

'I don't know but they said that if it was to be done, it was best done swiftly.'

'And you have no proof of who they were or why they wanted us dead?'

'None, Fat Jack. And you will have as much chance of finding them as you do the Radix Malorum.'

Cranston ignored the jibe as he roughly went through the prisoner's pockets. He smiled as he pulled out a purse and shook the gold coins into his hand.

'I have found this here, haven't I? Henry,' he shouted across at his chief bailiff. 'You are my witness. I have taken four gold coins which I will deposit in the Guildhall treasury. In the meantime,' Cranston straightened up, 'seal this place. It is now, together with all its movables, forfeit to the Crown on the proven charge of high treason by its former owner, who rejoiced in the name of Foxglove.' Cranston clapped his hands. 'Have the dead removed to the great charnel house of St Mary Le Bow. Then . . .' Cranston kicked the leg of Foxglove's chair, 'hang this bastard from his own sign.'

Cranston swept out of the tavern, Athelstan hastening beside him. They were forced to stop at the top of the alley; a horde of dark-dwellers had poured out of their filthy castles, the many cellars dug beneath the row of ancient houses. Ravenously hungry, the dark-dwellers had captured and slaughtered a wandering hog. They had built up the bonfire, burning the rubbish of the day so that they could roast and toast the meat. The night watch had arrived but the dark-dwellers insisted on cooking the slabs of meat laid out across the flames on makeshift grills. The air was a thick fug of smoke, fat and burning meat, and the sheer sweaty dirt of those feasting on their macabre bloody banquet. Cranston intervened to support the watch. Athelstan sheltered in a shop door and glanced up at a sign, a twisted bronze bar. Athelstan peered closer and he read the inscriptions around it and realized the house must belong to one of the many steeplejacks whose guild was always needed by the hundreds of city churches and their steeples. He recalled the sign of The Roaring Pig, and walked out of the doorway and stared back down the alley. The sight was gruesome. Foxglove had been hanged from the sign of his own tavern, and both sign and corpse twisted in the breeze.

Athelstan had offered the man the last rites. Foxglove, however, had simply spat on the floor, so the friar had given him a cursory blessing and followed Cranston out. Athelstan returned to the doorway. Flaxwith and his bailiffs, who had secured and locked The Roaring Pig, now joined Sir John and were trying to placate the dark-dwellers. Eventually some sort of peace was imposed. Cranston beckoned Athelstan over and placed a hand on his shoulder, peering down on him.

'As you would say, monk . . .'

'Friar, Sir John, and what would I say?'

'Sufficient for the day is enough evil thereof. The Lady Maude and the two poppets await me.'

'And my parish likewise, Sir John. I bid you goodnight but, tomorrow, I need to return to Westminster.'

'I'll send Tiptoft with both the time and place. In the meantime, two of my lovelies will escort you safely back to your beloved parish.'

PART FOUR

Lacche: to snatch

In the end, four days elapsed before Tiptoft arrived at Athelstan's house. Cranston's courier told him what he knew already. That news of the battle in The Lamb of God and The Roaring Pig had swept the city. Proclamations, providing lurid accounts of this fight to the death, were posted throughout Cheapside and beyond, alongside more taunting jibes at the coroner's inability to catch the Radix Malorum. Athelstan half listened to the messenger's chatter as he reflected on what progress had been made in the 'Great Hunt of the Lord'. In a word: none. The searchers had combed the church and were now concentrating on God's Acre, the death house, and even Athelstan's little cottage. Certain interesting artefacts had already been unearthed, including a tattered ledger of accounts for the parish. The manuscript had been slipped into a good calfskin pouch and, for reasons unknown to anyone, buried in an ancient tomb at the far side of the cemetery. Athelstan had leafed through its soiled paper, noting with amusement how members of the parish still figured prominently, even though the first entries were almost eighteen years old. The accounts must have been the work of the priest at the time, for the writing was clear and clerkly. Abbreviations had been used such as 'Wa. D. C.' for Watkin, the dung collector. Athelstan showed the ledger to Mauger, who confirmed the manuscript was the work of the priest at the time, adding that the ledger certainly pricked his memory on certain matters. Mauger said he could not recall them now but promised that, if he did, he would inform Athelstan.

'Brother, brother.' The friar broke from his reverie and smiled at Tiptoft's anxious face.

'I am sorry,' he apologized, 'I was lost in my thoughts.'

'Father, I have a barge waiting at Southwark Steps.'

'Then come, my friend.'

Cranston was in fine fettle when Athelstan met him in the buttery at the House of Secrets. The coroner was dressed in a dark blue, sleeveless cotehardie, over a jerkin of the same colour. Athelstan also glimpsed the snow-white rim of a cambric shirt. Cranston always dressed like this when he had received good news. The coroner was lounging in a seat at the top of the buttery table, on which he'd draped his cloak, sword belt and beaver hat. He sprang to his feet as Athelstan entered. They embraced and exchanged the kiss of peace. The coroner then served the friar a stoup of morning ale and raised his own in toast. Athelstan replied then stared around.

'What is happening, Sir John?'

'Nightingale, Thibault's man in Paris, has returned safely. The Chambre Noir was hunting him but he escaped, hale and hearty. He is now closeted with Thibault. Ah, I hear our master's footsteps.'

Thibault bustled into the room. He looked happier than before, one hand on the shoulder of a red-haired young man with a pale, narrow face and sharp eyes. He looked as if he had been freshly shorn, shaved and bathed. He was garbed in a dark murrey cotehardie, no jerkin beneath, just a simple shirt with a warbelt strapped around his waist. The man took this off, placing it on the wall bench.

'This is Thomas Rishanger,' Thibault declared, 'known to me and others as the Nightingale.'

Cranston and Athelstan shook hands with the new arrival, then took their seats.

'He is known as the Nightingale,' Thibault continued, 'because what he sings through the dark is always pleasing to us. Information about whatever mischief is being brewed in the Chambre Noir. However, that is now a thing of the past. Our Nightingale has fallen silent and his songs have stopped. But first,' Thibault held up a hand, 'Sir John, I have heard about all that happened at The Lamb of God and elsewhere. The murderous and treasonable attacks on you and Brother Athelstan by the felon Foxglove. I have shared this with Nightingale.'

'Undoubtedly,' the spy replied in a low, modulated voice. 'These rifflers were hired by the leader of a small battle group lurking here in London, known as Les Mysterieux, under their custos, the Key-Master. One of the reasons for my great haste here was that

I have learned that the Chambre Noir had ordered both of you to be killed.'

'Look,' Athelstan answered, 'Nightingale, I will call you that, but could you first describe yourself. What you do, as well as your perception of the challenges which,' Athelstan shrugged, 'confront everyone here.'

'Brother Athelstan, I am Thomas Rishanger,' Nightingale began, taking a sip from the tankard he had been given. 'I am the son of an English mother and Gascon father. I was trained in the service of the English Crown at the halls of Oxford and the schools of the Sorbonne. I am fluent in many languages, and skilled at cipher, whilst I have served in the royal array as a mailed clerk.'

'And Paris?'

'Nightingale was despatched by me,' Thibault intervened, 'about seven years ago in the retinue of Lord Audley. The good envoy returned, but Nightingale stayed to weave a web across Paris, including the Chambre Noir.'

'And what was this web?'

'Brother Athelstan, I gathered a "flock of birds" around me. Men and women who worked in the Louvre, the Palace of Fontainebleau, the Hôtel de Ville, and similar places. I collected chatter and gossip. I reaped a harvest of information, some of it useless, but other items most valuable. I despatched these to the House of Secrets here at Westminster.'

'And any replies?'

'They would be dictated by us,' Thibault explained.

'Is it possible,' Athelstan asked, 'if the traitor, or traitors, are those who bring such messages back and forth?'

'No, no, Brother Athelstan. If that was the case, we would soon discover who it was. Moreover, I doubt if a tinker or a chapman would be able to understand the ciphers we use. True, there could be Judas men amongst our many couriers.' Thibault sighed. 'But that is not the real problem.'

'So what is?'

'Master Thibault,' Nightingale intervened, 'has described me as spinning a tight web across Paris, particularly the Chambre Noir and the palaces of the Valois. Those I employed were bringers of secrets; men and women who work quietly, close to the lords of power in Paris. People who would scurry backwards and forwards deep in the shadows.'

'And?' Cranston repeated.

'And, Sir John, it is these who have been betrayed. Someone here at Westminster has informed the Chambre Noir of those involved in our enterprise – not just the names, but their work, where they live, what auberge and cook shops they frequent.'

'And?'

'These men and women began to disappear and continue to do so. I have seen my confederates hanged at Montfaucon or stabbed, deep in some filthy alleyway. This was the fate of our most recent casualty; my good friend, Jean-Luc. He worked in the Chambre Noir and heard about the decree for your total destruction.'

'Well, we are prepared for that threat,' the coroner replied. 'I have Flaxwith and his comitatus,' Cranston stretched out and patted Athelstan on the shoulder, 'and our good friar not only has my bailiffs, but also his parishioners.'

'A formidable wall,' Athelstan added wearily. 'But come,' he smiled at Nightingale, to whom he had taken an immediate liking, 'we have a traitor here at Westminster. He, she or they have broken through our guard to steal information which should be kept secure both here in the carrels as well as the arca below.'

'Correct,' Thibault whispered.

'And the real intent of our hidden enemy,' Athelstan declared, 'is to destroy – in fact I would say, *annihilate* – the web that Master Nightingale has spun over Paris and beyond.'

'Correct,' Thibault agreed. 'The names, dwelling places and other information relevant to all those who are part of our web. The problem is twofold. Our spies, but also the information they bring us.'

'Such as?'

'Brother Athelstan, troop movements around the English enclaves in France, the gathering of war cogs in their harbours. Some of what's handed over to us can be trivial, but all such information is drying up because the sources are being swiftly destroyed.'

'How many comrades have you lost, Master Nightingale?'

'I would say about thirty.'

'Thirty.' Cranston whistled under his breath. 'Satan's tits.'

'And there is at least the same number again fleeing for their lives or in hiding.'

'And how long since this crisis broke?'

'About two months,' Thibault replied.

'So we have it.' Athelstan tapped his sandaled foot against the floor. 'So we have it.' He repeated. 'Correct me if I am wrong, but the Secret Chancery is losing vital information. We are being betrayed. The Chambre Noir discovers all our secret designs, but the real damage is the total destruction of our cohort of spies in Paris. So, where do we begin?'

Nobody answered this question.

'Ah well, Master Thibault, Nightingale, can you explain this? I found it on Norwic's corpse.'

Athelstan dug into his chancery satchel and handed over the square of parchment. Thibault unfolded it, drew a candle closer and, with Nightingale looking over his shoulder, studied the cipher written there. Thibault smiled and glanced up at Nightingale.

'Hammes Castle,' Nightingale declared, retaking his seat. 'Hammes Castle in Calais. It's a report on what supplies and impedimenta are being stored there. Information which the French might find helpful if they were considering a siege, though not vital. What is more curious,' Nightingale glanced at Thibault, 'is why Norwic was carrying such a document. Look, it's out of date.' He pointed to scribbling in the corner of the parchment. 'The thirteenth of January – the Feast of St Hilary. So why,' Nightingale shook his head, 'was the principal clerk in the Secret Chancery keeping an out-of-date memorandum about Hammes Castle? Perhaps,' Nightingale pulled a face, 'he just picked it up by mistake, intending to destroy it.'

'Then leave it.' Athelstan took the piece of parchment back. 'Let us move on. Les Mysterieux, you've already mentioned them?'

'The Chambre Noir,' Nightingale sat back in his chair, 'have what I call battle groups: each has a Magister or master. Les Mysterieux, from what I gather, is led by an individual who calls himself the Key-Master.'

'And the number.'

'Each cohort or battle group has six to twelve members.'

'Both male and female?'

'Both male and female, Brother,' Nightingale replied. 'Each

member is a peritus, highly skilled in a certain art, be it ciphers or any form of mummery. Indeed, I use that word correctly. Les Mysterieux resemble some travelling troupe, their play a mystery, a masque, albeit a murderous one. I would say . . .' Nightingale paused, 'yes, from what I've learned, Les Mysterieux are probably the most skilled and highly dangerous.'

'They are certainly well named,' Athelstan murmured. 'Look,' the friar rose to his feet, 'Sir John, Master Thibault, my good friend Nightingale, I would now like to wander this cloister of secrets, this place of undoubted intrigue and murder. I want to watch and observe,' Athelstan shrugged, 'to get the very essence of this place.'

'By all means,' Thibault replied. 'If you wish, go down into the arca, Edmonton has the keys. And you, Sir John?'

'I have business here in Westminster,' the coroner pointed at the friar, 'but I know where to find you.'

The meeting broke up. Athelstan began his wanderings. He visited the carrels where the clerks were hard at work. Edmonton paused in his writing to inform Athelstan that the Blackrobes of Westminster had taken care of the corpses and funeral rites for their two murdered comrades.

'You believe both were murdered?'

'Yes, Brother, I do. Norwic knew how dangerous those steps were. Look, Brother, he went up and down them constantly. He was sure-footed, cautious and prudent. He must have been pushed.' He sighed. 'But for the life of me I cannot see how anyone could approach so close without alerting him. Norwic had keen sight and even keener hearing. He was a mailed clerk. Look at the floor of this building. Dust and gravel make it very difficult to walk silently, Brother. Ah well. Perhaps Norwic did hear something, whatever that might be, so he turned and slipped. But,' Edmonton crossed himself, 'God rest him, I believe Norwic was pushed. He was murdered.'

'Was Norwic distracted by anything in the days leading up to his mysterious death?'

'Distracted,' Edmonton smiled. 'Of course he was. Deeply smitten with the Lady Heloise. Brother, he could not stop talking about her. He was infatuated with her.'

'And she?'

'Likewise, Brother, he loved her and she him. I really do believe they hoped to marry, but I cannot say that for definite.'

'And Master Hyams?'

'It must be murder! Nigel was also smitten by Heloise, but she was not in the least interested. Strange man, Hyams. I believe his rejection by Heloise rankled deep.'

'Did it affect his relationship with Norwic?'

Edmonton closed his eyes, lips moving soundlessly. He then glanced at Athelstan. 'God forgive me, Brother, but I think Hyams was very jealous. He and Norwic used to be friends. I suspect they died enemies, though more than that I cannot say.' Edmonton pointed at the manuscripts on his desk. 'The candle burns and I must work.'

Athelstan continued his walk along to the door sealing off the steps down to the area. He studied the two locks and turned, going back to the buttery. The room was empty, so he continued out on to the cobbled bailey. The day was bitterly cold and a hoar frost still clung tenaciously to the stonework of both the house and wall. Dry leaves chased each other across the cobbles. Noisy crows flocked, screeching and cawing before disappearing into the mist.

Athelstan stared up at the parapet wall, where the Tower bowmen tried to remain vigilant whilst doing their best to protect themselves from the biting breeze. Braziers crammed with flaming red coal provided some warmth. Athelstan watched one of the Dies Domini, probably Jeudi, Thursday, also creep along the parapet wall with his sack and rough brush, which he used to sweep away the dirt, dead leaves and other debris. Athelstan watched for a while, then moved to inspect the fire pit, using its steel-edged pole to lift the heavy casing laid over the flames, which darted up and down like fireflies. Jeudi came down from the parapet. He emptied his sack of rubbish into the pit, then kept it open whilst he hurried off to collect a basket of discarded parchment, which he also fed to the flames. The scavenger grinned at Athelstan, lips curled back over filthy yellow teeth. The man lifted his hand and scurried off. Dimanche came out into the bailey with a small sack of rubbish, which he also emptied into the pit.

'A job well done,' he declared throatily. 'Good morrow, Brother.'

'*Pax et bonum*, my friend. Please assure your comrades that we have no case to present against you or them. Indeed, my grateful thanks for your assistance last Sunday.'

'Oh yes, the battle at The Lamb of God.'

'You cast about like a veteran cudgel-man.'

'Brother, you live in Southwark. You know how you must be prepared to defend yourself against all kinds of villainy. I am sure the likes of Watkin, the dung collector, would confirm the truth about this. Anyway, I need to press on but first, some refreshment.'

Athelstan watched him go and wondered if he should visit the Ghostman. He followed Dimanche into the buttery. The scavenger was now busy at the lavarium, washing his hands. He hastily pulled on his thick gloves.

'My apologies, Brother,' he declared hurriedly. 'I thought you might be Edmonton, or even Master Thibault.' He fell silent at the sound of footsteps outside.

Cranston swept into the room, accompanied by two strangers. Athelstan recognized fellow Dominicans, garbed in the usual black and white, though each of these also had a silver chain around his neck with a shimmering medallion. Athelstan swallowed hard, his mouth turning dry. He knew who these were.

'Brother Athelstan?' Cranston could hardly control his temper. He pointed to the taller of the two Dominicans, a bald-headed, harsh-featured man with a hook nose over thin, bloodless lips. 'This,' Cranston repeated, 'is Brother Thomas and his companion . . .' the coroner pointed to the second friar, pale and young, face oiled and shaven, hair neatly cut to display a perfectly formed tonsure.

'Jean de Cahors,' the Dominican replied swiftly, before Cranston could finish the introduction. 'Brother Athelstan, we are . . .'

'Inquisitors,' Athelstan muttered. 'You work for the Inquisition. You question possible heretics and schismatics. But what does that have to do with me? What province are you from?'

'The Inquisition!' Brother Thomas snapped back. 'We owe allegiance to our master general, as do you, and to his Holiness Pope Urban VI.'

'As do I,' Athelstan retorted.

'In Heaven's name,' Cranston grated. 'What on earth are you two doing here?'

'Outside,' Brother Jean answered, 'are two lay brothers

despatched by your superior, Prior Anselm, to ensure that you return with us to your motherhouse at Blackfriars.'

Cranston looked as if he was going to intervene. Instead, he turned on his heel, went out and brought back the two lay brothers.

'Have no worries,' he rasped. 'Brother Athelstan will go with you. Now,' he pointed around, 'you may be what you are, but I am the King's officer, not some featherhead. So,' he demanded, 'how will you go to Blackfriars: by barge, or walk along the riverside?'

'We arrived last night,' Brother Thomas replied, 'we crossed the Narrow Seas from Boulogne. That's where we have our house.' He forced a smile. 'The seas were very rough. So, we will ignore the river and go by road.'

Cranston didn't say a word. He lifted a hand in salutation to Athelstan and left. Once he had gone, the inquisitors, accompanied by the lay brothers either side of Athelstan, left the royal precincts of Westminster. Locked deep in his own thoughts, Athelstan was hardly aware of the vigorous walk. He wondered how this threat had emerged. He accepted that he enjoyed a reputation for promoting and defending the rights of the poor. He had openly sympathized with the Upright Men and the Earthworms who had led the Great Revolt the previous year. In addition, church officials such as Archdeacon Tuddenham were deeply suspicious of the way Athelstan sometimes flouted the strictures of canon law and the rights of Holy Mother Church. Athelstan accepted the world was changing. New threats and challenges were emerging to confront the Church. Different groups challenged the powers on high with their cry for the Church to divest most of its wealth, pomp and ceremony. Such debates raged within his own order. Many Dominicans lived and worked alongside the Earthworms. On the other hand, the Dominicans also emphasized their title, a play on the words '*Domini Canes*' – the 'Hounds of the Lord'. Some Dominicans saw themselves as the defenders of the faith and the hunters of any who dared infringe the rigid orthodoxy of the hierarchy. However, what had he done to attract their attention? Athelstan remained deep in thought, unaware of the weather, the gusty river breeze and the different smells it wafted.

Daylight was fading as they reached Blackfriars. They left the winding streets and entered the soaring mass of the Dominican motherhouse with its gables, tinted roof tiles and cornices sculpted in the shape of gargoyles, wodewoses, monkeys, angels and demons. They entered the inner precincts by a postern gate, the two lay brothers leading them into the cavernous chapter house with its oiled linen windows besides those filled with painted glass. Prior Anselm had already been alerted of their approach and was waiting for them in a small council chamber adjoining the main chapter room. The prior's ascetic face was wreathed in concern.

He glanced pityingly at Athelstan as they exchanged the kiss of peace, gesturing at the friar and his two companions to take seats either side of the table. A servitor hurried in to light more candles and rush lights, as well as move the capped braziers closer to those around the table. The rest made themselves comfortable. Athelstan stared at the bleak white plastered wall, bereft of any adornment except for a stark black crucifix. A door opened, wafting in the stench of the sulphur mixed with the mud outside. A man strode in, bowed at the assembled company and took the chair next to Prior Anselm, now sifting manuscripts on the table before him. Athelstan kept his face impassive even as he quietly cursed. The new arrival was Archdeacon Tuddenham, with whom Athelstan had often crossed swords, and it looked as if that was about to happen again. Prior Anselm rapped the table then intoned the '*Veni Creator Spiritus*'. Once he had finished, Athelstan sprang to his feet.

'What is all this?' he declared heatedly. 'Why am I here? What have I done?'

'Brother Athelstan, sit down,' Prior Anselm said softly. 'Please sit down.' Athelstan did so. The prior picked up a long sheet of vellum on the table before him and passed it to Athelstan. 'Read, Brother,' he demanded. 'Read carefully. Please note the costly vellum. The clerkly hand. The expensive ink. The language used, Norman French, the tongue of both court and Church. This document must be taken most seriously.'

Athelstan half listened as he swiftly read the allegations against 'Athelstan the Dominican parish priest of St Erconwald in Southwark'. As he read, Athelstan had to curb the fear curdling his belly. There was the expected accusation about him being a peasant priest, hand in glove with the likes of Parson John Ball, but then the indictment turned more vicious. Accusations were levelled that Athelstan was a secret supporter of the Leicestershire priest, John Wycliffe, who had tried to rewrite the theology of the Church. Wycliffe had also attacked the wealthy clergy, but then he moved on to more dangerous themes; Wycliffe rejected the temporal authority of the Pope and the pre-eminence of priests, which led him to deny the doctrine of transubstantiation: the power of priests to transform bread and wine into the body and blood of the risen Christ.

Athelstan could feel the sweat break out on him as he read quotations allegedly plucked from his sermons and homilies; untruths, lies, words cleverly twisted and thrust into his mouth. Wycliffe was dangerous, and so were his adherents the Lollards, with their demand that the Church should return to the evangelical poverty of its origins. The Lollards were ordinary working men such as Watkin, Pike and Moleskin. The authorities, however, were harsh. Any convicted Lollard, be they priest or lay person, could end up being burned alive at Smithfield. Athelstan sat staring down at the document, aware that the room had fallen deathly still.

'Words can be weapons.' He lifted his head as he tapped the table, then pointed at Prior Anselm. 'You don't believe this, do you?'

'No one does, Brother.' The prior forced a smile. 'However, let me inform you of the process which must be followed. The document you have read is written in a very skilled, clerkly hand. The vellum and ink are of the highest quality. Accordingly, someone—'

'Who is anonymous!'

'Yes, Brother, anonymous, but still someone well educated and learned.'

'As well as being a born liar!'

'I hope to God that's true.' Archdeacon Tuddenham abruptly spoke up.

'Listen, listen,' Prior Anselm soothed, 'John Wycliffe and the Lollards are regarded as deeply malicious by both Crown and Church. Someone highly educated and knowledgeable has accused you, Athelstan, of being a member of Wycliffe's coven. True, the document is anonymous, at least for the moment. However, your accuser may well reveal himself in the future.'

'I sincerely hope he does.'

'Be that as it may,' the prior continued, 'the document before you was copied to the Dominican House in Boulogne, which includes members of the Inquisition.'

'A copy was also despatched to my lord the Bishop of London,' Tuddenham declared.

'And a copy arrived here,' Prior Anselm added.

'How long ago was this?'

'Oh, just in the past few days,' Brother Thomas replied. 'Yes, Prior Anselm?'

The prior nodded his agreement.

'And this process?' Athelstan demanded.

'First you will remain here at Blackfriars . . .'

'So I am being detained?'

'You will be given a secure chamber; you will be well looked after. In two or three days' time . . .'

'Wait, wait . . .' Brother Thomas, who seemed the more senior of the two, tapped the table. 'I speak for Brother John, I am sure, when I say we would have no objection to Athelstan returning to his parish.' He smiled thinly at Athelstan. 'Your response to the allegations is most heartening and encouraging.' The smile widened. 'You are regarded as a good priest and a faithful friar. Your word of honour would satisfy me.'

'True, very true,' Brother John chorused.

Prior Anselm, now visibly relieved, turned to the archdeacon.

'I have no objection whatsoever,' Archdeacon Tuddenham declared, in a loud, clear voice. 'I doubt very much,' he continued, 'that the indictment is true. I am certain Athelstan will refute it.'

The meeting then ended. Athelstan rose and took his leave of Prior Anselm, who whispered that he was sure all would be well. Athelstan gave him curt thanks, however. He was still agitated as he strode through Blackfriars, trying to curb and calm the tumult of thoughts provoked by that deeply malicious indictment. He reached Blackfriars steps and was relieved to discover Moleskin had, at Cranston's request, brought his barge in and was waiting, but for what, Moleskin could not say. The coroner had simply paid him generously to stay until he was needed.

'Well, you are now,' Athelstan declared, stepping down into the barge. 'I just wonder,' he mused, taking a seat, 'what our good coroner is up to?'

'Father,' Moleskin replied, 'if I knew the high coroner's mind, I would be a wiser man. All I can say is that he is in a terrible temper, stamping off, as he put it, to confront the powers of darkness.'

'Which, in Sir John's eyes,' Athelstan replied, 'is anyone who upsets him. Let us go, Moleskin, my cot bed beckons.'

The barge master hastened to cast off. His six rowers strained over their oars, even as Moleskin's elder son, who served as poop boy, blew three blasts on his hunting horn. The barge pulled away. Athelstan murmured a prayer for a safe journey then sat back, reflecting on the day's happenings. He sensed a real threat confronting him, like some monster edging its way out of the gloom. Prior Anselm and Archdeacon Tuddenham seemed agitated but, there again, Athelstan ruefully concluded, the Inquisition and the charges those two fellow friars were dealing with, opened up a true path of thorns.

Athelstan's mind wandered on to other matters. He was making little progress on the business at Westminster, whilst he was growing impatient at the fruitless 'Great Hunt of the Lord'. So, what should he do? He returned to the indictment presented at Blackfriars. Was it the work of some great lord, many of whom had suffered grievously during the Great Revolt the previous year? The Lords of the Soil had hired mercenaries to protect themselves. The sweeping of foreign prisons. Sinister sinners, grim of face and hard of heart, professional killers, blood drinkers, they thronged into London at the behest of this lord or that. Athelstan had fulminated at the use of such men and those who hired them. Athelstan argued that some of the great lords and merchant princes were as wicked and lawless as the felons of London, be it the fraternity of the knife, the cackling cheats, the stall grabbers and all the rest. These men had no heart, Athelstan had thundered, so they would receive no mercy or compassion from God. Of course, such strictures would not go unheeded. And if it wasn't a great lord behind the present nonsense, what about those powerful clerics . . .?'

'Brother, brother.' Moleskin shook him. 'Brother Athelstan, we have arrived.'

The friar hurriedly blessed the barge master and his crew, and then carefully stepped ashore. Moleskin followed. He refused any payment and insisted that two of his burly oarsmen should see Athelstan safely home.

The friar followed his guides past the riverside gallows. The sun was setting fast, so the strangled corpses could now be cut down. Of course the hangmen charged a fee for their work, as well as a rent for a barrow to push the corpses to some mansion of the dead or city cemetery. All kinds of creatures swarmed here. Warlocks, with their long grey hair, desperate to pluck something from a bloated corpse for their own secret ceremonies of the deepest night. Sin-eaters prowled, touting for business; macabre wraiths with their dyed hair and garishly painted faces, garbed from neck to toe in horse-skin. The sin-eaters offered, for a fee, to eat bread placed on the chest of the hanged. In doing so, they claimed they would swallow the sins of the executed felon and take all of the guilt of the dead individuals on themselves. Friars of the Sack, who had a special ministry to the executed and their families, were fiercely protesting at such a pagan practice. They clashed with the sin-eaters, then a gaggle of whores in their motley-coloured rags joined the quarrel and the chaos deepened.

Athelstan's guides pushed their way through these. At last they reached the alleyway leading down to St Erconwald's. Athelstan duly noticed that The Piebald was already closed and shuttered against the night. The church too lay silent. Athelstan stared up to the top of the tower. He would love to spend just one night studying the stars against a cloud-free sky. But not now. He thanked his guides, blessed them, then made his way across God's Acre. He unlocked the door to the priest's house and revelled in its clean warmth. Everything was in place, everything was as it should be. He was about to lock the door when Bonaventure arrived, meowing hungrily. Athelstan let him in, locked the door and joined Bonaventure to toast himself before the fire. He slumped in the chair, falling into a deep sleep, when he was roused by a sharp knocking.

'Who is it?' he called out.

'Brother, it's Benedicta, I am sorry to intrude.'

Athelstan sprang to his feet and hurried to open the door. It swung back and Benedicta seemed to throw herself into the room. She stumbled and Athelstan caught her, just as Brothers Thomas and John followed the widow-woman through, slamming the door shut behind them. Athelstan took one look at them and his heart sank. Both men were still dressed in Dominican robes, but now they wore broad warbelts strapped around their waists, sword and dagger sheathed. Each carried a hand-held arbalest, already primed with a jagged bolt to rip flesh and shatter bone. Athelstan helped Benedicta to a stool. The widow-woman sat down, still clutching a bulging canvas bag. She slumped, eyes closed. Athelstan gently stroked her hair and turned on her attackers.

'You are no more Dominicans than Hubert the Hedgehog. In fact, he would make a better one than the sum of you two.' Brother Thomas lunged forward and punched the friar in the face. Athelstan stood, gasping at the pain, desperately trying to control the furious temper welling within him. He nursed his bruised face, studying this malevolent pair. He now realized what was happening.

'You're not Dominicans,' he declared. 'You are part of Les Mysterieux. You have been despatched by the Chambre Noir in Paris. Oh yes, there can be no other logical explanation.' Athelstan picked up a cloth from the drying stand on the hearth. Bonaventure, now shaken from his sleep, stretched and meowed. Athelstan crouched, stroked the cat, then turned back to his attackers, dabbing at his bloody lip.

'God knows where you're from,' he declared. 'I don't believe all that nonsense about Boulogne and Paris. You are part of Les Mysterieux battle group. You have probably been lurking in London for some time. You are skilled copiers, trained clerks. You can forge licences and letters of accreditation. Indeed, I am sure the Chambre Noir could forge any document it wanted. Create seals, buy the most expensive ink and the costliest parchment so you could write hideous lies about me in the clerkliest hand, carefully copied out and presented in a fashion no one could object to. Prior Anselm, Archdeacon Tuddenham were fooled.' Athelstan shrugged. 'And myself, Sir John included.' He took a step forward. Brother Thomas lifted his arbalest.

'What now?' Athelstan demanded.

'First, you will pack a fardee like the woman has. You must only include items of real value. You've already done so, haven't you, Benedicta?' The widow-woman simply nodded. Athelstan crossed himself.

'And then what?' he demanded.

'We will take you back down to the river. A boat awaits. It's the bum-boat of a French war cog *La Supreme*, anchored mid-river further down from Westminster.'

Athelstan nodded. The man was not lying. French war cogs were strictly watched and never allowed to dock or berth at any of the main quaysides such as Queenhithe.

'I see.' Athelstan strained his ears for any sound from outside but there was none, not even Thomas the Toad wandering with his little beasts.

'You see what, Friar?'

'How this deadly game is to be played out.'

'And how's that, Friar?'

'Ah well, the story will unfold. How the heretical, Dominican priest Athelstan, when confronted with his sins, gave his word to stay in his parish until the authorities conducted their own rigorous investigation into his ministry. Athelstan, however, as guilty as any Judas, decided to flee abroad with his paramour, Benedicta. He and his leman collected their precious possessions and fled. You have prepared well. Made careful study of me and mine.' Athelstan paused and stared at these grim-faced killers. They were professional assassins who, like Satan, could adopt the guise of an angel. 'Of course,' he continued, 'we will never reach France. We are to be killed, aren't we?' Benedicta gave a sharp sob.

Brother Thomas again raised his arbalest.

'What happens to you,' he snarled, 'will be decided later. Now we go. We douse the lights. We cross the tangle you call God's Acre. Our destination is that fishing enclave close to Southwark Steps. That's where our boat awaits. Athelstan, I warn you! Any sign that you intend to break free or alert someone we pass, and this woman will immediately die. So come.'

Wrapped in their cloaks, all four left the priest's house walking swiftly across God's Acre and into a tangle of alleyways stretching down to Southwark Steps. Athelstan, mouth dry, flesh clammy, prayed that he would meet someone, anyone who might help. But the hour was very late, the darkness was biting cold, few would be abroad tonight. Now and again dark shapes and shadows flitted across their path, but these were denizens of the underworld who could provide little assistance in dealing with these two burly killers. Cats and rats screeched against the darkness. Doors slammed closed. Shutters rattled in the wind and the mournful howling of some dog echoed chillingly. The only light was the lantern Thomas carried.

They reached the enclave, squeezing through, down the slippery, mildewed steps to the boat moored against the ancient, crumbling quayside. It truly was a bitter night, the icy breeze, full of different smells, was sharp on face and hands. Athelstan and Benedicta were bundled aboard the four-oared boat, which swayed sickeningly as the turbulent tide caught it. Thomas ordered the cast off. The rowers leaned against their oars and pulled back sharply as the boat nosed its way forward. Athelstan tried to control his panic. He understood enough from the likes of Moleskin to know how truly temperamental the Thames was. Sometimes placid, the river could very swiftly change and pose real danger, especially on a night like this. Athelstan gazed around. The boat now had eight aboard; it was too full and its roll across the waters was truly stomach-churning. He and Benedicta were seated close together in the stern. Athelstan thought Benedicta was lost in her own anguish but then she abruptly straightened up. In the poor light her face was drawn but resolute.

'Brother,' she hissed, 'if you see an opportunity, seize it.'

Athelstan grabbed her cold hand and squeezed.

The bum-boat was now lumbering across the waters. A thick, cloying mist closed in. Athelstan glimpsed the distant lights of other crafts and the warning peals of different boat bells. They made to turn and enter a bank of rolling mist. Suddenly it shifted. Athelstan exclaimed in surprise as the Fisher of Men's great war barge *Thanatos* broke through the murk, bearing down directly on them, oars rising and falling. The bum-boat shifted in a desperate attempt to avoid the sharp prow of the sleek black war barge.

Athelstan seized the opportunity. He leapt to his feet shouting, 'Harrow, harrow!' The general shout for help against any crime. The friar's powerful voice cut through the air. The war barge shifted slightly. Brother Thomas sprang between the rowers to close with Athelstan, but the friar lunged forward, knocking the arbalest from the assassin's hand. The oarsmen were now desperately shouting warnings. The bum-boat rocked. Thomas's accomplice tried to push his way past the oarsmen. The river swirled. One of those unexpected surges. The rocking boat promptly dipped to one side and then capsized. The water rushed in. Athelstan felt himself falling; he kicked out, loosening his cloak. He made to turn, searching for Benedicta, but the drag of the water pulled him into its black wetness. Athelstan panicked. He was not a good swimmer. He lashed out but then felt the back of his jerkin pulled as Benedicta grabbed him.

'Athelstan,' she screamed, 'let me push you.'

The friar tried to relax. He wondered where the *Thanatos* could be, then abruptly he was pushed against hard wood. He glanced up; lantern light floated above him. Ichthus, the Fisher of Men's henchman, was staring down, even as a rope ladder was thrown over the taffrail.

'Grab the bottom rung,' Benedicta yelled. 'Quickly now.'

Athelstan seized the rope ladder. He could still feel the pull of the river on his water-drenched clothes, but he grasped the rung and slowly forced himself up. Benedicta followed, shouting encouragement. Athelstan reached the top rung, even as Ichthus and another member of the crew threw down a second rope ladder, which they used to scale down the side of the barge to search for other survivors. Athelstan reached the taffrail, where he and Benedicta were pulled over the side and made to sit in the canopied stern. The black-garbed Fisher of Men barked out orders.

Athelstan and Benedicta quickly stripped and grabbed the clothes thrust at them. All modesty was ignored, Benedicta urging Athelstan to undress and get rid of the river-drenched clothing. He and the widow-woman were then given small warmers filled with strips of glowing charcoal from the capped braziers standing in the prow. Shivering and trembling, they also grabbed the pewter goblets of hot mulled wine thrust into their hands by one of the crew. Athelstan relaxed and stared around.

The Fisher and his strange retinue were now dealing with others. The two assassins had survived and now sat slumped against the far side of the barge. Apparently all the rowers had been lost, except for one, but he had been grievously wounded by a sharp shard of wood when their boat had cracked beneath the prow of the *Thanatos*.

Athelstan closed his eyes, trying hard to impose some form of calm. He could hear the noise of the river, the screech of gulls, the shouts of the Fisher and his crew, the creak of the barge and the rattle of rope. Athelstan was now warm, no wet clothes, whilst the strong goblet of posset warmed his belly. Athelstan crossed himself and called the Fisher over. He came and crouched before Athelstan, his lean face and hooded eyes looking even more sinister in the flickering light of the lantern he carried.

'Brother, what is it?' The Fisher ran a hand over the dome of his completely bald head. 'What happened?'

'Those two men,' Athelstan gasped, as his stomach abruptly clenched, 'they are assassins. They are to be held close and fast.'

'From your cries, I suspected as much,' the Fisher replied. 'So Brother, give thanks to God for your delivery.'

'And to you, my friend.'

'Friend indeed,' Benedicta echoed, stretching out to grasp the Fisher's wrist. He smiled and pointed further down the barge.

'And give thanks for Ichthus. He was the one who alerted us. He also saved your tormentors, and . . .' the Fisher pointed further down the barge, 'even more importantly, he rescued your baggage!'

Later the following day Cranston, escorted by his bailiffs and a company of Tower archers displaying the White Hart, the young King's personal emblem, arrived in St Erconwald's. Cranston ringed the parish church and God's Acre with these veteran bowmen. He also set up a temporary chain barrier across the alleyway, manned by his bailiffs, whilst he proclaimed through two heralds that the 'Great Hunt of the Lord' was now suspended until certain matters had been resolved. The coroner then joined Athelstan and Benedicta in the priest's house. Cranston had despatched Tiptoft to give his hosts clear warning of his pending arrival. Now, all tasks completed, he joined Athelstan and Benedicta around the table to eat a fragrant beef stew cooked by Benedicta and drink the small tun of Bordeaux that the coroner had brought with him.

Athelstan had spent the day recovering from the hideous events of the previous night. He and Benedicta had safely returned to Southwark, courtesy of the Fisher of Men, who also promised to inform the Lord High Coroner about what had happened. Now all had settled. Benedicta had quickly recovered and looked magnificent in her gown of blue, edged with silver bands, her night-black hair hidden beneath a white veil studded with small yellow stones. Around her neck hung a chain carrying a medallion from the Virgin's Shrine at Walsingham. Athelstan sipped at his wine. He caught Benedicta's gaze and winked, before returning to his study of the coroner, who sat strangely silent as he devoured the delicious stew.

'I didn't realize,' Athelstan declared, eager to break the stillness, 'how skilled a swimmer you are, Benedicta.'

'Brother,' she smiled, 'as you know, I was married to a sea captain.' Her smile faded. 'Until the sea seized him. Anyway, my husband always maintained that he was deeply surprised at how few people, including many who sailed upon the waters, could swim. One day, shortly after our marriage, he took me to Hollow Ponds, the freshwater lakes adjoining the Kentish Way. He said we should go swimming. I replied I couldn't.' Benedicta laughed, fingers fluttering to her lips. 'He took my clothes off and threw me in. Oh yes.' She added dreamily, 'I learned to swim as swift as any salmon.'

'And so to business.' Cranston, who had sat totally distracted, brought his goblet down hard on the table. 'Your abduction, as I am sure you have already deduced, was a clever, sinister plot by the Chambre Noir. Master Thibault believes they despatched those two false Dominicans, armed with the most skilled forgeries, to Westminster. They were probably also responsible for writing and despatching that indictment against you, Athelstan. Of course they then acted all tolerant; they wanted you back here so they could abduct you both.' He paused, rubbing his hands together. 'Believe me, Brother, Benedicta, the young King, Gaunt and Master Thibault are furious. I wager that the Bishop of London, Archdeacon Tuddenham and Prior Anselm will receive letters expressing the King's anger at what has happened. In my view it will be a long time, if ever, before they interfere in your affairs again. The only consolation they have, and it is deeply prized by Master Thibault, is that he now holds two members of the Chambre Noir as his prisoners. Those two assassins are now being racked and tortured, cruelly so, in the dungeons beneath the White Tower. As you can imagine, it is not a pretty sight. Thibault is desperate to learn as much as he can about the doings of his opponents in Paris. As for the rest,' Cranston shrugged, 'let us wait and see. But now it's time I was gone.'

'As must I be,' Benedicta declared.

Both of Athelstan's guests then left the priest's house. The friar bade them farewell and stood staring across God's Acre. He recalled the events of the previous evening and the murderous attempt on both himself and Benedicta. 'Why?' he whispered. 'Why was that planned, plotted and perpetrated? The only answer is that we must be very close, very close indeed to the truth.'

Athelstan closed the door and returned to his chair. He stared down at Bonaventure. 'Do you hear that, brother cat? We now confront Les Mysterieux and all their plotting. But who are Les Mysterieux? More importantly, what have we done to alarm them?' Athelstan paused to replace another piece of wood on the dying fire. He felt comfortable, warm and safe. Cranston had despatched the cream of the Tower garrison to protect him, as well as impressing on Flaxwith the need for constant vigilance. Athelstan rose, opened the door and just stood on the threshold. The weather had turned cold but God's Acre now looked far from deserted. Bonfires burnt fiercely. Braziers glowed, whilst cresset torches fixed on poles smouldered vigorously, tongues of flame licking the darkness. Athelstan sighed. He was safe. Cranston had not yet left St Erconwald's but stood deep in conversation with Flaxwith, close to the great lychgate. Athelstan did not want to interfere. He went back into the house, locking and bolting the door behind him. He then walked into the buttery and, as he did so, caught sight of the old ledger or journal that Mauger had found beneath a stone in God's Acre. He picked it up off the small table beneath the bed loft, cleared his chancery desk and began to study the journal page by page. The entries were legible, neat and clearly dated, some dating back sixteen or seventeen years, a few even before those dates. Some of the entries made him smile, whilst he found the different abbreviations difficult to decipher. He abruptly paused on one page which listed work on the church tower. Athelstan whistled under his breath and sat back in his chair as he recalled Cranston's description of Boniface and what the bounty hunter had said as he lay dying of a fever. Athelstan clasped his hands in prayer and gave thanks for the hard work of the bounty hunter. He made to rise. He needed to ask Cranston for help but then promptly sat down. 'No, no,' Athelstan murmured, 'let me think. Let me plot and plot again before I bring this masque to an end.'

* * *

Others gathered late that same day in The Wyburn Tavern, deep in the slums of Whitefriars. Les Mysterieux, under their Magister and Key-Master, assembled in the room he had hired. As always, they came hooded and visored, so it was very difficult to determine whether they were male or female, let alone to describe either feature or form of any of them. Their leader, the Magister, had organized wine and food and, once these were served, he tapped his boot hard on the floor and the whispered conversations abruptly ended.

'We are Les Mysterieux,' the Magister began. 'We are the emissaries of the Chambre Noir. We answer to no one except to the Luciferi, the lords of that chamber, and of course His most Christian Majesty, King Charles of France. Comrades,' the Magister, the Key-Master, continued measuredly, 'we have pierced the secrets of Westminster, but we are now being hunted by Cranston the coroner and his dog, the faithful friar. Our masters regard both of them as highly dangerous, Athelstan especially.'

'As they must,' one of the group called out, 'the English spy Nightingale. He inflicted terrible damage on us in Paris and I understand he has not been captured.'

'I agree,' the Magister replied. 'We know Nightingale is back in London and we should take care of him in the most appropriate way at the most suitable time. But now let us return to the reason for this conclave: Cranston and Athelstan.' The Key-Master paused, sipping his wine. 'Cranston is a royal officer. Now, bear with me. We have tried on two occasions to kill the coroner and his associate. The first was foiled by the sheer stupidity of those we hired. The second was cursed, so I understand, by ill-chance – an accident on the Thames. Fickle fortune spinning her wheel.'

'Thomas and Jean have been taken up.'

'Yes, they have been, and I am sure will be brutally tortured. But,' the Magister toasted them with his cup, 'that is a threat that each and every one of us must face.'

'Will they break, Magister?'

'Claude, I do not know. I know Thomas and Jean would rather die than confess.' He paused at the muttered curses of his comrades. 'Thomas and Jean,' he continued, 'know very little about us. They didn't need to know who we really are, where we live or what we do. True, they are part of our group and they receive direction from me, but more than that I will not say. In the end, we are royal clerks. We will act most prudently and, despite our failures, we will continue our good work. Now, to return to Cranston. The English Crown and its ministers now know that the Chambre were responsible for two attacks on Cranston's friar. We dare not make a further assault on Cranston himself. He is a royal official; he enjoys the personal support of the young King, Gaunt and Master Thibault. Any fresh attack on the fat coroner could well be construed as an act of war. Our masters in Paris would not want that. Moreover, Cranston will now be well guarded. Any attempt on him, either in the streets, the Guildhall or along the river, would be too dangerous to attempt.'

'So we leave both?' one of the coven called out. 'And why not? Magister, surely it is time we slipped away? We have prepared our path out. We have plotted and planned where to go, where to hide, and where to emerge like little innocents.' Claude's words were greeted with muted approval and quiet laughter.

'We are not finished.' The Magister's voice turned hard. 'We have been given a task; we should complete it.' He lifted a hand. 'Perhaps, when it is finished, we will hold a sumptuous hosting in La Delicieuse, just before we burn it down.' His remark provoked more laughter.

'But Athelstan?'

'Yes, my friend,' the Magister hitched his cloak over his shoulders, 'we can and we will take care of him. Athelstan is more vulnerable than Cranston, as well as being more dangerous. If Cranston is the dagger hilt, Athelstan is the blade. We must remove him for good and then, my friends, we shall take the pathway to a new, fresh life. We shall,' his voice shrilled with passion, 'devastate as we leave. The ladies at La Delicieuse must be silenced because they are traitors, and that sombre House of Secrets, like the tavern, burned to the ground.'

'But how? a voice called out. 'How do we remove that interfering friar?'

'Why, my friend, by the most subtle way known to man.'

Talbot, a serjeant in the Company of Tower Archers camped in and around St Erconwald's, reached the lychgate, the entrance to God's Acre. He took a swig from the wineskin he carried and continued on his patrol. A thick veil of mist had swept in from the river. Nevertheless Talbot, looking over the wall, could still see parishioners thronging around the entrance to the church, waiting for the door to open for morning Mass. Talbot walked on, continuing his circuit, aware that other parishioners were stumbling through the early morning mist, eager to get to Mass. Talbot paused, hitching his cloak closer around his shoulders. Once again, he peered over the wall at the ancient church.

'Strange place,' he whispered.

He and his comrades had been here for days, yet they could sense the fraught excitement of the parishioners: these were all deeply curious about recent events, with lurid rumours about a bloody affray in Cheapside and a violent clash at midnight along the Thames. The coroner had published very few details. On one matter, however, he had been blunt. The Great Hunt of the Lord, as the coroner declared, was to cease immediately. Talbot had since learned about the theft of the sacred relic, and the popular belief that it remained hidden in or around the ancient parish church.

'Ah well.' Talbot walked slowly on through the shifting mist, keeping the cemetery wall to his left. He eventually turned, passing the back of the church. The mist swirled, gathered then parted. Talbot paused. A hooded figure was walking towards him. Talbot relaxed as he recognized the earth-brown robes of a Franciscan.

'Good day,' the friar called out. '*Pax et bonum*, my son.'

Talbot drew closer. The friar extended his hand, which Talbot clasped. He started at the iron grip of the friar, who pulled him hard and swift on to the long dagger concealed in his other hand. Talbot struggled but it was futile. The assassin, disguised as a friar, watched as the blood bubbled in the archer's throat and the life light faded from his eyes.

PART FIVE

Layne: to keep silent

Brother Athelstan drew a deep breath and stared around the sacristy. All was in place. Mass had finished and now he had to make the usual journey across the sanctuary and out of the church. He knew the parish council would be waiting for him with their usual petitions and requests. Could they meet? What was happening? Why couldn't they continue the Great Hunt of the Lord?

'Because I do not,' Athelstan muttered to himself, 'wish to discuss that – not yet, not with you, and not until I am ready. And no, my beloved parishioners, I am not yet ready.'

Athelstan pulled his cowl close over his head. Outside was freezing, and he was determined to return as swiftly as he could to his studies. Days had elapsed since he'd seen Cranston, and he wondered what might be happening along the Secret Cloisters of Westminster. Athelstan crossed himself, left the sacristy and hurried across the sanctuary through the rood screen and down into the nave. He brushed aside Watkin and his coven, calling out to Mauger and Benedicta to join him. They left the church, following the twisting coffin path up through the thickening mist to the priest's house. Athelstan unlocked the door and waved his two guests inside.

'Would you like some morning ale, Father?'

Athelstan smiled at Benedicta. The widow-woman, like himself, had soon recovered from their ordeal along the river. Athelstan believed that it was an act of God that had saved him, though he would never forget his debt to the Fisher of Men and his motley crew. He'd already sent a message to the Fisher that, when the present business had finished, Athelstan intended to hold a special Mass for the crew of the *Thanatos*, followed by feasting and revelry at The Piebald.

'Father,' Benedicta repeated, 'do you want some morning ale? You're just standing there, staring at me.'

'Yes, yes.' Athelstan pointed across to the cauldron hanging on a tripod above the well-banked fire. 'And get . . .' He paused, gaping at the hearth.

'Father?'

'Bonaventure!' Athelstan strained his hearing, but he could detect no meowing or scraping. 'Bonaventure!' he gasped, 'Bonaventure should be here.'

'Father.' Mauger, sitting on the wall bench, sprang to his feet. 'Father, what is wrong?'

'It's misty outside,' Benedicta replied. 'Bonaventure never goes out when a fog sweeps in.'

'More importantly,' Athelstan shivered at a prickle of fear down the back of his neck, 'because of the mist,' he asserted, 'Bonaventure was here toasting himself when I left to celebrate Mass.'

'Yet you locked the door behind you,' Mauger declared. 'You must have. I saw you turn the key to let us in.'

'Someone,' Athelstan replied, 'picked that lock and opened the door. Bonaventure never likes strangers, and he may have also sensed danger. He would race from this room, mist or no mist. So,' Athelstan pointed to the cauldron, 'take that down and pile into it every single morsel of food and drink in this house.'

'Father?'

'Mauger, think! Someone skilled in picking locks turned the one on my door and entered this room whilst I was celebrating Mass. Bonaventure, all alarmed, fled. The intruder broke in here not to steal, not to damage or discover what I was doing.'

'But to kill you?'

'Precisely, Benedicta! And the most subtle device for that is poison. So we will remove the cauldron, the ale, the wine and the food and,' he paused, fingers to his lips. He then started at a sharp rap on the door, which Mauger, clutching a knife he'd picked up from the table, cautiously opened. The Captain of Archers strode in, shaking the water drops from his cloak.

'Brother Athelstan?' The captain swallowed, hard.

'What is it, man?'

'One of my company has been grievously slain, stabbed to death. He was supposed to patrol the cemetery wall. Anyway,' the captain took off his gauntlets to wipe the damp from his face, 'we eventually found Talbot's corpse thrust beneath a bush, stabbed through the heart. Nothing was taken, except for his jerkin, hood and tabard.'

'Of course,' Athelstan declared. 'And the tabard displays the White Hart?'

'Yes, Brother.'

Athelstan closed his eyes, trying to control his breathing.

'I suspect, Captain, that the sinner who murdered poor Talbot also broke in here and somehow, somewhere, laid poison down for me, as you would to kill rats.'

'Father, I think . . .'

'What?'

'The assassin has proclaimed himself.' The captain opened his belt wallet and drew out a thin scroll of parchment. He handed this to Athelstan who unrolled it and read the crudely scrawled message:

'Jack Cranston Lord of the Jakes,
Really should leave for all our sakes,
Mess after mess he crudely makes,
He would do better selling hot cakes.

'Signed and sealed by the Radix Malorum at his palace in the clouds.'

Athelstan carefully rolled up the parchment and slipped it into his wallet.

'Found on the corpse,' the captain offered. 'What does it mean, Brother, these doggerel verses? Of course I recognize the name, Radix Malorum. However, why should the assassin . . . what grievance does he have against us? Or the likes of poor Talbot?'

'What indeed?' Athelstan opened the door and stood on the threshold, staring out across God's Acre. The friar narrowed his eyes. Somehow, he thought, the assassin had made a mistake. He couldn't explain why or how he knew this, but the murder of poor Talbot was clumsy, haphazard. Moreover, it emphasized one important fact. The assassin, and Athelstan strongly suspected it was Les Mysterieux, whatever the message said, regarded him, in particular, as highly dangerous.

'Rest assured,' Athelstan whispered to the breeze, 'with God's help I shall show you how dangerous I can be.'

'Brother?'

Athelstan turned back to the soldier. 'Captain,' he declared, 'look after your dead comrade – Talbot, yes?'

'Yes, Brother, he hailed from Colchester.'

'Then God rest Talbot of Colchester. I shall offer a requiem for the repose of his soul.'

The captain thanked him and left. Once he'd gone, Mauger and Benedicta began to heatedly discuss what had happened.

'Come, come.' Athelstan clapped his hands. 'Let us not act like chickens trapped in a coop: that's what the assassin would like. Let's deal with his wickedness. Mauger, Benedicta, remove all the food and drink to the fire pit beneath the ancient sycamore. Benedicta, on second thoughts, Mauger and I will do that. I want you to seek out Ranulf the Ratcatcher. He is to go down into the cellars of The Piebald and bring two or three live rats in a cage to me at the fire pit.'

Benedicta left whilst Mauger helped Athelstan clear all the food into a barrow, which the friar then pushed across to the old fire pit. Athelstan murmured a prayer of thanks that a screed of bush and gorse hid them from being seen by anyone outside the church. Once they had reached the fire pit, they emptied the contents of the barrow into it. Then Athelstan went back to the house to clear any remaining food and drink, as well as to bring a flask of oil, a tinder and a rush light. Benedicta returned with a nervous-looking Ranulf who, with his constantly blinking eyes, pointed face and sharp, receding chin, looked even more like the three rodents scrambling around the cage he carried. Athelstan informed the ratcatcher what he wanted and Ranulf released the three rats into the pit; they immediately turned and twisted amongst the food. Athelstan did not have long to wait. He watched the rodents cavort at the banquet crammed around them. Then, abruptly, one leapt into the air and crashed down, gagging and squealing as his legs gave up beneath him. The other two rodents soon joined the poisoned rat in its macabre dance of death.

'I have seen enough,' Athelstan declared. He fetched the oilskin, poured it over the pit, lit the rush light and threw it into the pit. Flames erupted immediately, followed by a horrid squealing, then silence. Athelstan walked away, gesturing at the others to follow him back to the house. He thanked Ranulf, watched him go, then closed the door and sat down at the table, rubbing his face.

'Mauger,' he took his hands away from his face, 'please go and ensure my little flock are behaving themselves. Not a word about what has happened, though I suspect Ranulf will be gossiping like a squirrel on the branch.' Once Mauger had left, Athelstan turned to Benedicta. 'Please,' he urged, 'scour, scrape and clean everything in this house. I would do it myself, but other matters press hard on me. Do check on poor Philomel resting in his stable: he would appreciate a visit.'

Benedicta assured him she would, then watched as the little friar walked up and down, rubbing his hands, lost in his own maze of thoughts.

'Yes, yes,' he murmured, 'I need silence. I will leave this house to you, Benedicta.'

Athelstan collected his cloak and chancery satchel, exchanged the kiss of peace with Benedicta and left, striding, head down, along the coffin paths. He was so intent on his walking that he almost collided with Tiptoft.

'God forgive me, man,' Athelstan apologized. 'I was lost deep in my own worries.'

'And there's more,' Cranston's courier replied lugubriously. 'Sir John needs you at Westminster.'

Cranston, swathed in a heavy military cloak, a beaver hat pulled firmly over his head, was waiting for Athelstan. He hurried to help the friar out of the heavily armoured war barge. Grasping the friar's arm more firmly, Cranston almost pushed Athelstan away from the quayside into the light and warmth of The Pelican, a riverside tavern where a company of the coroner's bailiffs were busy supping ale. Cranston led Athelstan into a window seat and ordered two tankards of the best. Once this was served, Cranston leaned forward, eyes glistening.

'God save us, Brother, but Nightingale is dead. Murdered.'

'No.'

'Oh yes, my little friar, a true mystery. Last night he asked to remain in the House of Secrets. Master Thibault agreed. He trusted Nightingale completely.' The coroner half smiled. 'As he does you and me.'

'Why did Nightingale want to roam the House of Secrets at night?'

'Like you, Brother, he said he wanted to get to the very essence of the place, how it was arranged,' Cranston waved a hand, 'and so on and so on. Edmonton was told to leave his keys with Nightingale, as well as ensure his comrade had wine, food, and a makeshift cot bed. The Compline bell sounded. The House of Secrets emptied. Edmonton made sure Nightingale locked the door to the buttery. All was secure and safe, or so it appeared to me. The guards on the parapet walk, as well as those sheltering in the sheds and bothies around the fire pit, reported that all was well.'

'But murder made itself known?'

'It certainly did, Brother. The clerks of the Secret Chancery arrived just as the abbey bells tolled for the Jesus Mass. Edmonton and his companions knocked and pounded the door but there was no reply. Eventually they despatched a courier to Master Thibault. There is, as you may know, only two sets of keys to the buttery, to the passageway stretching past the carrels and, of course, the double-locked door leading down into the arca.' Cranston paused, shaking his head. 'Believe me, Brother, they had to unlock every door in that place. They shouted and called, but Nightingale failed to appear. Nothing was disturbed, no sign of violence or intrusion. The clerks scoured the House of Secrets but could find nothing amiss. Eventually they unlocked the door to the arca, went down the steps and found Nightingale slumped against a chest, dead from a dagger thrust straight to the heart.'

'In Heaven's name,' Athelstan whispered. 'We have a building with three fortified doors, all locked from within, yes?'

'Correct, Brother, and, before you ask, the keys were found on Nightingale.'

'So,' Athelstan declared, 'we have a royal clerk, a mailed clerk, all alone in a building locked from the inside. No alarm was raised. Nothing to signify any danger. No sign of a struggle or conflict. Nevertheless, this mailed clerk was found dead, stabbed to the heart. So how? How did the assassin enter and leave with such deadly skill, kill a man like Nightingale, and pass through locked doors?' Athelstan put his tankard down and rubbed his face. For a short while, both Coroner and Friar sat in silence.

'And you, little friar?'

'Oh, Sir John, what a tale I have to tell.' Athelstan then gave a pithy, blunt account of the attempt to poison him.

Cranston listened in astonishment. He just sat, nursing the miraculous wineskin. Once Athelstan had finished, the coroner took a generous slurp of his constant companion.

'Satan's tits,' he murmured, 'it cannot be the Radix Malorum. He's a thief, not an assassin.'

'I agree, Sir John. The attempt on me was the work of Les Mysterieux and their Magister, the Key-Master. They are trying to muddy the waters, mislead us, and create obstacles in our path, because we are closing with them. Sooner or later, Sir John, the truth will out. Now,' Athelstan pushed away his tankard, 'Sir John, I am not returning to St Erconwald's, not for the moment. I want to be lodged here in the abbey guesthouse.'

'Yes,' Cranston agreed. 'On one condition, where you go, Brother, four of my lovely lads will accompany you, whilst another will guard the entrance to your chamber. Now,' Cranston picked up his beaver hat, 'we must go. Master Thibault awaits. He will undoubtedly have learned about the most recent happenings at St Erconwald's.' Cranston paused. 'The murder of a Tower archer is a matter for his immediate concern. Especially if, be it true or not, the Radix Malorum is involved. Of course, we know he is not: that is a malicious piece of murderous mischief served up by Les Mysterieux. Anyway, our lord and master waits.'

Cranston, summoning his bailiffs, gave strict instructions for them to stay near and, once the coroner had left, keep vigilant watch over Athelstan. They all vowed to remain as close to the friar as a mother hen to her chicks. Satisfied, Cranston then led his entourage out into the narrow paths which snaked like ribbons through Westminster. They passed the magnificent soaring abbey church and entered the royal precincts.

The day was drawing on. Already lanterns, rush lights and candles glowed merrily through chinks, window and door. A boy and his sister were shepherding a gaggle of geese through the streets as two more children, armed with canes, drove away the hungry, feral dogs that prowled the area. They passed carts, fruit barrows and pack ponies almost smothered beneath the goods piled on them. A moon man stood on a barrel, reciting a poem about demons with glass eyes, razor-sharp teeth, and how these creatures of hell were gathering in the dusk. A funeral party, the coffin a mere arrow-chest, wound its way to a nearby chapel. Athelstan stared around. The scenes he glimpsed sharply reminded him of his own parish, as well as his determination to resolve the business of the Radix Malorum and its effect on his congregation. Athelstan now had well-grounded suspicions about the truth of that matter but, for a while, that would have to wait. They reached the House of Secrets. Thibault and his clerks were ensconced in the buttery. Cranston apologized for keeping them waiting, but he had to inform Athelstan about what had happened.

'And what do you think?'

'What do I think?' Athelstan replied, taking his seat. 'Master Thibault, I think nothing. Gentlemen,' he now turned to the anxious-faced clerks, 'Nightingale was one of your company. He now lies murdered. I need to see the corpse as well as speak to Dimanche, the Dies Domini, the scavenger responsible for cleaning here yesterday.'

'I have already summoned them all,' Thibault replied, stretching his hands over the chafing dish, crammed with sparkling pieces of charcoal.

Athelstan studied this sinister Master of Secrets. Thibault, he suspected, shared the same anxiety as his clerks. The House of Secrets was being torn apart. Thibault's sinister and powerful overlord, John of Gaunt, would not be pleased.

'Brother Athelstan.' Thibault again warmed his hands. 'You are silent, my friend.'

'Master Thibault, I am preparing myself.'

'For what?'

'To enter the meadows of murder. Now Sir John has informed me that Nightingale had asked to stay in the House of Secrets last night.'

'He said,' Edmonton spoke up, 'that he wished to wander, to observe and to reflect.'

'And, of course, you agreed?'

'Yes,' Thibault replied. 'I trusted Nightingale completely.' He shrugged. 'Edmonton cleared the House of Secrets, gave the keys to Nightingale and left.'

'And where did you go?'

'To La Delicieuse. We wanted to relax, at least for a while,' Sheffield replied, provoking murmurs of agreement from his companions.

'So,' Athelstan continued, 'you returned this morning.'

'Yes,' Edmonton replied. 'We knocked and shouted; we received no reply. I despatched Sheffield to Master Thibault's chambers in the palace.'

'I came,' the Master of Secrets declared. 'We opened the doors with my set of keys, nothing was disturbed. Nothing at all. We reached the door leading down to the arca, it was locked both top and bottom. We opened it.' Thibault cleared his throat. 'I sent Edmonton and Davenant down.'

'There was a lantern burning very low,' Davenant declared, his voice harsh and carrying. 'Nightingale lay propped against a coffer, his jerkin drenched in blood from a dagger thrust direct to the heart. He must have died instantly; his corpse still sprawls there.'

'Until Brother Athelstan views it,' Thibault responded. 'Once he has, Nightingale's corpse will be dressed and prepared for burial here at Westminster.'

'One question.' Athelstan gestured at Edmonton. 'You are sure that, apart from Nightingale, nobody else was here when you left?'

'Brother, I swear. Ever since Hugh's murder, we have all exercised great caution and prudence: this House of Secrets was made most secure last night.'

'So, only Nightingale was here,' Athelstan murmured. 'Enough for now. Master Thibault, Sir John and I need to view the corpse.'

'And swiftly,' Cranston added. 'Edmonton, you have the keys?'

'Go then.' Thibault flicked his fingers. 'The sooner the better. Oh, Sir John, I did what you asked. When you have finished with poor Nightingale, Dimanche and the Dies Domini will gather to answer any questions you have.'

'One thing I did notice,' Davenant spoke up, 'Nightingale seemed to be very interested in our scavengers. He declared that he liked them, found them amusing. I know that he questioned Dimanche very closely.'

'Did he?' Athelstan replied. 'About what?'

'Brother, I don't know, but I am sure Dimanche will tell you.

I just think that Nightingale was curious and wanted to learn as much as he could about this place.'

'I look forward to meeting Dimanche soon,' Athelstan retorted. 'First let's view poor Nightingale.'

Edmonton, carrying a spluttering torch, led them out of the buttery and along the passageway past the carrels. He opened the door of the arca and led them down into the cold darkness. Lanternhorns arranged across the arca illuminated the gruesome scene. Nightingale, eyes starting, bloodied mouth gaping, lay sprawled against a coffer.

'And nothing was disturbed here?' Athelstan murmured, crouching down next to the corpse.

'Nothing.'

'So,' Athelstan edged a little closer. He tapped the warbelt around the dead man's waist. 'Nightingale never even drew his dagger, yet the death thrust must have been from the front, but there is no sign either on the corpse or around here of any resistance, struggle or conflict. No clash of blade against blade.' He turned to peer up at Cranston. 'How was such murderous mischief perpetrated? How could Nightingale be so easily overcome?'

Cranston just shook his head. Athelstan could see the coroner was distracted, so he thanked Edmonton for his help and asked to be alone with Sir John. Once the clerk had left, Athelstan blessed the corpse, got to his feet and patted Cranston on the shoulder.

'Sir John, what is it?'

'My apologies, Brother. I admit, I am distracted. I am deeply worried by all this. Master Thibault is the same. The Commons are now learning of the murderous chaos here. News is also seeping in about the disasters in Paris and, of course, there's the public derision caused by the Radix Malorum.' Cranston smiled thinly. 'Even No Breeches has discovered nothing of interest.'

Cranston sat down on a three-legged stool placed between two of the chests. 'Gossip and chatter,' he continued, 'sweep this city like the wind. Merchants travelling from Paris are hearing this story and that: gossip about English spies being hanged out of hand on the public gallows. All this news is picked up and fed to the great lords of the city. The Commons smell blood and, like any hungry pack, they will turn on Thibault.'

'And then on you?'

'Of course, little brother – any or all of my past achievements will be forgotten. They'll summon me into the Commons, put me on oath, then ask whatever questions they like. Let's be honest, Athelstan, I know many of Thibault's secrets. I am at risk. The danger is great.'

'In which case,' Athelstan rose and patted Cranston on his bulky shoulder, 'let us trap those who hunt us. Come, Sir John. I want to stay in the House of Secrets tonight. Like Nightingale, I need to wander, to walk, to observe and, above all, to reflect. Four of your comitatus can stay with me, and two more will guard the door. We will need food, drink, palliasses, braziers and blankets. But first,' Athelstan tapped a sandalled foot against the floor, 'let us rejoin our friends.'

Thibault and Edmonton were waiting for them in the buttery. The Master of Secrets had dismissed the other clerks for the day. Edmonton handed over the keys then hurried out, as if desperate to escape. Thibault raised a finger to his lips for silence and left the buttery to bring in Dimanche and the five Dies Domini. Athelstan closely scrutinized these men. In truth they were no better than beggars in their tattered clothing, battered boots, hair and beards unkempt. They all took their seats and sat shuffling nervously. Once again Cranston, at Athelstan's urging, thanked Dimanche for his assistance in what he now described as the murderous affray in The Lamb of God. The coroner then asked, talking slowly and carefully, if they could throw any light on the murder of the clerk, Nightingale. His questions were greeted with shakes of the head and mumbled denials.

'Sir John,' Dimanche stumbled to his feet, 'we know very little. Indeed, and I speak for my comrades, it might be best if we left our duties here and you could then hire different scavengers. I mean,' Dimanche forced a smile, 'it is becoming highly dangerous here.' He stumbled over the word 'dangerous', and Athelstan concluded that these poor men were terrified out of their wits. 'We are sorry,' Dimanche raised a hand, 'we are very sorry to hear of Nightingale's death. He was kind.'

'You talked to him?'

'Oh yes, Brother Athelstan, he questioned me closely about the House of Secrets. He gave me a coin as a reward. I told him we knew nothing but still he questioned me. He did pay me for my trouble, though, that's all I can say.'

Cranston then asked a few more questions but couldn't elicit anything of interest. Dimanche and his retinue were dismissed and Thibault, clearly distracted, bade Cranston and Athelstan adieu, adding how the Captain of Archers would ensure that Athelstan was comfortable during his stay in the House of Secrets. Cranston declared that Thibault need not worry, his bailiffs would also be in attendance. Thibault left. Cranston and Athelstan waited until the Master of Secret's footsteps faded, then the friar swung his cloak about him, telling the coroner to do the same.

'Where are we going?'

'Why Sir John, to visit the Ghostman. He did not come to St Erconwald's, so I will go to see him. I have a question or two to ask.'

They left the House of Secrets, following the coffin paths which cut through the huddle of buildings in both the royal and abbey precincts; an eerie, silent walk. Night was gathering. Snatches of plainchant echoed different prayers and psalms. Voices shouted. Doors and shutters clattered. Shadowy shapes slipped through the murk, the pallid faces of monks and clerks illuminated by the small lanterns and capped candles they carried. Cranston and Athelstan reached the soaring mass of the main abbey church, following the path round to the crypt and the anker-hold built close by.

Athelstan was relieved as he glimpsed light glowing through both the leper squint and the narrow-shuttered window. He rapped on the door. The Ghostman demanded who it was. Cranston bellowed back that it was the closest thing to the Lord God Almighty, namely the King's own coroner in London. Bolts were hastily drawn, a lock turned, and the door swung open. The Ghostman, as strange as ever, beckoned them in. He closed the door behind them and gestured at the two stools to the right of the entrance. Cranston and Athelstan made themselves comfortable. The friar stared around. The anker-hold was surprisingly clean, neat and tidy. The cot bed was carefully made. Winter flowers in pewter vases adorned the tops of furniture. Crudely painted triptychs, together with coloured cloths, adorned the plaster walls, whilst threadbare but clean turkey rugs warmed the floor.

'What is it?' the Ghostman asked, pulling back the cowl hiding his skull-like face and head. 'I have been wandering,' he mused, 'among the ghosts who cluster in crowds around this place. I have also been wondering about you, Brother Athelstan. You disturb the ghosts.'

'Why, how?'

'You alarm the malignant spirits who hide behind their shield of lies and loose arrows against the virtuous.'

'Well, I don't know what you're talking about,' Athelstan replied, 'but I'm certainly happy to be of some use. Now look, sir, let us return to the question I posed last time we met. How the Lords of the Air, malignant or not, also have secrets. You said the same to the clerk Hugh Norwic, who now lies slain. Do you remember?'

The Ghostman, chewing his fingers, nodded in agreement.

'What did you mean? Let me explain. Norwic had a sheet of parchment undoubtedly from the Secret Chancery. I found it on his person when I viewed his corpse in the death house. Did you give him that? Is that what you meant? Have you found pieces of parchment littered around the abbey and the royal precincts? Scraps blown by the wind where your so-called Lords of the Air reside?'

'Now I remember,' the Ghostman replied. 'Brother Athelstan, you are correct. I found other scraps culled from the wind and stuck to brambles.'

The Ghostman leapt to his feet and crossed to a battered coffer. He opened the concave lid and brought out a handful of parchment scraps which he thrust at the friar. Athelstan took them and asked Sir John to bring the chipped candle spigot closer so that the glow illuminated the strange signs on the different pieces of vellum.

'Undoubtedly a cipher,' Athelstan murmured. 'And you found these outside?'

'Oh yes, where the Lords of the Air blew them.'

'But do you know where they came from?'

'Why, Brother, the Lords of the Air.'

'Yes, but why did you inform Master Norwic about these fragments? And you gave him one. You knew those scraps had something to do with the House of Secrets where he was a principal clerk. You visited him there; we know that.'

'Yes, that's the truth, Brother Athelstan. But it came to nothing.

Norwic, like everybody else, was not interested in me or what I have to say. I do wander the abbey grounds. I do find pieces of parchment. I handed one of these to Norwic, but the only person really interested in what I found was you, Brother; that's why the spirits take such an interest in you.'

Athelstan glanced at Cranston. The coroner smiled faintly and shook his head.

'All we have, Brother,' he murmured, 'are pieces of parchment. Probably from the House of Secrets, but why they were found outside or how they came to be there is a mystery. I don't think we can make any further progress here.'

Athelstan agreed. The Ghostman's replies were jumbled and incoherent. The friar doubted whether the poor man's wits could even stand close questioning. He and Cranston rose, thanked the Ghostman, and made their way back to the House of Secrets. The coroner then had words with the four bailiffs, ordering them to keep strict guard over Athelstan. He exchanged a hasty kiss of peace with the friar and left. Athelstan watched him go. He then told the bailiffs to make themselves comfortable whilst he walked up and down past the carrels, sifting through what he had learned.

'First here,' Athelstan murmured, pausing to stare at a triptych depicting Michael Archangel's battle against Satan. 'That's what we have here,' Athelstan murmured. 'A conflict between the truth and lies in this House of Secrets. Another world, far removed from the holiness of the abbey, which manifests itself in treachery, betrayal and murder. Here, the secrets of kings, princes, popes and prelates are jealously guarded. Once fought for with a fury and passion, now they are all quietly locked away in iron-bound chests and coffers.'

Nevertheless, Athelstan mused to himself, despite all the secrecy, all the guarding and protection, this House of Secrets was a dripping wound, most hurtful to King and council. Confidential information was being fed to the enemy, who acted on it most cruelly. English spies in Paris were being decimated, secret places uncovered, all to cause chaos and harm, but who was responsible for it? Only the royal clerks in this House of Secrets had access to such information, yet they seemed honest, upright and faithful. They watch each other closely, even as Master Thibault watches them all. So far there has been no sign, no evidence or proof of any treason or treachery by these clerks. True, they resorted and relaxed in a French brothel but, to be honest, there was no sign of anything irregular, except for the murder of one clerk: Hyams. And how did he die in a locked chamber, drinking wine that was proved to be untainted, with no evidence whatsoever of a possible source for the noxious potion he took? So how did he really die, and why? Who was responsible? Hyams had been absent from La Delicieuse the evening Norwic was murdered. Was there a reason for that? Was it part of the mystery or just a coincidence? And why did Hyams visit La Delicieuse so soon after Norwic's death? Were he and Norwic rivals for the hand of Heloise?

Athelstan closed his eyes and reflected on what he had found on Hyams's corpse. Nothing but that small green silk purse, a strange item for a mailed clerk to own. What use would he have for it?

'Brother, Brother?'

Athelstan opened his eyes and smiled at the bailiff facing him.

'Brother, are you all right? I heard you talking and then you fell silent. I thought you were asleep.'

Athelstan reassured the man, telling him that all friars talk to themselves. The bailiff grinned, Athelstan thanked him for his care and continued his walk. He reached the fortified door leading down to the arca. Athelstan lit the refurbished lanternhorn and carefully managed the steep steps. He reached the bottom and sat down on a coffer, staring into the inky darkness. Nightingale's corpse had been removed to the abbey death house, but did the spirit of that resolute spy still linger?

'What happened here?' Athelstan whispered to the emptiness. 'I call on you, Hugh Norwic. How were you pushed, and I think you were, down those razor-sharp steps? You were a fighting clerk, used to the fury of battle. Yet you never even drew your dagger. And why were you murdered? Had you seen something amiss? Did you entertain your own suspicions?' Athelstan rubbed his eyes. 'I am becoming tired,' he murmured, 'yet these matters press hard on me.' He crossed himself. 'And no more so than your murder, Nightingale. Who silenced your song? How did your assassin enter this place when you had locked all the doors? How could they approach you so close to deliver that deadly heart wound and then disappear through locked doors? Did you see your assailant? A man who should never have been here in the first place, whose very presence would alert you to danger. God save me,' Athelstan paused, 'help me trap the killer of these two men.'

Athelstan returned to the buttery and the palliasse now laid out on the floor together with bolsters and blankets. He thanked the bailiffs and they left for their own makeshift beds set up in the different carrels. Athelstan slept for a while and woke abruptly from a dream. He sat up praying the 'Mercy Psalm', then clambered to his feet. He felt refreshed.

'It's time, Friar,' he murmured to himself, 'that you concentrated on the monsters lurking in the murk of your mind.'

He poured himself a small morning ale and ate some of the bread, cheese and ham laid out on a platter beneath a linen covering. He walked over to scrutinize the red circled hour candle before moving to the lavarium to wash his hands and face. He did so slowly, cleaning the ink stains on his writing finger and abruptly paused. Athelstan recalled something occurring at this very lavarium. He stood staring down at the water bowl.

'Oh, sweet Lord,' he breathed. 'I saw that, I know I did. And the memory of it remains because what I glimpsed was a contradiction of something else. Oh Lord, I need to think.'

Athelstan finished his ablutions. He then opened his chancery satchel and set out his writing implements. He unrolled a parchment scroll, placing small weights on each corner. He then sat, recalling the advice of the ancient friar who taught him logic.

'In all matters, Athelstan, let your mind float. You will see, hear and feel things which, at the time, mean nothing, but later acquire a significance all of their own. As you reflect, let your mind sift the chaff from the wheat. No matter how small the piece, keep it in mind. Above all, try and connect cause and effect. If you see something out of place, something which is not logical, don't be impatient. Your mind will clarify matters. Above all, recall what you saw at the time. Remember what you felt, then move down to a conclusion which, however ridiculous it may seem, is the only acceptable answer to the mysteries challenging you. A logical conclusion is, in the main, always the truth – or at least part of it.'

Athelstan closed his eyes, recalling all that he had learnt about the horrid murders here at Westminster. He drew a deep breath and suppressed the excitement he always felt when the hunt for the truth gathered pace. Athelstan stared down at the parchment as he played with the quill between his fingers.

'The problem is in three parts,' he murmured. Then he paused at the pealing of the bell summoning the Blackrobes to prayer. He resisted the urge to join them in the hallowed darkness of the abbey church. 'Wait a while,' he murmured. 'This too is God's work. The relentless pursuit of the sons and daughters of Cain. To trap and catch them, brand them as murderers, assassins, slayers of the innocent.'

Athelstan began to write. First, there was Hyams in that chamber. Secondly, Norwic in the arca. Thirdly, Nightingale, also killed in that cold dark chamber beneath the floor. Athelstan drew a square on the parchment with a stick figure in the middle.

'How does someone murder you?' Athelstan whispered, scoring a line beneath the figure. 'The square is firmly locked. You have the key, yet someone gets in, kills you then leaves, going out through locked doors.'

Athelstan chewed the corner of his lip as he half listened to the rise and fall of the plainchant echoing from the abbey church.

Hyams's murder was different from the other two. Hyams had locked himself in that chamber, the wine left there was untainted. In addition, Argentine was of the firm belief that Hyams could not have been poisoned before he entered that room. According to that skilled physician, the poison used was swift-acting. 'Therefore,' Athelstan whispered into the darkness, 'Hyams must have swallowed it himself. But why? How could that be?'

Athelstan sat sifting through what he had discovered, both now and when he viewed Hyams's corpse and possessions. He abruptly felt the coldest of chills, so swift and clammy that he rose to warm his hands over a brazier.

'Oh yes,' Athelstan murmured to the spluttering coals, 'Hyams's murder is quite distinct from that of Norwic's or Nightingale's. There is a link, a chain of events which connects all these mysteries, but each is quite unique. As for poor Norwic . . .'

Athelstan left the buttery and walked down past the carrels where the sleepy-eyed bailiffs were rousing themselves. Athelstan bade them good morning and continued on to the door to the arca. He unlocked this and carefully made his way down to the fifth step where the lantern was stored. He then left, locked the arca, and opened the door to the jakes closet. Once again, he noticed how well-oiled the hinges were, whilst the smell of wine was still very strong. He left the closet and stood staring at the arca door.

'How?' he asked himself. 'How were those clerks murdered when they were protected by doors locked from the inside? They carried the keys, the only other set being held by Master Thibault. So how?' Athelstan momentarily recalled the attempt to poison him in his own priest's house. 'I shall return to that,' he whispered, 'but not yet.' Athelstan stood for a while reflecting, then made his decision. He returned to the buttery and swiftly wrote a note to Sir John, which he handed to one of the bailiffs to deliver as a matter of urgency. Athelstan then decided to celebrate his Jesus Mass in the chantry chapel of St Edmund, deep in the shadowy nave of the abbey church.

Afterwards, with the bailiffs walking behind him, Athelstan adjourned to the great refectory and broke his fast before returning to the buttery to continue his constant listing as the indictment he envisaged began to take shape. The clerks arrived, going to their carrels. They were followed by Dimanche and one of the Dies Domini, who immediately began to carry out the constant sweeping of the House of Secrets. Athelstan was pleasant and cordial to them all, determined on his studies, his quill pen racing across the parchment in his own secret cipher. He paused for a time to reflect on matters at St Erconwald's: the mist around that mystery was certainly beginning to clear. He now suspected the truth, but that would have to wait for a while.

The day wore on. Cranston arrived an hour before Vespers and, as arranged, the coroner met Athelstan well away from the House of Secrets. Sir John had been given the Abbot's Parlour, a fairly lavish chamber, its walls decorated with gold and silver; bordered tapestries depicted scenes from the life of St Benedict and his sister Scholastica. Cranston handed over the schedule of documents that Athelstan had requested, then left, returning with a sallow-faced, hollow-eyed individual, well dressed in sombre jerkin hose and boots.

'This is my good friend Picaloc.' Cranston patted his companion on the shoulder. 'He has another name, but Picaloc is what he calls himself, so fair enough.'

Athelstan gestured at Cranston and his companion to sit on the chairs placed before the fire, before taking his own.

'I asked for the best, Sir John.'

'Brother Athelstan, Master Picaloc is fairly unique, or so I think. Once he was a master locksmith, the beloved of his guild. Picaloc's star rose high in the firmament and then, like Satan, he fell like lightning from Heaven, never to rise again.'

'All very intriguing.' The friar smiled at the close-faced Picaloc. 'So, what caused your fall from grace?'

'Brother Athelstan, I decided to use my skills on other people's locks. It was so easy.' He pulled a face. 'I was a widower. I married again. A younger lady, most vigorous in bed, but demanding in wanting all the world might offer. In the end . . .'

'In the end you were caught.'

'Yes, Brother,' Cranston replied. 'I seized him myself. Bound for a hanging he was, but I obtained a royal pardon because Picaloc, as he surely will demonstrate, can prove very useful to the Lord High Coroner. Can't you, my friend?'

'And you are sure,' Athelstan asked, half laughing, 'that Picaloc is not the Radix Malorum?'

'Oh no,' Picaloc protested. 'Sir John thought the same. But not me. Nor would I insult the Lord High Coroner.'

'Oh, at the time,' Cranston declared, 'I was suspicious, but the Radix Malorum could climb like a squirrel. Our good friend here has a great love of standing on terra firma. He was skilled in opening doors, but only those which he could easily approach.'

'Which is why we need you here,' Athelstan declared. 'Look Picaloc, or whatever your true name is, I am going to leave you – well-guarded, mind you – in the House of Secrets.'

'And?' Picaloc swallowed nervously.

'Simply put, my friend, once you are there, I want you to open as many locks as you can. You have brought whatever tools you need? I asked this in my letter to Sir John?'

'Oh yes I did.' Picaloc patted the satchel on the stool next to him.

'Good.' Athelstan handed the keys over to Cranston. 'Sir John, we need your authority. Take our mutual friend here over to the

House of Secrets. Clear it completely. Make sure you do, then lock Picaloc in with his satchel of tools and bring the keys back to me.'

'Are you sure?' Cranston and Picaloc's reply was almost a chorus.

'I am certain.'

'And you, Brother?'

'Well, Sir John, the day is drawing on, and for the moment all I can say is that there are locks and there are locks.'

'Meaning?'

'I too have a problem to resolve.' Athelstan smiled gently. 'Sir John, you still look downcast.'

The coroner sighed noisily.

'You mentioned the Radix Malorum, Brother. Well, the bastard has posted another taunting proclamation, claiming he will soon make his presence known all along Cheapside.'

'Will he now, Sir John? Let us see.'

Athelstan sketched a blessing over Picaloc's head. 'Go, my friend,' he urged, 'do what you have to do, as I will here. Sir John, hurry back. God is growing impatient. I will wait for you in the abbey choir.' Athelstan picked up his chancery satchel and patted it. 'All that I need is in here.'

Cranston and Picaloc left. Athelstan heard them go then, escorted by the bailiffs, made his way out into the cold darkness. He followed one of his guards, who lit a sconce torch, its dancing, sparkling tongues of flame hungrily kissing the gathering dark. They entered the abbey church through the Devil's door. The bailiffs remained in the nave, warming their hands over a brazier and discreetly sharing a wineskin and a linen parcel of food. Athelstan went up into the choir stalls and sat down on a lowered seat. He stared around. Lanterns had been lit and hung on hooks. Candle spigots glowed and shared pools of dancing gold. The light seemed to bring to life the carvings along the wall opposite his choir stall: grey-stone faces of saints and angels, as well as the smirking, snarling mouths and eyes of babewyns and a myriad of grotesque, macabre gargoyles. Athelstan relaxed, reciting snatches from the psalms, pleased for the opportunity to seek God's grace and support. The friar eventually closed his eyes. He must have been asleep for an hour before being roused by a grinning coroner.

'Brother, Picaloc is safely ensconced in the House of Secrets. I never imagined that I, as the Lord High Coroner, would allow a former felon to wander such a place and open anything he could.'

'A strange world indeed, Sir John. And now it's going to get a little stranger. Come.'

Athelstan got to his feet and stood for a while, stretching his muscles to ease the stiffness. Once ready, he and Cranston and the escort of bailiffs left the abbey church.

'Where to now, little friar?'

'Oh Sir John, no less a place than La Delicieuse.'

Despite the late hour, they found the taproom of the tavern ablaze with candlelight. Puffs of perfumed smoke rose from the herb-scented braziers and sweet logs crackling on the fire in the great hearth. Stygal offered to show them into the tavern's private parlour, but Athelstan brusquely refused, demanding to be taken up to the chamber where Hyams had died, adding that Mistress Heloise should join them immediately. Once she had, Athelstan gestured at her to take the seat opposite. He studied Heloise's beautiful face, noting the dark shadows which now ringed her eyes, her smooth brow slightly furrowed and lined, her full lips dry and unpainted.

'You have been waiting,' Athelstan demanded, 'for me to visit you again, haven't you?'

She nodded and quietly exclaimed as Athelstan removed from his chancery satchel the small green silk purse he had found on Hyams's corpse.

'You recognize this, mistress? I can, if I want, break into your private chamber and search it. If I did that, I am sure I would find purses such as this, fashioned out of silk and neatly embroidered. Small enough to carry a medal or a pilgrim's badge, not to mention some precious stone. Or, indeed, anything small which needs to be preserved and protected. If you examine it carefully, as I did, you will detect small grains of some substance. I cannot test these. I dare not. You follow my drift, mistress?'

'Yes, I do. So what?' she asked archly.

'My first question, is this your purse? Yes, or no?'

'Yes.'

'Why did I find it on Hyams's corpse?'

'I don't know. Perhaps he picked it up.'

'Where would he pick it up, mistress? In your chamber? And why should he do that? Would you like to taste these tiny morsels?' Athelstan stretched out his hands holding the silk purse. Heloise just glanced away. 'Very good.' Athelstan schooled himself for a lie which was necessary. 'Sir John sprinkled a few of these grains on a soft manchet loaf: the starving rat released to feed on it died in agony.'

'What,' Heloise stammered, 'has this to do with me?'

'Everything, mistress. I shall tell you.' Athelstan pointed a finger at her. 'Listen well. God bless you both, but Hugh Norwic was deeply in love with you and you with him, yes?'

Heloise turned away, brushing at her tear-filled eyes.

'You loved him deeply. You both tried to hide your passion but, as is common enough, such fervour is always noticed by others. In this case, Nigel Hyams, another clerk in the Secret Chancery, who was also deeply smitten with you.'

'But I had nothing to do with him.'

'Of course not. And so, we move to the very heart of this tragedy. Norwic was murdered in the House of Secrets. A deadly push down steep, sharp steps. Hyams, unthinking, uncaring, realized his rival had left the field for good. He cannot believe his good fortune, so he hastens here full of false hope.'

'False indeed.'

'Oh yes, Hyams could hardly hide his elation at the abrupt change in circumstances. He simply failed to realize the sheer tragedy of what had happened and its effect on you and others. Hyams was one of those individuals who are so bound up in themselves, they have no thought of the other. On his arrival here, he could hardly hide his delight, completely ignoring your feelings. Hyams opened his heart to you. You, however, were stricken, cut to the heart by your lover's murder and now by Hyams's open joy at the brutal slaying of your beloved.' Athelstan paused, collecting his thoughts. 'Who knows,' he continued, 'so deep was Hyams's glee that you may well have begun to wonder if Hyams was responsible for Norwic's death. After all, he showed no remorse, no mourning, no sorrow. Whatever, you decided you would have justice over him, as well as silence his spewing mouth. You brought him up here, a well-furnished bedchamber. For a while you performed your own murderous masque, sheer mummery so as to deceive Hyams and coax him towards his death. You promised to return to this chamber where you would . . .' Athelstan paused, trying to choose the right words. 'Yes, yes, you would entertain him! You arranged for wine to be brought, a jug and a goblet, adding that you would bring your own when you returned. God knows what delights you promised Hyams. However, you did offer him an aphrodisiac, no bigger than a small sweetmeat, only this was pure poison.'

'And by chance I would be carrying such an item on my person.'

'Oh come, mistress. You knew why Hyams had come here and what he wanted. Sometime during his visit, you slipped out to your bedchamber, where I am sure such deadly substances are secreted away. If we search your room, and I shall order that if necessary, we would find many different substances. Indeed, a wide variety, as plentiful as any apothecary shop.'

'We shall search,' Cranston intervened. 'Your room and any other place we deem necessary. Mistress, the case against you presses hard. I urge you to think about that as well as your refusal to plead or confess.'

'Why should I? This is all nonsense.' Heloise's voice rose, quivering with fear.

'Nonsense, mistress? How is it nonsense?'

'Brother Athelstan, why should I offer Hyams an aphrodisiac? More importantly, why would he take it?'

'Let me repeat what I have said already.' Athelstan jabbed a finger at her. 'Whatever you pretend this place to be, it is in fact a brothel; and, I suspect, it is also a storeroom of many substances and potions. You are the owner of this place. You are the mistress of this brothel. I am sure what happens in the chambers here is faithfully reported to you by your bevy of ladies.'

'Such as?'

'Oh, personal preferences, what each customer likes or demands. You keep careful watch to see that none of your ladies are harmed or injured in any way. You also learn about, how can I put it, a man's ability to perform between the sheets; who is impotent, who is not, who needs an aphrodisiac, and so on.'

'You seem to know a great deal for a priest.'

'Mistress, being a priest is no protection against the demands of the flesh. I am a sinner and I am not judging you or yours, I am simply proposing a resolution to a murder. Now, is what I am saying the truth?'

Heloise refused to answer, now very pale-faced and visibly agitated, she simply stared at Athelstan as if in shock.

'You gave Hyams that poisonous sweetmeat in this little green purse. You told him to consume it sometime after you left.' Athelstan paused, as if listening to a bell tolling through the gathering dark. 'Mistress, let me summarize why this case presses so heavily against you. First, Argentine, the physician, stoutly maintains the poison was swift-acting. Consequently, Hyams could not have consumed the poison before he came into this chamber. Secondly, you were the last to see him alive. Thirdly, you had to deal with his elation, even joy, at the death of your beloved Norwic. Fourthly, I maintain you gave him that silken green purse containing poison. Furthermore, why was Hyams waiting in the chamber? Who or what was he waiting for? We all know the answer now. He was waiting for the lady of the house to return. Finally, we could, and we certainly will, search your chamber. I think we will find what we are looking for: potions, powders, and small silk purses. Consequently, Sir John here will leave a guard to ensure that you are confined here until our return. Mistress, face the facts. You had both the means and the motive to kill Hyams. You probably knew he had some impairment for which he needed an aphrodisiac; he also wanted you. He would take the potion without a second thought.' Athelstan got to his feet. 'Reflect on what I have said, mistress. We have other business elsewhere but we shall return for your confession.'

'Be careful,' Cranston warned. 'You will be detained in this chamber. One of my men, Grumbel, will lock and guard the door. When all is ready, you will be taken to Newgate Prison and be questioned more closely. Mistress, you murdered a royal clerk and for that you must answer.'

They left the chamber. Cranston locked the door and gave the key to Grumbel, with strict instruction not to open it until they returned. News that something significant had occurred had already swept the tavern. Some of the ladies were agitated, desperate to know what was happening. Cranston and Athelstan politely ignored them and made their way out into the cold, darkening streets. They stopped at an alehouse for Cranston to refill his miraculous wineskin before continuing their journey back to the abbey church, where Athelstan wished to light tapers in the Lady Chapel. Once they had, they crossed to the royal precincts and into the House of Secrets. The bailiffs on guard at the entrance looked slightly embarrassed, whispering to Cranston and pointing to the buttery door.

'What is the matter?' Athelstan demanded.

'He says that we are in for a surprise, so let us see.'

They entered the buttery and Athelstan exclaimed in surprise. Picaloc sat sprawled in a chair, a tankard in one hand, in the other a manchet loaf smeared with honey and butter. As Cranston and Athelstan entered, he gulped this, draining the blackjack and lurching to his feet.

'I'm glad you made yourself comfortable!' the coroner declared.

'Sir John,' Picaloc bowed. 'I was waiting for you. Please, follow me.' He led them through the open door then on to the gallery, passing the carrels, along to the door leading to the arca. This now hung open and Picaloc, trying to hide his air of triumph, led them carefully down the steps to the arca, where two small coffers had been pulled out, and their concave lids raised to reveal the scrolls lying inside. Cranston, mopping his face, sat down on one of the chests, Athelstan beside him.

'How?' the friar demanded. 'How did you do it? You opened the door from the buttery, then turned both locks on the door to the arca and then came down here to open two coffers.'

'I could have done more,' Picaloc answered smugly.

'Impossible! So swift!'

'No, Brother, listen carefully. I am a locksmith. I was born one. I was raised by my father and trained to be the best. Of course, we create a tremendous mystery around our art. Locks are complex, difficult. People such as myself love to promote our skill as something almost miraculous. But, in fact, it is very simple. Listen Brother, Sir John: what is a lock?' Picaloc used his forefinger and thumb to form a circle. 'That's what a lock is, a hole specially fitted into the wood. A small circle of steel, and inside that circle are clasps and catches. If you insert a needle or rod, its sides and tip specially crafted, you can catch those clasps and so release the lock or close it.'

'So, all you need is that special rod?'

'Well, Brother, that's the tool you use. Of course, it requires great skill, but as long as that rod is delicately manoeuvred it will clasp the catch and fasten on to it. It's a question of cunning, skill and patience.' Picaloc opened his belt wallet and took out what looked like a small arrow, except there was no point, just small catches and hooks along the side. 'You turn this in the lock,' Picaloc continued. 'Do it carefully and delicately, and you will eventually fasten the head as you would the key. Once you have done that, the lock is free. Keep it inside, remove what you came for, be it in a chamber or chest, and so you have it. Look.' Picaloc crouched by one of the large crates with three locks across the front. Squatting down to make himself more comfortable, Picaloc inserted the special rod, turning it delicately, listening carefully. He sighed noisily as he heard a sharp click. Then he skilfully removed the rod, turning to the second and third locks to achieve the same result. He tipped the lid back and got to his feet, his face wreathed in a smile. 'As I said, Brother Athelstan, all you need is this rod, along with skill, keenness and patience. Oh, by the way . . .' Picaloc sat down on a chest, wiping his hands on the front of his jerkin, 'I am not the first to try my skill here, both on the door to the arca and these coffers.'

'What do you mean?'

'Sir John, I am a locksmith to my very marrow. I have, and still do, study locks and keys. Accordingly, I can tell from small marks and cuts around a lock if it has been forced as I have just done.'

'But that could be the result of a key being inserted and withdrawn many times?'

'No, that's highly improbable. A key just slides in and turns. However, with the rod,' he grinned, 'what I call the "Rod of Aaron", it's different. You have to push, scratch and scrape around. True, I concede, a key might leave some mark, but on all the locks I've examined? No. I would go on oath, Brother, someone else has also tried their skill on these locks.' He shrugged. 'How successful they were, I cannot say.'

Athelstan nodded and stared at the paved floor, lost in thought, as if listening to the silence of this ghostly place.

'Brother?'

'Sir John, how was Norwic killed? Am I correct in my line of logic? There's evidence enough to move forward.'

'Brother? What are you talking about?'

'Pardon me, Sir John. If you and Master Picaloc would return to the buttery.'

Cranston murmured that he would. Athelstan watched them go, then sat reflecting on the two clerks murdered here. Norwic's slaying now rested on a logical sequence of events. But Nightingale's? Why and how was he killed so swiftly by a deadly thrust to the heart? Athelstan contemplated the possibilities, sighed, then smiled to himself. 'On your knees, Friar,' he exclaimed. 'Time to get on your knees.' He went up the steps, then turned and stared down, imagining Norwic standing with his back to the door whilst he tried to light the lantern. He murmured a requiem and crossed himself whilst wondering how he could empty the House of Secrets for a few days. He reached the buttery. He told Cranston and Picaloc not to be alarmed, then, holding a small lanternhorn, he got to his knees. Athelstan edged backwards and forwards across the paving stones which stretched past the carrels down to the arca door. Now and again he would pick at the dirty cracked stone and peer at what he'd gathered up on his fingernail. At last, satisfied by what he'd seen, he returned to the buttery.

'What on earth was all that about, Brother? A new method of praying?'

'In a way, yes, Sir John. However, I now need you to persuade Master Thibault to clear and close the House of Secrets of all its clerks. You must persuade him to do this and, when I say so, arrange a meeting. Please . . .' Athelstan paused at a sharp rap on the door. It flew open and Grumbel, the bailiff, almost fell into the room.

'Sir John,' he gasped, 'Brother Athelstan, there was nothing I could do about it.'

'Good Lord man, what is it?'

'The woman, Heloise. Brother Athelstan, she's dead.'

'Christ have mercy on her,' Athelstan exclaimed. 'I think I can guess how she died. Poison?'

'Yes, Brother Athelstan. Shortly after you left, so Physician Argentine maintains. I knocked but could hear nothing,' Grumbel continued in a rush, 'so I summoned Stygal. We broke down the door. The woman lay sprawled on the floor.'

'Did she leave a note, a message? I recall there was a small chancery desk beneath the window.'

Grumbel nodded, muttering his apologies as he opened his wallet.

'Calm down, my friend,' Athelstan soothed. 'All will be well.'

'There was a message, here.' Grumbel took out a thin roll of parchment and handed it to Athelstan, who read the short message before passing it to Cranston.

'*Sic habes*,' the coroner murmured. 'You have it. A phrase lawyers use when conceding a point before King's Bench.'

'We have it indeed,' Athelstan replied. 'The closest thing to a confession by that murderess. God knows I feel sorry for her, and I shall certainly recite a requiem.'

'Do you feel guilty, Brother?'

'No, Sir John, I feel sad. Three lives ruined. Three lives ended. Norwic, Hyams, Lady Heloise, and yet the source of their deaths and misfortune has its roots in love. Truly a tragic commentary on the way of all flesh. We wish well, we want to do well but then, as with fruit, a rottenness sets in and all comes to nothing.'

'For her it must have been a relief,' Cranston declared. 'To take the quiet way out. Brother, I take no pleasure in saying this, but she would have been imprisoned, abused, arraigned before the court and condemned to a horrible death.'

'I will pray for her,' Athelstan declared. 'I will pray that she goes towards the light, that she meets the love her life, poor Norwic. God have mercy on them all.'

'*Corona locuta, res finita*.' Cranston quoted another legal phrase. 'The Crown has spoken, the business is finished. Now, my little friar, the House of Secrets and what you want done . . .'

PART SIX

Entouche: poison

Brother Athelstan sat in his priest's house. Across the table opposite, Benedicta stared wonderingly at him.

'So, you know the truth?' she stammered. 'In God's name, Brother Athelstan, if what you say is true, and I know it must be, they could all be hanged. Even worse. Master Thibault and Sir John would be besides themselves with rage. Are you sure?'

'No Benedicta, I am certain. True, my evidence consists of small items which, when woven together, form an indictment strong enough to summon the suspects before the royal justiciars at Westminster or the Guildhall. Firstly, we have the twisted iron bar. Secondly, we have the rostra for the scavengers, detailing who these were and where they worked on certain specific dates. Thirdly, we have the findings of the late Boniface the bounty hunter.' Athelstan used his fingers to emphasize his different points. 'In particular, Boniface's often repeated phrase: how the first three letters of each revealed the identity of the Radix Malorum. I have shown you what these are. Fourthly, we have the poem to St Erconwald and the reference to the bishop and the corpse, and how these two knew where the Redstone was. I now realize what all these references truly mean. Fifthly, we have all that nonsense in the city, which was a cunning diversion. Oh yes Benedicta, you, like me, sense the truth of the situation.' He shifted, listening to sounds outside. 'Ah.' Athelstan rose to his feet. 'Our guests have arrived. Say nothing, Benedicta, until the end. Just sit and wonder.' He was about to turn away when he caught a glint of mischief in the widow-woman's beautiful eyes. 'Benedicta, do you know something I don't?'

'Rest assured, Father, perhaps I do. But as you say, not now. I will let you deal with the mischief in hand.'

A short while later, Athelstan invited his guests – Watkin, Pike, Radulf and Malak – into the house, indicating they should sit on the wall bench just inside the door. Benedicta served morning ales whilst Watkin mumbled news about the parish.

'Yes, yes,' Athelstan interrupted. 'As you know, I arrived back yesterday morning. Benedicta has kept me fully apprised on what has happened since I left. I, however, now have more pressing business with you.' He paused. 'The Redstone! You haven't found it, have you?' In any other circumstance, Athelstan would have burst into peals of laughter. The expressions on the faces of all four men spoke eloquently of their guilt. 'Do not,' Athelstan pointed at Radulf, 'waste my time or that of God or the King, as these are truly weighty matters and must be resolved. All of you could hang, and your only protection against that is me and the truth.'

'Father,' Watkin gasped, 'what is this?'

'Sit still and listen, as will my witness Benedicta. The Radix Malorum,' Athelstan began, 'was a shrewd, skilled and most cunning housebreaker. You not only stole . . .'

'You?' Radulf broke in. 'Who's you?'

'Not the best way to talk to me,' Athelstan snapped back. '"You" refers to yourself, Malak, and of course your two accomplices, Watkin and Pike.'

'Never!'

'Shut up, Pike,' Athelstan warned. 'Just shut your mouth and listen. You stole and you gloried in your crimes. Now the people love names and titles, especially the poor. This is very true of the situation I am now describing. The Earthworms openly revelled at all the stories about this cunning sneak-thief plundering the wealthy lords of Cheapside. You assumed the name from an ancient axiom "*Radix Malorum, Omnium est Avaritia*". The root of all evil is avarice, the love of money. Very apposite for the avaricious wealthy, losing some of their riches. The first three letters of your name, Radulf, leads into Radix, whilst the first three of your name, Malak, initiates the word Malorum. The first three letters of each. The legend of Radix Malorum was born. You trumpeted the name even as you robbed, and then you baited poor Jack Cranston about not being able to catch you. No wonder, you were very well protected. You, Radulf, are a skilled steeplejack, a member of the guild whose insignia you wear on a chain around your neck. I saw it and asked you about it, do you remember?' Radulf glanced away, shamefacedly. 'Do you remember?' Athelstan persisted. 'You claimed it was a gift from the Vagabond King in Paris for a favour you did for one of his coven. Utter nonsense! Now, to return to the indictment. You are most skilled in climbing church steeples, so a three-storey mansion in Cheapside would offer little difficulty.' Athelstan shook his head. 'You kept that skill well-hidden, didn't you? It's not something you like to proclaim for all to see and hear. I certainly cannot recall you ever telling me about it. No, no, you are just Radulf, who mends this and that – best not proclaim what you really do.'

'I-I . . .'

'No, Radulf, now is not the time for lies. Your job as a steeple-jack is one you kept very quiet, though one which you used in your travels. You have further protection. Malak here is your assistant, your guard. He keeps alert for any danger; that's important when robbing a house. You need to be warned in good time that the watch might be swinging by on their nightly circuit. Anyway, once you seize your plunder, you climb down. You join Malak and then wait for further help.' Athelstan pointed at Watkin and Pike. 'Two city scavengers, who by chance are working close by. Oh, don't tell me I am wrong. Your names appear on the rostra kept at the Guildhall.' Athelstan took a sip from his morning ale. 'Sir John Cranston provided such information. You see, I was confused. I racked my brains about how the Radix Malorum could move his ill-gotten gains. Well, first there is the evidence of the rostra, and secondly there is what happened after the Redstone was stolen. On that occasion you, my precious twins,' Athelstan gestured at Pike and Watkin, 'were actually stopped and searched.'

'They found nothing,' Pike protested.

'True, they found nothing, because you had already moved the ruby from your cart to some nearby lay stall, along with the tools used to break into the palace. In fact, that's where the tools were stored before the actual break-in occurred. Who would want to search among mounds of human shit? Oh no, the Radix Malorum stole the Redstone, then gave it to you to hide. You did so, then came back later to collect it. You played the part well. Two hard-working scavengers, cleaning the streets and the lay stalls, arms deep in human ordure and other hideous filth. Radulf, I must admit,' Athelstan smiled, 'I was intrigued by how close you and Malak were with these two precious parishioners of mine.'

'We have always been comrades.'

'Nonsense,' Athelstan snapped. 'You were conspirators as well as comrades. I shall come to that soon enough. Now, to go back down the years to the theft of the Redstone. God knows what really happened that night, but you two thieves fled, later to be joined by your fellow conspirators, Watkin and Pike. All four of you reached St Erconwald's. It was dark but you still had to be careful. I must be truthful, I don't know all the details but somehow, heaven knows for what reason, the Redstone was hidden away in a place you later couldn't recall. Now I know that, fifteen to sixteen years ago, confusion reigned at St Erconwald's, with parish priests coming and going. Many of these were mediocre, a few a downright disgrace both to God and man. In the intervening years, these priests and pastors made changes, especially in God's Acre. I have done the same myself. I have rebuilt the death house, cleared away crumbling headstones, crosses and funerary slabs. Graves were flattened. Gorse and grass cut back. You know that, you witnessed it; in fact you took part in it.' Athelstan fell silent. He stared at the four accused. He could tell by their demeanour that they were guilty, and he sensed that they would be desperate to escape the dire consequences of their crimes. 'The theft of the Redstone,' Athelstan continued, 'also marked the end of your thieving forays. You had crossed a line. You had provoked the wealthy and the powerful too far, too much. The city was deeply disturbed. Vigilance increased; more patrols organized. Lavish rewards were posted for information. Spies, Judas men and bounty hunters were also encouraged to join in the hunt for the Radix Malorum. You had lit a fire and its flames burst out of control. It was time for Radulf and Malak to disappear. Matters were not helped – were they, Radulf? – by your wife's sudden death, but not before she had given birth to twin girls. Ever the merry minstrels, you both decided it was time to travel and off you went. Well away from the traps being set for you in Cheapside and elsewhere.'

Athelstan cleared his throat. 'The years passed; you lived the wandering life, finding work where you could. Life then grew hard, so you returned to St Erconwald's with your so-called precious relic. Oh, you are feted and welcomed as the returning heroes. You have come, so you say, to visit your beloved daughters, as well as to show your miraculous, wondrous relic. In truth, however, you also returned to search for the Redstone, and you set the stage for your masque, the "Great Hunt of the Lord". Sheer mummery. Shadow play. A device enacted so you could basically ransack St Erconwald's both within and without. The main thrust of your argument was that your relic must be concealed somewhere around here. At the time I was distracted. I never really probed why you should think that. Oh, you gave reasons, but why should it go on for so long and so intensely?' Athelstan rose and refilled his tankard. He turned and winked at Benedicta, who had sat fascinated by what she was hearing. Athelstan also caught the merriment in her eyes, and he truly believed she was nursing some great secret about the proceedings in hand. He held her gaze. Benedicta just shook her head, indicating she wished to remain silent.

Athelstan returned to his chair. 'You certainly planned the hunt. You even enjoyed it. You also returned to your game of publicly baiting Sir John Cranston, Lord High Coroner of the city, though there was also a devious reason for this.'

'Sweet Lord!' Watkin moaned.

'Sweet Lord indeed,' Athelstan replied. 'You trumpeted your return. You promised more daring thievery. This was all part of the masque. You wanted Sir John and others to concentrate on the city, the old hunting ground of the Radix Malorum. You agitated the wealthy and, more importantly, roused the Judas men, as a huntsman would whip in his pack of hounds. You provided both bait and lure and all these Judas men cheerfully obliged, coursing like lurchers all over the city, searching for you, desperate to secure the rich rewards offered. Consequently, the hunters confined themselves to the city, well away from Southwark. You then roused your own hunters, but their quarry was different, the Redstone! My parishioners were to find that for you.'

Athelstan's voice shrilled with anger. 'You had the likes of Benedicta here, searching high and low.' Watkin was now groaning, rocking backwards and forwards. 'I was at a loss to explain,' he continued, 'and I really did wonder what was happening, when I discovered a possible key to all this mystery. After the theft of the Redstone, generous rewards were offered for the capture and indictment of the Radix Malorum. Boniface was a most skilled bounty hunter. I cannot vouch for what path he followed but, like any good lurcher, he kept to the scent. Boniface was a strange character; shrewd and cunning, very skilled at hunting men. He concluded, for what reasons I cannot say, that the Radix Malorum would not be found in the city. Perhaps he learned that from the lords of hell who rule London's underworld. He would find nothing except that the Radix had carried out robberies. Nothing about who he might be, how he dressed, where he lived, who his confederates were, nothing. Now, Boniface knew that Southwark – and St Erconwald's in particular – was a place where outlaws, wolfsheads and other felons would congregate, and he began to wonder if that's where the Radix Malorum might be found. You remember him visiting the parish, surely?'

'A true dog of a man,' Pike grated. 'A lurcher in human flesh. We kept well away from him.'

'Of course you did. Boniface knew the likes of you would not help him, so he searched around and he came across an old parish ledger from your previous time in the parish. You did good work here, didn't you, Radulf? Repairing the church tower and roof, not to mention the old mortuary and other buildings. Entries were made, including some abbreviated to "Rad." and "Mal." The priest who wrote in the ledgers at that time used these abbreviations. Boniface studied such entries and, being the most inquisitive of men, he also came across a poem detailing a conversation between Bishop Erconwald and the corpse of a man who had come back from the dead. Boniface made reference about this to Sir John Cranston as he lay dying of a fever at St Bartholomew's. In his confused mind, he claimed the bishop and the corpse had the truth about the Redstone. Boniface had come to believe that the whereabouts of the Redstone was here in St Erconwald's, hence the bishop of the poem, whilst the corpse was a reference to our cemetery. To conclude, I suggest Boniface believed that you, Radulf, and your accomplice, Malak, were the Radix; that you had stolen the Redstone only to flee the realm without it. Consequently, it might still be in or around St Erconwald's parish.'

'Straws in the wind,' Malak protested. 'Nothing but fragments.'

'Which, when put together, do form something quite possible.'

Athelstan spread his hands. 'Of course, I have only described what is possible, but I have also argued that it is also probable, and I think it is.' He stared at the four men. 'For the love of God,' he continued quietly, 'can you imagine what will happen if I lay this indictment before Sir John, not to mention Master Thibault? All four of you would disappear into the Tower. Quite recently, and I learnt this from Sir John's courier Tiptoft, two French spies – yes, those disguised as Dominican friars – were arrested and locked in the Tower. Well, Sir John informed me that both were questioned closely, and tortured, and both are now dead.'

He paused as Watkin groaned, whilst Pike stifled a scream. Radulf and Malak just sat, slightly forward, ashen-faced. Athelstan could see they were terrified. He glanced at Benedicta. She sat, apparently at peace, lost in her own thoughts. She glanced up swiftly and smiled at him. Once again, Athelstan caught her strange mood, as if she too had her own secret thoughts on this matter. Abruptly she shook her head, as if to free herself from her reverie and gestured at the four accused.

'Father.' Watkin and Pike would have slid to their knees to beg for her help, but Benedicta rose quickly to stroke both of them on the head. That gesture determined Athelstan and he made his own decision.

'Benedicta,' he called out, 'what do you think I should do?'

She returned to her chair, sat down and winked at Athelstan.

'Father . . .' Pike pleaded.

'Yes, yes Pike, I know what you are going to say and I agree. All four of you are my friends, fellow parishioners. I cannot, I will not see you taken up by Thibault's creatures. So, Benedicta, what do you propose?'

'Well,' the widow-woman replied, 'Radulf, Malak, you must draw up fresh proclamations. Oh yes,' she insisted, brushing aside their muffled protests. 'These proclamations will be very different from the others—'

'Oh, by the way,' Athelstan interrupted, 'on that fateful Sunday afternoon when I left to meet Sir John in The Lamb of God, I did notice parishioners busy in the hunt – but no sign of you four. Strange, yes? But of course only later did I reflect on what might take all four of you from a so-called hunt on a Sunday?'

'Posting proclamations!' Benedicta retorted. 'Now you will do the same,' the widow-woman continued. 'Only this time you will declare that Sir John Cranston, Lord High Coroner of London, is too much for you; too strong, too cunning an opponent. Accordingly, the Radix Malorum will be leaving the field of combat, give up the tourney, withdraw from the tournament. You will vow to sink into obscurity, never to reappear.'

Athelstan nodded in agreement, though still intrigued by Benedicta's strange mood.

'You will also find the holy relic,' Athelstan declared, 'the alleged sacred image of Our Saviour's face.' He laughed, 'You hid it, so you know where it is – that won't be difficult. You will bring all the nonsense about the "Great Hunt of the Lord" to an abrupt end. I would also recommend that both of you go on pilgrimage, a well-proclaimed one to Walsingham or some other northern shrine. Oh, by the way,' Athelstan added, 'you will leave your sacred image entrusted to your two accomplices in mischief. They can supervise those who wish to pray before it and collect all monies.' Athelstan paused. 'All monies that will, I repeat, be handed over to Mauger the bell clerk for the relief of the poor in the parish.'

Athelstan rose and went to stand over them. 'You will also take an oath to keep secret all that has happened here.' Athelstan pointed to the psalter on the small lectern close to the hearth. 'A most solemn oath on God's own word.' Athelstan steeled his face. 'To break such an oath would incur punishment in this world and the world to come.'

All four quickly agreed and each of them took the oath, repeating every sentence Athelstan gave them. Once they were finished, the friar waved them back to the wall bench.

'Very well.' Athelstan pointed at Radulf. 'You have now learned what I have described, and I believe it is God's own truth. Now, let me hear it from you.'

Radulf glanced swiftly at his three companions, who simply shrugged and returned to stare fixedly at the floor.

'It is true,' he began, clearing his throat. 'I am a most skilled steeplejack. I can climb any mansion. I am skilled in opening clasps and locks.' He rubbed his sunburned face. 'Malak is my most vigilant guard. Watkin and Pike took what I stole and placed it in their cart to take to the nearest lay stall. They also took care of any tools I used both before and after I broke in. No one would want to search a shit heap.' He grinned. 'So, Brother Athelstan, you are correct. I admit I grew heady with my success and I boasted. I took great pleasure in baiting the lords of the Guildhall, Sir John in particular.' Radulf shuffled his booted feet. 'Oh yes, there was another motive: a deep, curdling resentment. My wife died in a street accident caused, I was told, by Thibault's mercenaries, who were cantering too fast along some narrow street. I had scores to settle with both him and the Lord Gaunt.'

'So you decided to steal the Redstone?'

'Yes.' Radulf took a deep breath. 'Father, I am most skilled at climbing walls, however high they may soar. I discovered where the Redstone was kept, how it was guarded – not very securely. We chose a night when Watkin and Pike were on the rostra close to the Palace of the Savoy. Yes, I stole the ruby. I gave it to Watkin, who hid it first in his cart then in a lay stall. Of course, he and Pike were stopped and searched, their cart ransacked. Nothing was found and they were allowed to go on their way, returning to collect the ruby, which they duly did.'

'So what went wrong?'

'I did,' Watkin grated. 'I made a terrible mistake.'

'Oh, you certainly did, my fat friend,' Radulf spat back.

'What?'

'Oh Brother, you won't believe me.'

'Oh yes, Watkin, I will.' Athelstan glanced across at Benedicta. He knew her moods and realized she was bubbling with laughter over what she was listening to, yet she seemed determined to hide this at least for now. Athelstan turned back to Watkin. 'Well?' he demanded.

'Father, I was drunk, completely mawmsey. I was so relieved to escape those searches. Anyway, I kept the Redstone on me even when we entered the parish. We visited The Piebald Tavern and drank blackjack after blackjack of Joscelyn's best ale. After that I cannot remember a thing, except wandering around St Erconwald's looking for a place to hide the ruby.'

'We were in no better shape,' Pike interjected. 'Father, we drank too much, we could hardly stand.'

'I don't remember anything,' Watkin wailed. 'I cannot recall a thing except, and I might have dreamt this, going in and out of the church, stumbling through God's Acre, where I collapsed into a deep sleep.'

'And that is it,' Radulf declared. 'Amen to our attempt to seize the Redstone. We returned here to find the Redstone under the guise of searching for my relic. We were determined not to keep it, but to find it and claim the most generous reward.'

'Of course,' Athelstan breathed. 'The law of treasure trove would ensure a rich return for your discovery: the work of good, honest yeomen who happily stumbled on the ruby whilst searching for something else.'

'Yes, yes,' Radulf agreed.

Athelstan sat back in his chair. 'Benedicta,' he called out, 'do you have anything to say?'

'No, Father.' The widow-woman kept her head down. 'Nothing for the moment.'

'This is all finished,' Athelstan murmured. He then repeated what he had decided and made them promise once again to carry out what had been agreed. Athelstan then gave them all his most solemn blessing and bade them farewell. He locked and bolted the door behind them and returned, moving his chair closer to the fire, stretching out his hands towards the warmth.

'Well, Benedicta, what a tale, eh?' The widow-woman rose, clutching the battered chancery satchel Athelstan had once given her. She moved her chair to sit beside him in front of the fire. 'Ah well,' Athelstan sighed. 'In the end, the Redstone's whereabouts will remain a mystery.'

'Not so!' Benedicta's smile was now impish.

'In Heaven's name, my friend, what do you mean?' He turned to face her squarely. 'Benedicta, you look like Bonaventure when he's cleared a bowl of cream.'

'Because I have the bowl and the cream.'

She rose, made sure the door was locked, and returned to her chair. She opened the chancery satchel and drew out a leather pouch. She untied the knot around the neck and shook out the ruby. The precious stone almost blazed as it caught the light. As big as any egg and similar in shape, the ruby shimmered and glimmered, as if it contained tongues of darting fire. Benedicta handed the ruby to Athelstan, who held it up so it caught the light.

'I see,' he murmured. 'I glimpse its pure beauty.'

He handed the ruby back to Benedicta, who slipped it into the small leather pouch, tying the knot fast before getting up and walking over to the lectern, where she put the stone beside the psalter.

'How, Benedicta? How did you achieve that?'

'Quite easy, Brother. We are not as witless as Radulf and his coven believed. From the very start, I was deeply suspicious about the "Great Hunt of the Lord", and the determination of Radulf and his coven to find the alleged holy relic. After all, Father, who would steal such a thing? To use for themselves? News would spread, the thieves would be caught and severely punished. I thought, I reflected, I prayed, and finally I reached the conclusion.' She grinned. 'As you so often put it, Father, that Radulf was not searching for the holy image. He was looking for something else, and the Redstone is the only logical explanation.' She pulled a face. 'Which in turns means that Radulf and his coterie were responsible for the theft in the first place. Of course, I knew nothing about the details, but I became certain that the ruby must be somewhere in St Erconwald's.'

'Clever, clever.'

'Thank you, Brother. I searched the one place they overlooked. Dark and dingy, with a myriad of cracks and crevices in the wall.'

'Which is where?'

'Philomel's stable.'

'Of course,' Athelstan whispered, 'the wall against which it is built has more gaps and holes than spikes on Hubert the Hedgehog.'

'Well, that's exactly where I found it, Father, behind a loose brick.'

Athelstan rose, walking up and down rubbing his hands, laughing to himself. He went and stood by Benedicta, one hand on her shoulder.

'I will give the ruby to Sir John. He can make up whatever story he wants. How he conducted his own search and, using his wit, his ever-so-sharp wit, he found the ruby. He can act all mysterious and secretive. I'll help him spin a tale. Gaunt and Thibault won't give a fig. They will be delighted to have the ruby back and trumpet Sir John as their noble coroner, the powerful champion of the law. Oh yes, Jack will be drenched in the praise and favour poured out over him. At the same time, the Radix Malorum is also proclaiming the shrewd subtlety of Sir John, his mind and wit, so sharp that the Radix Malorum vows to leave the field to him. Oh yes, Jack will become the toast of the city. Meanwhile, here at St Erconwald's, Radulf and his coven won't be able to say a word. If they did, they would face the most dire consequences. Oh yes,' Athelstan walked closer, 'you, Benedicta,' he bent down and kissed her on the head, 'are the light of my life. However, I have one great favour to ask of you.'

'Father?'

'I want you to leave right now and discreetly search out Moleskin the Bargeman. I desperately need his help. I want him to bring his barge around to that rotting quayside where those two assassins placed us in the bum-boat, intending to take us out to that French war cog. Yes, I still have nightmares about that myself. Take Crim with you. Once you have met Moleskin and secured his agreement, send Crim back to me with a message. I will then come and join you.'

'Father, what—'

'Benedicta, I will tell you when we meet. Now the day is drawing on, I must have Moleskin's advice. I want to set a trap, a lure, a bait, at the very place those ruffians tried to push us out of this life.'

'But that's not all, Brother, is it?'

'Oh, Benedicta, it's just something Sir John and I are dealing with at Westminster: treason, treachery and murder. I believe there is a very strong connection between the assassin at Westminster and that war cog *La Supreme*. Now find Crim and go. I will meet you there.'

Athelstan unlocked and unbolted the door and watched Benedicta leave. He then placed the Redstone into the coffer beneath the bed loft, banked the fire, poured Bonaventure's milk and waited. The flame on the hour candle had almost reached another circle when Crim, all breathless, pounded on the door, shouting for the friar. Athelstan rose, swung on his cloak, looped the strap of his chancery satchel around his neck, grasped his walking stick and opened the door to find Crim leaping about like a flea on a hot pan.

'Benedicta sent me, Father,' Crim shouted, wiping the snot from his nose on the back of his hand. 'She's with Moleskin and they're leaving now.'

Athelstan spun the boy a penny, and strode down the cemetery path to the lychgate. He kept his head down, quietly praying, verses from this psalm or that. Thankfully he was left alone. It was mid-morning, a clear bright day, so most of his parishioners were up and busy with their own affairs. Athelstan continued walking when he heard his name called. He paused, closed his eyes and turned. He then smacked himself on the side of his face as he stared at the four bailiffs, led by Grumbel, who stood staring accusingly at him.

'You,' the bailiff wagged a finger, 'were supposed to tell us when you left. Sir John would have the skin off our backs if we let you go without us.'

Athelstan bowed, struck his breast as a mark of sorrow, gave the bailiffs his most solemn blessing and profusely apologized for his oversight.

'I am glad you are coming with me,' he said, 'because I am going to visit a nightmare place.' Athelstan walked on. Memories of that dire evening, of himself and Benedicta being pulled by those assassins, were still very real; pointed and disturbing. Athelstan had walked these streets and runnels time and again as he visited parishioners, but the horror of that night made everything more vivid. He instinctively knew what turn to take, following the dark cobbled alleyway down to the crumbling quayside. He climbed on to a stone plinth and stared out across the river. No mist had curled up, so he had a clear view of the surging waters. He felt the bitter spray on the sharp breeze, coupled with the usual smells of rotting fish, tar and salt.

'Father?'

'Yes, Grumbel.'

'Sir John said this was the place those assassins took you. Why have you come back?'

'Do you know anything about cogs, Grumbel?'

'No, but I am sure he does.'

Athelstan spun round and stared back. Moleskin's barge was now rounding a bend in the river, the three oars on either side rising and falling. Lanterns glowed in the stern, whilst Moleskin's eldest boy brayed on his hunting horn. Athelstan glimpsed Benedicta sitting in the canopied stern. He got down off the plinth and watched as Moleskin brought his barge in to moor at the very same place the assassins had docked their boat.

'Father, what's so urgent?' Moleskin, pushing back his tarred leather hood, climbed out of the barge on to the soft shale.

'Do you know the river, Moleskin?'

'Better than I know my wife!'

'Then tell me, how far up the river is the war cog *La Supreme*?'

Moleskin made a face.

'Father, because it's a French war cog,' he replied, 'it has to stay on the Southwark side, midstream, down-river. I've seen it a few times – been refurbished it has, Father, all buckled for war.'

'So what's it doing here?'

'It's on guard, Father. On watch for any threats to French shipping. It's to protect their merchantmen, both coming and going. They set up watch on the Thames, ever ready to lift the anchor stones and cast off.'

'What is it, Father?' Benedicta asked, as she joined Moleskin to sit on one of the many plinths that littered the shale-covered water's edge. She wrapped the thick military cloak around her, thanking Moleskin for the loan, and peered searchingly at the little Dominican, who sat like a statue staring across the river.

'To echo what Benedicta asked, Father, what is it, what are you interested in? What do you want?'

'Just some answers, Moleskin.'

'Then go ahead, Father – ask the questions.'

'So, *La Supreme* is anchored further down river?'

'Yes.'

'Can its crew come ashore?'

'No, they can't, Father. They are termed aliens or foreigners. People who might well be hostile to both the Crown and kingdom. They man a French cog of war. They would need a licence to disembark and I am sure none has been given.' The barge master turned and roared at his son to bring warming dishes, small earthenware pots crammed with fiery charcoal and sealed with a metal cap. The boy did so. Athelstan took his, nursing it closely.

'So,' the friar continued, 'how do they provision themselves?'

'Oh Father, for goodness' sake, all the river people provide a market. You've seen the like, Father: wherries, barges, boats, fishing smacks. All kind of craft gather around some majestic cog such as *La Supreme*, offering to sell everything: water, vegetables, meat, drink and, with certain ladies, themselves.'

Athelstan laughed softly and agreed. 'So you are sure the crew of *La Supreme* cannot go ashore? They buy what purveyance they need from the river people, who offer a floating market, with barges and boats rather than stalls?'

'Correct, Father.' Moleskin paused to offer both Athelstan and Benedicta the wineskin he and his crew were sharing. Both shook their heads.

'So,' Athelstan demanded, 'let us say the captain of that cog wishes to send urgent messages to his masters in Paris. What then?'

'Again, Father, you've seen the Venetian galleys, long and sloping, many-oared and with powerful sails. We call them the greyhounds of the sea. They can pick up what they wish from that cog and, given good weather, leave the Thames for the Narrow Seas and across to some port such as Boulogne.'

'And then even swifter couriers pound their way to Paris and the Chambre Noir.' Athelstan smiled. 'Don't worry, Moleskin, none of this is to do with you or the sea or the river.'

'In which case, Father, with all due respect, what are we doing here?'

'Visiting a nightmare place,' Athelstan replied absent-mindedly. 'But Moleskin, never mind, the day passes, let me continue. If I was the master of *La Supreme* and I wanted to send and collect messages from someone ashore, how would you advise I do that?'

'Why Father, if it's a regular occurrence, then simply arrange for your friends ashore to be at a certain place at a certain time.'

'And how would I discern that?'

'Father, pardon me, but do you wish to trap someone?'

'He certainly does,' Benedicta retorted. 'Father, I am getting cold, please tell us what it is you are looking for?'

'Very well, I trust you both.' Athelstan rose and beckoned at Benedicta and Moleskin to join him further up from the water's edge so the oarsmen couldn't hear what he was about to divulge. Once they were well away from the barge, Athelstan lifted a hand, as if taking an oath. 'My friends, what I say is a matter of great importance. To be blunt, if I was the master of *La Supreme* and I wished to receive secrets from a spy ashore, a traitor in our King's household, how could I do this without hurt or harm if none of my crew can disembark?'

'Oh, that's very simple, Father,' Moleskin replied. 'If that was the case, I would advise you to choose some lonely spot where the traitor ashore would come at a certain time as tolled by the city bells. I'd advise the spy to carry a shuttered lantern so you have the place, the hour and the signal. The cog would then lower its bum-boat.'

'Of course, of course,' Athelstan murmured. 'And that's how the exchanges are made. Very simple to organize, with little danger to anyone. Who would notice a bum-boat being lowered in the dark, and rowed with muffled oars to some lonely place along a desolate river bank? The time and place already decided, the lantern drawing them in. Yes, now I understand. Very well, Moleskin my friend. I know, as indeed does all the parish, that you are most skilled in bringing in wine, clothing, spices, herbs and other items. Indeed, all kinds of provender and purveyance.' Athelstan tapped Moleskin on the shoulder. 'And you pay no customs.'

'Really, Father?'

'Yes, really Moleskin. But that does not concern me. John of Gaunt's taxes are unjust and onerous. He can spare a penny or two. Anyway, listen Moleskin. Tonight, I want you to bring *La Supreme* under very close scrutiny. Watch it without being seen yourself, and then report to me what you see and hear. Don't worry,' Athelstan tapped the barge master on the chest, 'you will be well rewarded. A silver piece for you and each of your crew. Three extra pieces if you bring back the information I seek. Moleskin, I know you can do this. You will be a veritable shadow on the water. You can move your barge as if it came from the realm of ghosts like Charon across the River Styx. I've heard of your reputation. "Moleskin the Smuggler" is the toast of the river people. Only this time, don't worry, the Lord High Coroner will extend his protection and, more importantly, make sure you are rewarded "for services to the Crown".'

Moleskin grinned his agreement and clasped Athelstan's hand, promising that he would fasten on to *La Supreme* like a rash.

'But don't be seen,' Athelstan warned, 'and whatever happens, do not intervene. Be vigilant, as what I suspect will transpire, will happen as swiftly as a thief in the night. I bid you farewell. Oh sorry, just one final task, Moleskin. Take your barge across river, search out Sir John Cranston, but do not discuss with him what I have talked about with you. I intend to surprise our noble coroner.'

'So what do you want me to do, Father?'

'Tell Sir John I need urgent words with him at my house this evening. He is to be my guest at a small but splendid banquet cooked by my good friend here, the lovely Benedicta.' Athelstan glanced quickly at the widow-woman, who shrugged and smiled her consent.

She and Athelstan watched Moleskin leave and they walked back to the priest's house. Once there, Athelstan repeated his invitation for the evening, to stay and cook a meal for both of them as well as for their guest, Sir John Cranston.

'I need him here, Benedicta,' Athelstan murmured, crouching before the fire, his fingers out to its warmth. He looked over his shoulder at her. 'But Benedicta, not a word about the Redstone, please. This is not the time or the place. So,' Athelstan got to his feet, 'let me plan, let me plot.'

The evening drew on, Athelstan busy over his chancery desk, Benedicta bustling about in the buttery, leaving the house for a short time to buy certain produce. She returned, laughing to herself.

'The news is now being proclaimed,' she declared. 'Radulf has apparently found the holy image and so the "Great Hunt of the Lord" has been cancelled. They are all assembling in The Piebald to rejoice and celebrate.'

'I'm sure they are, Benedicta. It doesn't take much for my parishioners to rejoice and celebrate. Anyway, where was the relic allegedly found?'

'Buried beneath a gorse bush – the soil carefully arranged. Radulf has proclaimed that he had a dream, a vision of its whereabouts, so he and Malak responded. Very fitting, yes Father, the "Great Hunt of the Lord" brought to a successful conclusion by an Angel of the Lord. Goodness, if you believe that, you'll believe anything!'

'Sweet heavens, Benedicta, what fanciful webs my beloveds weave.' He laughed quietly. 'On the surface they are simple rustics. In truth they are devious, manipulative, creative, and never lacking in their determination for mischief, which is why I love them so much. Now, talking of those we love, let us prepare for Sir John while I pray for Moleskin.'

The coroner arrived just as dusk settled. He came up from the river with an escort of bailiffs, whom he despatched to The Piebald to eat, drink and relax but, he warned, no trouble with Athelstan's beloved parishioners. The coroner still looked despondent. Athelstan sensed this as the coroner exchanged the kiss of peace with Benedicta and himself, before taking off his cloak, beaver hat and warbelt, which he slung over the wall bench. The coroner sighed noisily as he sat down at the table. He took his horn spoon out, polishing it with his fingers, then filled three goblets from the miraculous wineskin. Benedicta and Athelstan served the meal: tender strips of roast lamb, along with dishes of spring vegetables and the softest white bread and wafers from Merrylegs's cook shop. Athelstan recited grace, then proposed a toast to that 'ever-green cook', Mistress Benedicta. For a while they ate in silence.

'Wonderful,' Cranston murmured. 'I could smell the richness of this dish even before I knocked on the door.'

'Lord Jack,' Athelstan retorted, 'you eat well, yet you still seem troubled.'

'Oh, the pot is beginning to bubble over.' The coroner put down his goblet. 'Gaunt wants answers, Thibault can't give them.' He paused as the city bells began to toll for Vespers, the hour for all good citizens to return to their homes and pray for God's mercy.

Athelstan crossed himself, bowed his head and prayed fervently that the bells now tolling would also bring him the proof he so desperately needed. He stretched across and tapped Sir John on the back of the hand.

'My friend,' the friar insisted, 'trust me, deliverance is close at hand. If all goes well tonight, then tomorrow night we will spring our trap and the morning after that we will close with our enemy. Now, Sir John, let us leave all this and discuss what the Commons are complaining about. Above all, what is Thibault doing to save his skin and that of his Master Gaunt?'

Cranston happily obliged. They sat and chatted, Athelstan keeping an eye on the hour candle, its flame turning the wax to liquid as it moved down to the next mark. The flame had almost reached the red circle when there was a pounding on the door. Athelstan answered it and Moleskin, all excited, strode into the room, clapping his hands in glee. Athelstan made him calm down and sit with them, serving the barge master a heaped platter with a generous goblet of wine. Once finished, he pronounced himself satisfied and beamed across at the friar.

'You were successful, Moleskin?'

'Successful indeed, Father!'

The following morning, Athelstan rose early to prepare himself for the coming confrontation. He washed, shaved and changed his clothing, before hastening, through the mist-hung morning, down to the church to celebrate the Jesus Mass. His congregation was rather meagre, only a few of the committed gospel greeters were present; these included Benedicta and Moleskin. The barge master still looked ever so pleased with himself. Benedicta, however, showed her real fears over what had been discussed, plotted and planned the previous evening. Even Sir John had left cheerfully, laughing quietly to himself, adding that he would return tomorrow evening with his escort, who could be billeted in the parish church. All they would need would be himself, Moleskin, Flaxwith and the barge master's oarsmen. He maintained that these would be enough to carry through what Athelstan had suggested. Athelstan now prayed it would be so.

Once Mass had finished, Athelstan excused himself, reassuring Benedicta all would be well, whilst whispering to Moleskin that he must be ready at the appropriate time.

The day passed quietly enough. The parish woke up late, still immersed in the celebrations around the discovery of the relic of the Holy Face, and the successful end of the Great Hunt of the Lord. Athelstan kept well away from this. He knew that the jovial mood would soon pass and his parishioners would return to the thorny problems of daily parish life.

Athelstan kept to his cottage for the rest of the day, reviewing the indictment he was drawing up. He believed he had the truth of the situation; now all he needed was more telling evidence, sure proof, which he knew would send people to the scaffold.

Cranston arrived as the light turned to dusk. He and his escort of Flaxwith and five bailiffs collected Athelstan, and they walked down to the ancient quayside where Moleskin and his barge were waiting. Cranston dismissed the other bailiffs, then he, Flaxwith and Athelstan clambered on to the barge, cloaked and cowled against the biting river breeze. They cast off and made their way across the Thames then changed tack to move down past Westminster. Eventually they rounded a sharp bend in the river, close to the Devil's Sandbanks, which reared up like some ancient river monster. Moleskin ordered his oarsmen to rest. Lamps and lanterns were doused, oars swiftly muffled with rolls of filthy cloth. Once ready, they continued through the gathering night. They rounded another bend, moving more into midstream and eventually stopped. The French war cog, *La Supreme*, was now in full view. A tangle of wood, sail and rope, black against a clear sky, made brighter by the full moon which hung rich and low.

'Will they see us?'

'No, Father,' Moleskin replied, 'we are low in the water. The darkness shrouds us. As long as we make no carrying noise and keep all light extinguished, we will be safe.'

Athelstan quietly prayed that they would remain so. They had made good, swift passage along Southwark bank and on past the buildings, churches and quaysides of Westminster. They were now free of the city, with stretches of wild countryside either side of the Thames. A most suitable place for a French war cog to ride at anchor, as well as being an ideal place, as Athelstan pointed out, for the ship's crew to indulge in mischief. The friar took out his ave beads. He was reciting the final 'gloria' when the bells of the city began to toll for Vespers, the powerful pealing booming out from the city. Athelstan tensed. Moleskin ordered his eldest son up into the poop.

'Peterkin has the keenest sight,' the barge master whispered, 'he's as sharp as any hawk on the wing.' The young man scampered up as high as he could, nodding at his father's whispered orders to watch the bank off the starboard side. Peterkin hissed back that he had a good view. Moleskin urged the others, Cranston included, to watch *La Supreme* carefully. Athelstan slipped the ave beads back into his wallet. The Vespers bells still boomed out, drowning the screeching and cries of the river birds and the constant slap of the river as it swirled peacefully down to the sea. They watched and waited.

'There!' Peterkin hissed. 'Look, look, on the bank, on the bank!'

Athelstan narrowed his eyes, darkness hung like a heavy curtain. He could just make out trees, bushes and gorse, which crowded down to the waterside. Again he looked, brushing away the salty spray as he glimpsed lantern light, flashes of brightness, as whoever was holding the lanternhorn open and closed its shutters.

'And the same from the cog,' Cranston whispered, 'watch now.'

Athelstan stared hard. *La Supreme* moved slightly, pushed by the current, and he glimpsed the bum-boat being lowered, followed by two men clambering swiftly down the rope ladder into the waiting skiff. For a while this tipped and turned as it was caught by the river. Eventually the two oarsmen brought it under control, turning it slightly, before pulling out to the river bank. Athelstan edged forward.

'Ignore whoever is on shore,' he declared. 'Indeed, I do not want him or them alarmed. They must return to report that all is well: that is most important.'

'And those in the boat?'

'We must intercept them, Sir John, swiftly and silently. They are not important, but what they might be carrying will be. So, Moleskin, how do we trap the boat people?'

The barge master stepped closer.

'I hear what you say,' he declared, 'so, we must wait for whoever is on land to first disappear. The boat people will beach their skiff as high on the shore as they can. They don't want the river pulling their craft away. Once they have done what they came to do, they will turn the boat as swiftly as possible for the journey back to *La Supreme*. We should not sail directly for the shore, but cross and turn in the shallows, then wait. We will be deep in the shadow of the trees, the darkness will help, but we must get as close as possible to that bum-boat.'

'And remain silent,' Athelstan warned. 'Those aboard *La Supreme* must not be alerted to what we are doing. We must seize those boat people with as little sound as possible.'

'Oh, don't worry about them,' Cranston replied. 'Yes, Flaxwith?' The chief bailiff murmured his agreement.

Moleskin ordered his rowers back to their seats, and the barge, silent as a shadow, cut through the waters, hidden by a cloak of darkness, as well as a deepening river mist, for which Athelstan gave grateful thanks.

They reached the shallows close to the bank then turned, with Moleskin whispering instructions to his crew. His rowers dipped their muffled oars into the water; the barge slowly and quietly edged its way forwards. Now they were so close to the shore that the sounds of the night echoed more sharply: the constant shriek of gulls were answered by the hoot of the owl and the bark of foxes. Athelstan sat tense. He could not see much, but Peterkin, still high in the prow, whispered back what he could glimpse.

Moleskin ordered his men to rest on their oars. They were now close enough to hear noises as the bum-boat reached the shore, scratching on the shale with the clatter of oars. Athelstan caught snatches of conversation in French, as well as the harsh sound of bracken breaking under someone's boot. This was followed by silence, eventually shattered by fairly loud farewells and some short, sharp laughter. Again, the sound of bracken snapping and cracking under booted feet.

'Their visitor is leaving,' Cranston whispered.

'I agree,' Moleskin replied.

'In which case, Master Moleskin, for God, our King and St George.'

Cranston snapped his fingers at Flaxwith. 'Henry, let's get ready.'

The chief bailiff nodded. He opened the sack between his feet and took out two handheld arbalests. He handed one to the coroner, then both men hastily primed their weapons, winding down the winches and inserting the thin, barbed bolts. Moleskin whispered fresh orders. The rowers leaned on their oars and, at their captain's instruction, pushed forwards together. The barge abruptly surged, racing forward, cutting through the water, coursing through the shallows so swiftly, so silently that Athelstan could hardly believe it. The mist cleared. Athelstan realized that they were aiming directly at the bum-boat which had just turned towards *La Supreme*. Moleskin's barge crashed into the skiff; a resounding crack echoed sharply, followed by silence. The bum-boat's two occupiers were flung into the river, their cries and calls easily stifled by the water. Cranston and Flaxwith now crouched on the side of the barge and, before Athelstan could intervene, loosed their bolts, killing both men, who were floundering so close that their corpses were swiftly hooked and pulled aboard.

'Silence now,' Cranston ordered.

They all sat listening, staring into the dark. Athelstan wiped the sweat and spray from his face. He felt his stomach pitch, a queasiness caused by the sheer speed and horror of the attack. Those two French sailors had been sitting in that bum-boat and, within a few heartbeats, they had been tossed into the water before being slaughtered and hooked as if they were fish.

'All quiet now,' Cranston breathed, coming to sit beside Athelstan. The crack of the boat, the cries and shouts of those two men, had all been cut off. 'I doubt if anyone on *La Supreme* heard anything amiss and, if they did, they would dismiss it as sounds of the night.' He nudged Athelstan. 'Strange things happen along the river, little friar.'

Athelstan didn't reply. He just rose and made his way, stumbling, to the stern, and the two water-soaked corpses heaped there. He muttered a requiem as he blessed the dead men and returned to sit on the bench next to Cranston. Moleskin was now rapping out orders at the coroner's instruction, telling his oarsmen to pull away, keeping as close as possible to the river bank until they reached Westminster. Then they would turn towards King's Steps.

'What's the matter, Athelstan? Are you upset, little friar, at those sudden deaths? Please remember they were our enemy; they were forbidden to leave their ship and come ashore here or anywhere else. We could not let them escape. You've already told me the reason why. More importantly, and we will examine the corpses when we reach Westminster, if they had been given time, I am sure they would have disposed of whatever they were carrying.'

'Yes, yes,' Athelstan sighed noisily, 'Sir John, I agree. Thibault would have hanged them out of hand, anyway. I just pray that we find what I suspect they were given.'

'The captain of *La Supreme* will be suspicious.'

'I don't think so, Sir John. They will wait for that bum-boat to return and, when it doesn't, they will begin a search. But for that, they must wait for daylight, and that's hours away. By then, we shall have sprung our trap, and there's nothing *La Supreme* or the Chambre Noir can do about it. Indeed, Sir John, I believe that cog, *La Supreme*, is in fact the Chambre Noir, a warship specially devoted to certain enterprises, crewed by men who have already taken an oath of total loyalty to the French Crown.'

Cranston took a generous swig from his wineskin, then thrust it into the friar's hands.

'Take a slurp, little friar. Let me see if I can bring you a present.' And before Athelstan could stop him, Cranston stood and made his way to the stern, crouching before the corpses.

Athelstan sat, head down, clutching the wineskin. He did not want to drink. What had happened on the river was only the beginning, not the end. He looked up as Cranston shouted in triumph. The coroner stumbled back and thrust a small leather sack into Athelstan's hands before giving the friar a fierce hug.

'Well done, Brother,' Cranston declared. 'Well done indeed. You were correct. What we've found tonight will definitely despatch traitors to their just reward.'

Athelstan opened the leather sack and took out the small scroll-container. He loosened the copper lid and shook out the manuscripts. By now Moleskin had relit the lanterns, and Athelstan asked the barge master to bring one closer. Once he had, Athelstan undid the scroll and smiled at its contents.

'Oh yes,' Athelstan murmured. 'Sir John, we have it. Once we have reached the quayside, let us seek urgent audience with Master Thibault. War cogs must be despatched to keep *La Supreme* where it is and to ensure no one either enters or leaves that ship. We need more time to put our pieces together on the chessboard, then we will make our final move.'

'Very good, Friar, an excellent night's work. Time to relax, time to rejoice at The Lamb of God.'

'First we must tend to the dead, Sir John. Have the corpses removed to the death house where we can examine them more closely.' He brandished the small leather bag. 'We have enough here but there may be more.'

They berthed at a quayside near King's Steps. Cranston immediately disembarked, staring around, but it was still the early hours with hardly anyone about. Just the occasional lay brother from the abbey going about this errand or that. Satisfied they were not being watched, Cranston returned to the barge and asked Moleskin's oarsmen to bring the corpses, as discreetly as they could, to the abbey death house. The barge master then instructed the oarsmen to wrap the two dead men in the canvas sacking he kept in the hold of his craft. Once ready, Athelstan told Moleskin to wait whilst he led what he called 'the funeral cortege' into the abbey precincts. Surprisingly enough, the death house had not closed. Athelstan glimpsed chinks of light between its shutters and under the heavy, forbidding door, which swung open as the Keeper of the Dead, looking even more skeletal in the flickering light, beckoned them in.

'An early hour, Brother Athelstan.' He peered over the coroner's shoulder. 'And I suspect you've brought more guests for my tavern of eternal night.'

'Brother,' Athelstan replied, 'we need you to keep this discreet and confidential. The cadavers are two Frenchmen killed in a fight on the Thames. They were where they were not supposed to be, and carrying something that was not theirs. Sir John and Master Flaxwith had no choice but to kill them.'

'Come in, Brother. I am not concerned about why people die, but what I must do for them when they are dead. Come, come.' He led them into the hall of corpses and pointed at two tables. Moleskin's oarsmen undid the canvas sacking and placed both cadavers on the tables next to each other. The Keeper of the Dead exclaimed quietly at the horrid wounds to both men: a crossbow bolt embedded deep in each of the men's skulls.

'It will take some time,' he murmured, 'to remove those. I won't do it now, Brother. It is sickly – in fact, it's disgusting; brain, blood and bone will pour out. So, now they are here, what else do you want with them?'

'To search their corpses.'

'Very good. Then I will leave that to you.'

Athelstan and Cranston searched the clothing of the two deceased sailors. They found some silver coins which they handed to the principal oarsmen. Cranston said he could find nothing else, but then Athelstan drew out another leather bag with costly leather twine tied at the neck. He cut this and emptied the scroll out. Unrolling it carefully, he studied the well-written cipher.

'God knows,' he breathed, 'what information this is. But, Sir John, we certainly have enough.'

He turned to the Keeper of the Dead.

'My friend, dress both corpses for burial. Have one of the good brothers sprinkle holy water, then have then interred in the poor man's lot. Any costs you incur will be met by Sir John Cranston here.'

'Submit all bills to the Guildhall,' the coroner declared. 'For my friend,' he clapped the Keeper of the Dead on the shoulder, 'you have certainly earned your fee. Now, Brother, my bed awaits, and I am sure so does yours. I said we could adjourn to The Lamb of God. Of course I had forgotten the hour, whilst Mine Hostess, after what happened there, is extremely wary about opening her hostelry at such an early hour.'

'Sir John, it's time we retired. Now you know what to do.'

'I don't really, Brother. However, I am sure, when you have refreshed yourself, you will tell me what you intend, what you need and what you want. Until then . . .'

They exchanged the kiss of peace and left the death house. Cranston lifted his hand in farewell and stomped away, whilst Athelstan and the oarsmen rejoined Moleskin on his barge.

Two days later Athelstan, accompanied by Flaxwith and a cohort of bailiffs, left Southwark in Moleskin's barge, to meet – as arranged – the Lord High Coroner in the Abbot's Parlour at Westminster. Once they had exchanged the kiss of peace and broken their fast on morning ales and strips of bread toasted with cheese, Cranston assured the friar that all had been arranged.

'We shall meet,' he said, 'in the small chapter house. Thibault will join us at the Angelus. He will be accompanied by his Spanish mercenaries. I have a company of Tower archers, not to forget Flaxwith and his comitatus. We will be well protected. Master Picaloc will also be there. I received your messages. Those on your list whom you wanted to be invited to this banquet of murder are all on the way. Everything is as you asked. Now, Brother, what is all this?'

'In a short while, Sir John, all will be made manifest. However, in the meantime . . .' Athelstan drew out the small leather pouch from his pocket, undid the knot and gently shook the Redstone on to the table. Cranston, crowing like an excited child, seized it in both hands, raising it high as a priest would the host during Mass. The coroner then slumped down, staring at the Redstone, turning it over, moving it from hand to hand before gasping out a veritable litany of questions which Athelstan adroitly fended off, insisting that Cranston must now compose what he would say to Thibault. The coroner swiftly understood what Athelstan was intent on.

'This has nothing to do with your beloved parishioners and the bubbling pot of intrigue and mischief they constantly stir?'

'Sir John, I assure you they have nothing to do with your great present for Master Thibault. So, what I want you to do is listen carefully. You will take the ruby back to him. You will proclaim that you found it. I have thought long and hard about a possible tale and I give you this. I understand in Cheapside, close to the Standard, there used to be a goldsmith's house.'

'Yes, there was. I remember him well, Pendle, an old miser, a collector of precious stones. But Athelstan, he's dead, long gone to God. And, if I understand correctly, his house is all boarded up both front and back.'

'Precisely, Sir John. Now you will tell Thibault that Pendle was not above receiving precious stones stolen from their rightful owner. You wondered if he had anything to do, not with the theft of the Redstone, but with its disappearance. Anyway, you visited the house using your authority. You broke in and searched it but found nothing. You then went out into the garden where you noticed, yes, something amiss. You investigated and found that leather pouch with the Redstone inside. So, Sir John, you will have to pay a visit to that garden and use your imagination to further this tale. But you will find something. You will then argue that Pendle received the jewel from the thieves and hid it away, intending to sell it at the appropriate time in the safest way. Embellish the tale if you must but, I assure you, Thibault and Gaunt will be so pleased that they won't give a fig about your story or about Pendle. They'll care for nothing except for the ruby's safe return.'

Once he was satisfied that Sir John had the tale word perfect, Athelstan excused himself to pray at the prie-dieu placed beneath a triptych depicting the Virgin and Child. Athelstan quietly intoned the '*Veni Creator Spiritus*', asking for guidance in the coming confrontation. He closed his eyes and, lost in the words of the prayer, gently dozed until the sound of harsh mailed footsteps aroused him.

Cranston deftly put the ruby away, saying he would inform Thibault once he had visited Pendle's house and garden. The Angelus bell was tolling as Thibault and Evangelios, his Spanish henchman, along with a comitatus of hard-bitten, harsh-faced veterans, swept into the Abbot's Parlour. Thibault was insistent on questioning Athelstan, but the friar gently fended off the spate of questions, asking Thibault if all was ready in the small chapter house. Once assured it was, Athelstan insisted that they go there immediately.

The chosen room was a half-circular building, nestling between the great cloisters and the abbey church. It consisted of a range of stalls, built against the concave wall, six on either side of the aisle, which swept up to the lectern where the abbot or prior would direct proceedings.

Athelstan took his place there, staring around the chamber. It was busy and bustling now, yet everything was as he had asked. The four clerks of the Secret Chancery sat in stalls to his right. The stalls on the other side being taken by Dimanche and his five scavengers. All looked highly nervous and agitated. The scavengers in particular, combing hair and beard with dirty fingers, shuffling mud-encrusted boots as they talked amongst themselves. Braziers glowed whilst the fire in the mantled hearth, built against the outside wall, roared noisily up the chimney stack.

Cranston and Thibault sat at a table to Athelstan's right and, behind them, arranged in an arc, Tower bowmen, arrows notched, whilst Thibault's mercenaries mixed with Flaxwith and his bailiffs near the doors and windows.

'What is this?' Edmonton called out.

'Quiet!' Athelstan shouted back.

'Silence, Master Edmonton, or I'll have you in chains. And,' the coroner added, 'that applies to everyone else who interrupts proceedings.' The coroner turned in his chair. 'Brother, do begin.'

'So I shall,' Athelstan declared in a ringing voice. 'A few days ago, I asked Sir John Cranston and Master Thibault to close the House of Secrets, its clerks being confined to their chambers or, if they wished, the La Delicieuse tavern. Sir John proclaimed his reasons for this. How we believed a precious key, a very important one, had been lost; gone missing. As you know, only Dimanche and the Dies Domini were allowed in. No one else. Their task was twofold: to clean the House of Secrets in preparation for spring, and to find that key. Dimanche?'

'We certainly cleaned but,' Dimanche rose and raised his hands, 'we found no key.'

'Of course not,' Athelstan replied. 'That's because there isn't one. We lost no key. It was all a fiction.' Athelstan's reply stilled all clamour. Dimanche, mouth gaping, stumbled back into his stall.

'I don't, I . . .' he spluttered.

'Silence!' Athelstan demanded, staring around. The atmosphere in the chapter house had suddenly changed. An air of anxious expectation, of fear creeping like a mist across the chamber. 'Very well. Let me continue.' Athelstan pointed towards the door. 'Bring in Master Picaloc.' The locksmith was marched in. He took the oath, placing his hand on the Book of the Gospels held by Cranston, before turning to face the rest. 'Master Picaloc,' Athelstan began. 'You are a master key-smith, yes?'

'Yes, I certainly am.'

'Locks and keys hold no mystery for you?'

'Very little, if any.'

'And over the last few days, you have examined many of the locks and keys . . . But ah!' Athelstan held up a hand. 'I hurry ahead of myself. On the first day of the closure of the House of Secrets, you smeared the locks to its doors, as well as those of the chests and coffers held in the area?'

'Yes, I used a soft spot of grease, which is harmless enough. It is, as you say, translucent. Something you would miss seeing and, if you did catch sight of it, something you would dismiss as being caused by the locks or the keys that opened them.'

Athelstan stood silently, gathering his wits and thoughts for the coming confrontation. He had met Picaloc soon after he had disembarked at King's Steps, and received his news which would unlock this mystery.

'So,' Athelstan pointed at the scavengers, 'you were the only ones allowed into the House of Secrets. You, or one of you,' Athelstan now pointed at Dimanche, 'seized the opportunity for mischief and the trap was sprung.'

Dimanche lurched to his feet, hands waving, lips mouthing protests. He took a step forward.

'*Captain!*' Cranston roared; a yard-long shaft whistled through the air to smash into the wall behind the scavengers.

'I will be blunt. You,' Athelstan gestured at Dimanche and his comrades, 'are not who you claim to be. I shall prove this, thanks to my good friend Picaloc here.'

'This is impossible,' Edmonton shouted. 'They are the lowest of the low: simple rustic men.'

'They are French spies,' Athelstan retorted. 'So let us start from the beginning. This is the House of Secrets; it is a place where important documents are drawn up and recorded. We have the writing carrels for the clerks and the arca, a secure repository for all the important and confidential memoranda and letters of our King and his ministers. There are six clerks, or rather there were – senior officials under the direct supervision of Master Thibault here. Now, one of the problems of any record office or library is the way vermin swarm, and these are anathema to parchment, vellum, wax, quill pens, and all the other paraphernalia of the chancery. They can cause great damage so there's a constant need for cleanliness. Yes, Master Edmonton?'

'Of course. Of course.'

'However, another problem is: how do you keep a building such as the House of Secrets clean, without making it vulnerable to those who would love to know what is stored here. Yes, Master Thibault?'

'It stands to reason, Brother Athelstan.'

'So, it is essential that those who are hired to keep this place clean are illiterate, uneducated. Such men would pose no threat to the security of this place. However, to take matters even further, Hugh Norwic, at Master Thibault's persuasion, decided to hire five simple scavengers, one for every working day, as well as a custos or keeper to supervise their work throughout the week. He would advertise and proclaim what he required in the usual places: St Paul's Cross, or the Great Conduit in Cheapside, or the approaches to London Bridge. Now, unbeknown to anyone, except for the dark masters of the Chambre Noir, a French battle group, a "*cohors damnosa*", had been despatched to London on board a French war cog, *La Supreme*. Now I believe that vessel is not only a floating fortress, but a chancery chamber for this battle group, known as Les Mysterieux, which consists of very skilled spies, mailed clerks, veterans under their leader or Magister, who calls himself the Key-Master – that is you, Dimanche. In fact, you are all, I am sure, as educated and learned as any Oxford clerk or master in the schools. As I have said, you have probably all seen military service, fully trained in the ways of the chancery, fluent in English and, above all, as skilled at mummery as any strolling player. Les Mysterieux land here, courtesy of *La Supreme*, which exploits the ordinance of the English Crown that French war cogs must stay well clear of both the city and Westminster. They must ride at anchor along some lonely stretch of the river. At least six of the group lands; this includes their Magister, though I am sure *La Supreme* housed, and still does, other members of the battle group, including those two assassins disguised as Dominicans. The ship's hull also contains potions and poisons and a wide choice of weaponry. Now, on landing, Les Mysterieux have changed, slipping from one guise to another. Old masks are doffed and new ones assumed. No longer the sharp, keen-witted clerks, shaved and shorn, instead they have become shambling English labourers, garbed in filthy rags, with hair, moustache and beard more tangled than a bramble bush. Once landed in some desolate part of the river bank, you searched out possibilities. You must have gone on your knees in thanksgiving when you read Norwic's proclamations, trying to recruit scavengers for the King's chancery. You and Norwic meet.'

'But why should he appoint them?' Edmonton shouted.

'Oh, I think the logical answer to that is simple enough. Dimanche, as he is called, promised to recruit a scavenger for each day of the week. Now, we all know that few scavengers would accept only one day's work, and would much prefer to work all five days of the week.'

'But Dimanche himself would be here for weeks on end.'

'True, Master Edmonton,' Thibault called out, 'but we need at least one, not more, to supervise these scavengers, to be their custos.'

'Correct,' Athelstan declared. 'There had to be some continuity. Dimanche provided that. As for the other five, Dimanche probably argued that his small coven of scavengers would be busy elsewhere, but each could spare one day in the week. I admit,' Athelstan spread his hands, 'I felt a slight unease when I learned this. I was uncomfortable with that arrangement. However, at the time I had no context for it. Now I do. Norwic must have been beside himself at such success.'

'He certainly was,' Sheffield called out. 'He was delighted.' The other clerks murmured their agreement. 'I remember,' Sheffield continued, 'the day we met Dimanche and the five scavengers. We coined those names for them. Of course, I was – we were – completely duped.'

'Oh yes,' Athelstan shook his head, 'three months ago Norwic did not appoint scavengers. In fact, he appointed spies, members of Les Mysterieux. French spies, fluent in English, who disguised themselves behind an appearance of being the most wretched, poverty-stricken denizens of this city. They didn't have to speak much and were confined to simple tasks: cleaning rubbish, brushing steps and emptying baskets. The sheer banality of such tasks was their best protection and disguise. So it was and so it is.' Athelstan sighed. 'Dimanche and his cohort thrived here. They penetrated deep into the House of Secrets of our King. At first, however, they would work faithfully, dutifully, honestly, creating no trouble or any suspicion.'

'They were excellent,' Edmonton intervened, 'we had no complaints. They would arrive at the proper hour and leave at the appropriate time. They were like shadows or ghosts. I never really noticed them. All I was aware of was how the House of Secrets was always clean and tidy.'

'Naturally,' Athelstan replied. 'They wanted to humour you and, above all, soothe you.'

'And they duped us.'

'Yes, Master Edmonton, they certainly did.' Athelstan paused, collecting his thoughts. 'Now,' he continued, 'when I began my investigation, I was utterly baffled at how very important information could leave the House of Secrets and be found in the Chambre Noir. The clerks who walk and work in these secret cloisters are all good and true in their loyalty. There is not a jot of evidence or the slightest suspicion about their integrity. Of course, they consort with the French ladies at La Delicieuse, but that issue was thoroughly investigated. In addition, everything in the House of Secrets is kept very firmly under lock and key. The scavengers could hardly be viewed as a threat. Totally illiterate, each worked only one day a week. They are watched as they work and searched when they leave. Well . . .' Athelstan paused to take a sip of morning ale and quickly stared around the room. He was pleased; all the assembled were now fully attentive, absorbed by what he was describing. 'Well,' he repeated, 'when I first began to follow my suspicions, I did wonder if the stolen secrets were somehow connected to the rubbish collected from the chancery baskets kept in each carrel. Of course, I soon realized that little, if any, secret matter could be found in mere scraps of parchment. Nightingale talked of his web in Paris being cut, hacked and sliced. No, I concluded. Someone was fishing in deep waters to catch the largest fish. Eventually I reached the logical conclusion that, if I am in the arca and I wanted to steal from one of its coffers, the only way I could do so was with a key. However, I don't have one. The keys, two sets in all, are held by Master Thibault and his principal clerk. I prayed, fasted and reflected. If I didn't have a key, was there a way I could still open a sealed coffer or casket?' Athelstan went over to Picaloc and clapped him on the shoulder. 'I decided to summon a peritus, an expert, a veteran locksmith, and my hypothesis was proved correct. The coffers could be unlocked with the correct tools by someone of consummate skill. You, Dimanche, call yourself the Key-Master, and you certainly are. This is a very blatant reference to what you do.'

'You have it wrong. I do not—'

'You are the Key-Master,' Athelstan flatly replied. 'As highly skilled as Picaloc here. Now, Edmonton, correct me if I am wrong, but when the House of Secrets is cleaned, the door to the arca is unlocked so the scavenger can carry out his duties?'

'Of course.'

'I thought as much. In which case, imagine Dimanche going down those steps. He is confident in doing so because he has one of his fellow conspirators sweeping the passageway above or busy cleaning the nearby jakes closet. Moreover, everyone knows how dangerously steep that staircase is. Dimanche is armed with a lantern—'

'Of course,' Cranston intervened. 'He would have taken the lantern with him. Anyone else who wanted to go down those steps would have to find a fresh lanternhorn, so giving the scavenger on guard, as well as Dimanche himself, plenty of time to ensure matters were as they should be.'

'I agree,' Edmonton called out. 'Only a fool would hurry down those steps without a light.'

'So,' Athelstan continued. 'Dimanche is below. He can search as he wants, which is easy enough. The index posted on each coffer clearly states what is held there. Dimanche searches and takes what he needs before locking the coffer with the same skill as he opened it.' Athelstan patted his own wallet. 'Dimanche now has some valuable information but, I wondered, how does he smuggle it out of the House of Secrets? I have an answer. Even before my suspicions took root, I noted how the scavengers also cleaned the parapet walk around the curtain wall. I now believe that the scavenger took what had been stolen from the arca, put it in a leather sack, easily carried, and dropped it over the wall to be collected.'

'And then it took wing to France?' Dimanche scoffed. He lapsed into silence, aware, as everyone now was, that the tone of his voice had radically changed.

'Oh no, it did not take wing to France. Why should it? Once darkness had fallen, you or one of your coven slipped through the night to stand on that lonely stretch of the river bank opposite *La Supreme*. Carrying a shuttered lantern, you informed the cog of your arrival at the usual place and the agreed hour: when the city bells tolled for Vespers. Once the signal had been made, the captain of the cog would lower the bum-boat with two rowers. They would reach the shore, where their confederate would hand over whatever secret document had been filched from the arca, as well as receive the one which had been read and deciphered. The bum-boat leaves with its prize, whilst the scavenger would give what he had collected to Dimanche, who would return it to its proper place.' Athelstan pointed at the accused. 'I wager that *La Supreme* houses its own secret chancery, the workplace of the most skilled clerks.'

'The Salamander,' Thibault intervened. 'They have a clerk named the Salamander, who is most skilled in deciphering hidden writing.'

'In which case,' Athelstan replied, 'I am sure the Salamander is on board. He, along with others, goes through the stolen information. They take what they want and, once finished, it's ready to be taken back to the House of Secrets, and none of us are the wiser. I am sure the Salamander is most pleased.'

'The Salamander can go hang. They can all go hang,' Thibault exclaimed, as if unaware of others around him. He rubbed his face, eyes blinking, lips moving wordlessly. Athelstan sensed the Master of Secrets was deeply perturbed. Thibault glanced up and stared around, then quickly asserted himself, tapping the arms of his chair. 'Brother Athelstan, this indictment is most serious, a matter of life and death. Foreign hostile forces threatened our young King and his realm, which is why, Sir John, at your insistence, I have despatched the *Saint George* and the *Osprey* to keep *La Supreme* under close watch: that ship will not leave without our permission. Brother Athelstan, do continue.'

'These French spies had developed a simple yet very effective way of penetrating our House of Secrets.' Athelstan pointed at the accused. 'There was no real danger to you. You were responsible for cleaning the parapet walk, and one of you would go up with your barrow, brush and pick. You would clean but you would also drop that sack over the side of the curtain wall for collection later: that is where you made a stupid mistake. One or more of these sacks opened and pieces of parchment were caught up in the wind. Some of it became entangled in the gorse, bramble and wild grass. The Ghostman found some of these. He may well be fey-witted, but he is sharp enough.'

'Proof!' Dimanche yelled. 'I have yet to see any evidence or proof.'

'Quiet,' Cranston roared back, 'or I'll have you gagged.'

'We know,' Athelstan continued, 'that the Ghostman came into the House of Secrets to speak to Norwic about what he'd found. Of course, he took some of these scraps of parchment with him. You, Dimanche, along with one of your minions, eavesdropped on those conversations.'

'Proof?'

'In a while, in a while. Now you, Dimanche, realized the crucial importance of what the Ghostman had found and what he'd say to Norwic. Norwic, however, did not. He thought it was some accident; perhaps some rubbish intended for the fire pit which had broken loose to be tossed about here and there by the breeze, what the Ghostman called the "Lords of the Air". Now, this definitely occurred sometime before suspicions were aroused about the possibility of treason being committed in the House of Secrets.

When these suspicions did emerge, you, Dimanche, realized it might be only a matter of time before Norwic connected the two. The senior clerk in the Secret Chancery might have begun to speculate about all the possibilities. However, he suffered one great weakness. Norwic was deeply distracted, totally absorbed, with his love for the fair Heloise. Nevertheless, soon after Master Thibault stated his fears about a traitor in the House of Secrets, Norwic would reflect deeply on what had happened. On the night he was murdered, he opened the door to the arca and prepared to go down those deadly steps. As I said, Norwic was not his usual sharp-witted self; he was totally unaware of his death creeping close behind him. Naturally, he had to prepare the lantern before he went down that treacherous staircase. He would be on that step, preparing the wick, when you, Dimanche – armed with a long-poled brush, the type used to sweep floors – crept silently behind him. You held it like a spear and delivered a blow to Norwic's back. I can only imagine his shock at such an attack. Of course, he tried to save himself, but it was futile. Norwic stumbles and falls to a cruel death.'

Dimanche held a hand up to speak, glaring under heavy-lidded eyes at Athelstan.

'You are alleging that somehow I stayed hidden in the House of Secrets, or entered it illicitly. I made no noise. I did not alert Norwic to what I intended. He goes down those steps. He obligingly stops for me and I hit him with a broom handle and he falls to his death. Would any Justice accept such nonsense?'

'Oh, but you know how you did it. The House of Secrets was locked that night. Everyone had left. You could have entered using your usual skill, but you decided that was not really necessary. What you did was go along to the arca and hide in the jakes cupboard close by in that same enclosure. You had your brush, you had your wine, and above all you made sure that the hinges to that closet were very well oiled. Now I examined that closet closely, I scrutinized it when I first came here. The hinges were well coated – and whose task was that?'

'His,' Edmonton shouted. 'Dimanche was responsible for oiling the hinges on every door. But, Brother Athelstan, what would have happened if Norwic had wanted to use the closet?'

'When I inspected that closet, Edmonton, it reeked of wine.

Dimanche had splashed that on himself, probably, as well as down the jakes hole. In such an enclosed space, the wine would certainly reek. Now, if anybody had opened that closet door, all they would see was a poor drunken scavenger. They would make a story up about it – how this miserable wretch went to relieve himself, drank a belly-full of coarse wine and promptly fell asleep. Of course, Dimanche would act the part, which you are so very good at, and wait for another opportunity. Oh, by the way,' Athelstan pointed at Dimanche, 'your own mouth betrays you – your voice has a clipped tone and you use a more sophisticated vocabulary – words such as "allegations" or "illicitly". You plead you are not a Frenchy spy; you certainly are not a scavenger.'

Athelstan walked closer to Dimanche and repressed a shiver of fear. The accused just stared arrogantly back at him and the friar once again realized he did not fully understand what motivated a man like this. What vision did he follow? Dimanche gave Athelstan a smirk and turned to his comrades, talking to them in a patois Athelstan could not understand. He continued to do so until Thibault got to his feet, stamping the floor and gesturing at Athelstan.

'Brother, please continue. The murder of Nightingale?'

'Oh yes, poor Nightingale. He came back from Paris tired and depleted. He had seen his friends, his comrades, disappear into torture chambers or be hanged on the gallows at Montfaucon or elsewhere. Nevertheless, Nightingale was a man of sharp mind. I think he believed, long before I did, that the House of Secrets was the source of all his troubles. Someone in the Secret Chancery was a "dyed-in-the wool" Judas. Nightingale decided to concentrate on that building. He walked the length and breadth of the House of Secrets, as I myself did. He talked to the scavengers and he also talked to you, didn't he, Dimanche? Now if Nightingale was keen enough, you certainly were. You realized this very dangerous spy posed a real threat to you. My interference was bad enough, but Nightingale's even more so.' Athelstan cleared his throat. 'Nightingale knew that the Magister, the custos, the keeper of the Les Mysterieux was called the Key-Master. Was that, he may have wondered, the solution to the problem? Did he, whoever he was, resemble our Master Picaloc here? A man most skilled in opening locks. I do believe that he may have reached the conclusion that the secret coffers in the arca were being opened and their contents plundered. After all, each coffer has an index attached to it, so the spy, the traitor, could pick and choose what he wanted whilst one of his minions stood guard at the top of the steps.' Athelstan laughed sharply. 'It would be like choosing what you wanted from a market stall. Did you watch him, Dimanche? Did you see him examining locks and clasps? Nightingale had to be silenced. As I've said, he was a real threat to you. Moreover, he had provoked the Chambre Noir with his web of informants across Paris. They tried to capture him there, but he was too swift, too cunning. He avoided their clutches and arrived at what he thought was the safety of Westminster. But the Chambre Noir had not finished with him. The masters there had a number of grudges to settle with young Nightingale. You knew that, and so you plotted how to murder him. Now, watch this.' Athelstan called over Flaxwith and asked him to stand as close as he could. 'I am a Dominican friar,' he smiled, 'not a dagger man, Henry. But you are. If, God forbid, you wanted to stab me without provoking me to retaliate or even defend myself, you would draw as close as you could, like this?'

'No, Brother.' Flaxwith shook his head. 'To draw your dagger, you would have to take a step back, even more, to unsheathe your blade.'

'So how?'

'Like this.' Flaxwith drew his knife but kept his dagger hand concealed, hanging down by his side. 'See how I would do it, Father? I would approach you as if we are friends. Once I have, it is simply a matter of raising my hand and thrusting the blade into your belly, a savage wound which would open your stomach. Death would soon follow.'

'As I thought.' Athelstan thanked Flaxwith and returned to the lectern. 'Nightingale would stay in the House of Secrets until he had the truth. He would cast about searching for any clues; anything that could resolve the mystery of what was happening there. Now, Dimanche, you are a consummate actor. You ingratiated yourself with Nightingale, you were seen conversing with him on a number of occasions.'

'How could I get close to such a man, a mailed clerk?'

'Oh, but you did. I suspect that you invited yourself back into the House of Secrets on the night the murder took place. You probably told Nightingale you had privileged information. Perhaps you wanted to show him something in the arca or one of the carrels. You would make up some story about not telling him, but letting him draw his own conclusions of what you had discovered which, of course, was nothing. All you had to do was to meet Nightingale alone. I admit I have no evidence. God only knows what a farrago of nonsense you told him. Perhaps, about something amiss in the arca? You see,' Athelstan paused to take a sip of morning ale, 'Nightingale was following the same path as I was. Something was very wrong in the arca, and what Dimanche wanted to show him might prove useful. Intrigued, Nightingale agreed to a meeting with you. You left the House of Secrets but you didn't go far. You informed me when I first arrived in the House of Secrets that you often slept in one of the bothies out in the bailey. In itself a minor matter, if you truly were a poor scavenger, utterly illiterate, locked out from the formidable House of Secrets.' Athelstan turned. 'Captain of Archers!' he shouted. 'Is that true? Am I correct? Can you recall Dimanche bedding down in one of those bothies?'

'He certainly did,' the captain replied. 'But Brother Athelstan, I cannot be specific about which nights he stayed, but he certainly did quite regularly.'

'Good. Now imagine, if you can, that night-shrouded bailey. A heavy river mist has floated in. Dimanche sneaks out of the bothie, one shadow amongst many. Nightingale probably specified the hour; perhaps when the Compline bell sounded. Whatever, you stand by the door to the House of the Secret Chancery and Nightingale admits you. Now, bearing in mind what Master Flaxwith has told me, I did at first wonder if you struck immediately. The door opens, you step in as close as you can to your intended victim. As with Master Flaxwith, your dagger is concealed. You abruptly bring it up for that deadly stab. Opening a door to someone who simply wished to help you could have left Nightingale very vulnerable. However . . .' Athelstan crouched and crept forward, picking at the floor. He then got up. 'Dirt,' he declared, 'nothing but dirt. It was the same when I crawled the paving stones in the House of Secrets. I found no blood, nothing to indicate that Nightingale had died in the doorway and his corpse was dragged down to the arca. No, Dimanche, you followed Nightingale past the carrels and down into that most secret place. I can only suggest what happened. You crouched down beside a coffer, then asked Nightingale to take a look. Once he did, you'd get up and distract him with something else behind him. Nightingale gets to his feet, turns and, like the dagger man you are, you thrust a blade straight into his heart.' Athelstan paused as Thibault called out and beckoned him closer.

'Brother Athelstan,' he whispered, 'I fully follow the logic of your indictment. However, if we are to arraign these criminals before the King's justices, we need more proof, sound evidence.'

'In a while, Master Thibault, in a while. I do have a few surprises.' Athelstan returned to the lectern.

Dimanche raised his hand to speak. Athelstan noticed that he and the other scavengers still wore their battered gauntlets.

'I need to speak,' Dimanche declared. 'Brother Athelstan, Sir John Cranston, you forget I was with you in The Lamb of God in Cheapside. I helped to defend you from assassins. I fought as courageously as any retainer would for his lord.'

'No, no,' Athelstan protested. 'In Heaven's name, do not quote that. We have the truth of it. You hired a cohort of killers from Foxglove, one of the Lords of Hell. You visited him in his filthy tavern, The Roaring Pig. You gave him good gold for our lives. Foxglove has now gone to his eternal reward. He paid for his mistakes, for he chose badly, sending ruffians more interested in filling their bellies and slaking their lusts. You arrived at The Lamb of God, so you said at the time, to plead your innocence and that of your comrades, in the chaos at the House of Secrets. It was no coincidence that the assassins arrived at about the same time you did. However, you swiftly deduced, as we stood poised outside that kitchen, that what you had plotted was going to be severely frustrated. So, you exploited the opportunity. You would turn the tables, depicting yourself as faithful and loyal. You also did your best to ensure that not too many of the assailants survived to tell their tale. Now of course, our stout, sturdy coroner completely frustrated that attack on us. The assassins were killed and, a short while later, their masters followed the same path out of life. As for the second attempt on my life, we have the Dominicans. I am sure that both were crew members of *La*

Supreme, where hair can be tonsured, robes, sandals and daggers supplied, not to mention documents cleverly forged and sealed by the likes of the Salamander.' Athelstan paused as Thibault called his henchman, the Castilian Evangelios, to stand near him. He whispered to the mercenary then gestured at Athelstan to continue.

'The attack of those two killers, disguised as members of my order, completely failed, but that was more due to God's good grace than anything else. Anyway, you decided on one final attempt. You tried to poison me. I am sure you brought that noxious potion as you crossed to Southwark, slipping through the mist like the great sinner you are. You murdered poor Talbot, the Tower bowman. You also tried to be clever. First, you left a proclamation indicating that the individual responsible for the death of poor Talbot was that great criminal the Radix Malorum. You left a doggerel verse mocking Sir John. Absolute nonsense! No one really knows who the Radix Malorum is. More importantly, that skilled housebreaker was and is not a killer. He's more interested in stealing your jewels than taking your life. Finally, you seem to know a great deal about St Erconwald's. You know your way around the church, God's Acre, my house.'

'I know nothing about that filthy place. Be it your squalid little house or your gloomy church.'

'Oh, but you do. On at least two occasions, when talking to me about the scavengers, you made reference to Watkin, the dung collector. How did you learn about him? Watkin may be many things, but he is hardly a notable of the city. A man who only crosses London Bridge to work. Oh no, Dimanche, I would wager you know a great deal about me and mine and the life I lead. Whatever, to continue. You murdered Talbot, then cut towards my house. The day was foggy, the light poor. It would be easy enough for an assassin like yourself to creep through the mist. You reached the door; the lock would be no defence against your skill. You enter my house and pour poison, probably into the cauldron hanging over the fire. Again, God intervened and saved me through – of all things – my cat; a very wise one indeed. You made a mistake. Bonaventure would never have left that house for the wet, misty cemetery unless he was truly frightened. And, of course, he took a great dislike to you.'

'Cats, poison,' Dimanche retorted, 'your homily is very

interesting, Brother Athelstan. Quite fascinating, indeed, but where's the proof, the evidence?'

'Yes, yes, it's time I came to that. First, there's the sheer logic of my indictment. You and yours, Dimanche, are spies, assassins despatched by the Chambre Noir. Now, remember, the Secret Chancery and its cloisters have been closed for a week. Only you and your scavengers were deployed for your own secret purposes. Now we know that the war cog *La Supreme* is really a vital part of the Chambre Noir. It is both a listening place and a command post, like the tower of a castle. The cog has two purposes: directing you, and reporting back to Paris with letters and missives carried by swift-sailing galleys belonging to either the Chambre Noir or Venice.'

'But *La Supreme* does move,' Thibault declared. 'I know it takes position down-river; it rides at anchor . . .'

'Of course, it has to,' Athelstan replied. 'It has other duties, and it does not want to provoke suspicion. So, the cog will leave for the estuary and patrol the approaches to both the Thames and the Narrow Seas. I suspect that – during its absence – some other vessel, a French merchantman, will berth at Queenhithe, where it can give and receive messages and whatever else might be needed. The days pass and *La Supreme* eventually returns to carry on its secret meetings with the accused. Master Edmonton, look at this.' Athelstan picked up his chancery satchel from a nearby table, opened it and took out the manuscript he had seized on the Thames. He beckoned Edmonton closer and insisted that he sit next to Master Thibault. 'My good friends, I want you to read this.'

The clerk shrugged, took the manuscript, and went to sit where Athelstan directed him. A strange silence descended, broken only by the muttered curses of Thibault and Edmonton.

'Brother Athelstan, what is this?'

'Why, Master Edmonton, do you recognize it?'

'Yes, I certainly do. I drew it up about two weeks ago. It is a very important summary of reports on the King's envoys in Bordeaux, regarding the deployment of the wine fleet after Easter. It is, or it was supposed to be, highly confidential. How did you get it?'

'I found it on the corpse of a member of *La Supreme*'s crew. Someone stole that document from the arca in the Secret Chancery and went down to the banks of the Thames, where he met someone from *La Supreme*. The purpose of that meeting was to hand over that manuscript you now hold. I cannot and will not, at this moment in time, give an exact account of what actually happened. Suffice to say, I seized the manuscript, which should never have left that arca. As regards that, well, you all know that the Secret Chancery was closed. The clerks were made to stay away, and the only people admitted were the scavengers. They would be delighted. You accepted our explanation for the closure which was really a farrago of nonsense. You were left in that place and you must have had a merry time, helping yourself to this and that. How did you work? Was it one item every evening, or did the Chambre Noir name a document it might need?'

'*Bastards!* I know what you must have been searching for.' Thibault's statement, blurted out in an enraged shout, silenced proceedings. He wagged a finger at the accused. 'I know what you were after, and you will never ever get hold of it.'

'My Lord?' Cranston queried.

'Nothing, nothing,' the Master of Secrets replied.

Athelstan glanced quickly at the accused and caught the sly grin on Dimanche's face.

'To hurry on,' Athelstan declared in a ringing voice. 'You, the accused, have the truth of what I said. My father was a farmer. Every night he used to wash his hands of the day's dirt and grime. He'd often say that you could tell a man by his hands. You are scavengers, your hands should be coarse and rough, but they are not. Dimanche, I once watched you washing your hands in the buttery. I saw clean, smooth flesh, but only reached the implications of this when you and your coven provoked my suspicions. I also recalled how all of you wear gauntlets and never take them off. At least not in my company. I now order you to do so or I'll have Evangelios and his men do it for you. Show me the soft, pink flesh of your hands, which will eloquently testify to your true status as clerks, not scavengers.'

'Better still,' Thibault shouted, 'Evangelios, take one of the accused, not Dimanche. Bring him to me.' The Castilian and some of his ruffians moved towards the stalls and dragged one of the scavengers to his feet, pushing and shoving him towards their master, who now sprang to his feet, speaking swiftly in

Spanish to his henchmen. Athelstan caught Cranston's eye. The coroner just shook his head, a warning for Athelstan not to become involved. The prisoner was dragged close to the lectern. Evangelios, at Thibault's insistence, pushed one of the wheeled braziers closer, its heated charcoal now turning into a glowing red mass. Athelstan watched in horror. The scavenger, who realized what was going to happen, redoubled his screams and struggles. Dimanche and his comrades were now on their feet, but a cohort of Thibault's bodyguards kept them herded together. Cranston remained seated, shouting at Flaxwith and his bailiffs not to get involved.

The prisoner was pushed up against the brazier: his captors, at Thibault's shouted command, grabbed the man's arm and dragged off the battered gauntlet on his right hand. One of the mercenaries then grasped the man's naked hand and thrust it as deep as he could into the fiery charcoal. Others helped, keeping the prisoner still. Athelstan slumped down on the stool. The prisoner's piercing screams echoed like some hellish hymn, chorused by the shouts and cries of Dimanche and his comrades. The stench of smoking, burning human flesh trailed across, a sickening odour. Thibault and his coterie, however, mocked the prisoner. Cranston leapt to his feet.

'Athelstan,' he called, 'listen.' The friar did so. The prisoner was still screaming but no longer in his customary, coarse patois but clear Norman French.

'Enough,' Thibault shouted. 'Who,' he added mockingly, 'has heard of a London scavenger speaking fluently in Norman French?' Thibault's words were drowned by the growing chaos and clamour in the chapter house. Matters were getting out of hand. Athelstan tensed as he heard Dimanche shouting in that patois, no longer protests at what was happening, but more like orders to his comrades. The tortured prisoner, his right hand now a peeling mess of burnt, scorched flesh, slumped to his knees, screaming with pain. The wounded man edged closer to the brazier. Then, staggering to his feet, he kicked the brazier over and the burning charcoal, a ribbon of fire, trickled towards Thibault, who immediately screamed orders at the archers behind him. Arrow shafts sang through the air, piercing the tortured scavenger in chest and belly.

Chaos now descended. Cranston drew his sword as flames licked at the edge of turkey rugs and a collection of cloaks thrown over a stool. Dimanche and the rest of his comrades drew concealed daggers, clashing with the Spanish mercenaries. Two of these now lay sprawled in spreading pools of blood. Athelstan hurriedly seized his own cloak and chancery satchel. Thibault was shouting for his mercenaries to stand firm. Cranston, bellowing at the archers to choose their targets carefully, edged forward. Dimanche, however, followed by his cohort, had now broken through, picking up fallen weapons as they went. Athelstan made to withdraw but then tripped over a small footrest behind him. He stumbled to the ground, only to be seized by Dimanche and the scavengers. They pulled the friar to his feet.

Dimanche, grinning like a gargoyle, pressed the tip of his dagger into the friar's throat. Athelstan, hiding his fear, remained still. He felt someone pushed up beside him and turned slightly. Edmonton and Sheffield had also been taken hostage. Cranston, together with his bailiffs, now guarded the door, the coroner yelling that the Tower archers were not to loose, for fear of hitting the hostages. Thibault, protected by a screed of his mercenaries, shouted the same, calling his men off as Dimanche roared that he and his be left alone or all three prisoners would suffer the consequences. A Tower bowman, however, confused by the chaos, believed he had a clear target. He notched and loosed in a matter of heartbeats. The arrow cut through the air just above their heads. Dimanche screamed an order and one of the scavengers, pinioning the hapless Sheffield, drove his dagger straight into the clerk's exposed throat. Sheffield sagged, eyes rolling, mouth gagging on the blood spurting from throat, mouth and nose. The hideous gurgling of the dying man, the jerking of his body, stilled all clamour. Cranston, who had already guessed what was about to happen, broke the silence as he ordered no one to move.

Athelstan felt the dagger point prick his throat. He turned slightly, staring into Dimanche's clever eyes.

'Take your dagger away,' Athelstan hissed. 'Whoever you really are, you have my word.'

Dimanche nodded, lowered the dagger, but kept one hand on Athelstan's shoulder.

'Listen,' Dimanche shouted, 'the friar and Master Edmonton here will surely die if my orders, my safety and that of my comrades are ignored in the slightest way. First, my men will arm themselves.' The scavengers, carrying weapons they had already seized, took some more, along with warbelts and four small arbalests. Dimanche, still gripping Athelstan's shoulder, pointed to the corpse of the dead scavenger. 'I leave him,' he declared, 'to the mercy of Holy Mother Church, for he is past all human help. Now, me and mine, together with Athelstan and Edmonton, will adjourn to the quayside. Sir John, your Captain of Archers, having divested himself of all weapons, will join us. On our way here I noticed the bold Moleskin and his barge. We will take that barge and journey down-river to join our comrades on *La Supreme*. Master Thibault,' Dimanche pointed to a crucifix nailed to the wall, 'you will swear, and I mean swear, on the Cross of Christ that we will not be interfered with in any way. Not here, or on the river, or as we board *La Supreme*. Once we are aboard that cog, the King of France's vessel, its crew and any passengers will remain sacred. If you so swear, if you keep your word, Brother Athelstan and Edmonton will disembark safely before *La Supreme* sails for the open sea. Remember the oath you take is the most solemn. You will swear on Christ himself. If you break this, both of these prisoners will die. I will, I shall execute them.'

Thibault needed no further urging, Cranston whispering heatedly in his ear. The Master of Secrets took the oath under the pain of excommunication, in this life and the life to come. Once completed, Dimanche pushed Athelstan into the care of two of his coven and took the same oath, with the same eternal penalties if that solemn vow was broken. Dimanche then led his party out of the chapter house, following the Captain of Archers, now divested of all weapons. They walked quickly, a tight huddle of people hastening across the royal precincts, skirting the great abbey and down to King's Steps. Once there, the Captain of Archers had urgent words with Moleskin. Athelstan, now virtually ringed by Dimanche and his coven, could see Moleskin was agitated. The bargeman leapt to his feet, gesturing at his crew, but the Captain of Archers remained insistent. Athelstan watched as the bargeman and his crew nodded their acceptance before collecting their personal belongings and leaving the barge. Dimanche ordered everyone forward. As they climbed into the boat, Athelstan caught Moleskin's stare and quickly sketched a blessing in his direction.

'Father?' the bargeman cried plaintively.

'Don't worry,' Athelstan shouted back. 'All will be well, and all manner of things will be well.' He could say or do no more, as one of the scavengers pushed him stumbling across the barge.

Dimanche ordered the Captain of Archers to join Athelstan and Edmonton sitting in the shrouded stern. Once they had all assembled, they cast off. The scavengers manned the oars whilst Dimanche sat facing his hostages. The rowers proved skilful enough and the barge turned and turned again until it was midstream, heading down-river. The day was cold but clear of any mist. The Thames flowed fast, its swirling current thrusting the barge forward. After a while, Edmonton abruptly nudged Athelstan.

'We are not alone,' he whispered. The friar glanced up. 'Sir John moves swiftly.' He murmured, 'Dimanche, you have company.'

The custos turned on the bench, glancing over his shoulder.

'So I see,' he declared.

'So do I,' Athelstan retorted, narrowing his eyes to study the two war barges, displaying the royal arms of England, cutting through the water behind them.

'As long as they keep their distance, all will be well,' Dimanche smirked. 'To quote you, Brother Athelstan. This should end well, and if not, that is a matter for Master Thibault. He has sworn the most solemn and holy oath. By evening, God willing, you will be ashore. I and mine will be on *La Supreme*, heading out across the estuary for the Narrow Seas.'

'You will kill us,' Athelstan stated. 'You will take two innocent unarmed men who have done nothing but their duty, and execute them if Thibault does not do exactly what you want.'

'Reluctantly, Brother Athelstan. I have no choice. So let us pray,' again Dimanche grinned, 'that all will be well, and all manner of things will be well.'

Athelstan went back to his reverie as the barge moved on, breasting the occasional turbulence and keeping to its course. This part of the river was quiet, apart from the occasional fishing smack, herring boat or merchant cog carefully making their way to some London quayside.

They rounded a bend in the river. Athelstan recalled his previous visit here, a crucial part of his investigation. *La Supreme* still rode at anchor, sails reefed, flags, pennants and banners all folded.

However, on either side of *La Supreme*, no more than a mere bow shot away, rode two English ships, the *Osprey* and the *Saint George*, magnificent war cogs all armoured for war. Athelstan could see the archers and men-at-arms on the decks of both ships. He could also smell the smoke from the fiery braziers which stood beside the catapults, all primed and ready for attack. The *Osprey* turned, moving slightly, as if to block the barge from reaching *La Supreme*. The Captain of Archers, however, standing as high as he could on the poop, called out who they were and why they were here.

'I understand,' a voice bellowed back, 'that French pirates or spies, enemies of our King, hold two of his loyal subjects – three if you include yourself, Captain – as hostages. I also recognize the threat, so you have safe passage to *La Supreme*. However, Brother Athelstan, I must know one thing. Are you and the other clerk hale and hearty?'

'We are,' Athelstan yelled, stumbling to his feet, one hand resting on Edmonton's shoulder as protection against the barge's constant sway. 'We are,' he repeated, 'hale and hearty.'

'Then go forward. However, let those malefactors who hold you, as we have informed the master of *La Supreme*, realize that we will not allow that ship or its crew to sail without the direct command of our sovereign King and his worthy uncle my Lord of Gaunt.'

The *Osprey* then gently veered away. Athelstan sat down, wiping the spray from his flushed face.

'Well done.' Dimanche leaned forward, pointing up at the shrieking gulls circling above them. 'During your speech,' he mocked, 'even the birds fell silent. The English cogs seemed well warned!' he continued.

'Of course they would be,' Edmonton retorted. 'I am sure as we made our way down to King's Steps, Thibault was ordering his fastest horseman to gallop along the bank to alert both the *Osprey* and the *Saint George*.'

Dimanche shouted at the oarsman to take great care as they approached *La Supreme*. The barge moved alongside the cog, the river battering it against the wooden hull. Dimanche shouted who they were and why they were here. A rope ladder was quickly dropped. Athelstan and Edmonton were forced to climb up to the taffrail, where they were roughly seized, pulled over and made to squat on the other side of the deck. Dimanche came last. Once he had boarded, he leaned over the rail, shouting at the Captain of Archers that he was free. If the captain wanted, he could take the barge either across to the bank or to the nearest English cog. However, if he boarded either ship, he must remind the captain that any attack on *La Supreme* would mean the summary execution of both Athelstan and Edmonton. Dimanche then swaggered across the deck, shouting at one of the crew to bring a wineskin and three goblets. The scavenger leader filled all three. Edmonton took his and drank greedily. Unable to converse, he seemed cowed and shocked by the violence which had erupted in the chapter house. Athelstan thanked Dimanche and sipped carefully. Two men came towards him. Athelstan put his goblet down and scrambled to his feet as Dimanche introduced the master of *La Supreme* and the ship's principal clerk, popularly known as the Salamander. The captain was a rugged, weather-beaten mariner who sarcastically welcomed his guests aboard. The Salamander, on the other hand, was small and pert, thin as a beanpole. He had the smooth face of a baby but sharp, keen eyes, and a mouth which moved continuously, as if he was chewing something. He muttered a welcome, smiled at Athelstan in a rather sinister way, then turned and walked off.

'He does not like tail-wearers,' the master laughed, using the common insult hurled at the English by the French: a sly, subtle way of reminding them that they were no better than monkeys. 'Whatever,' the captain added, thrusting his face forward. 'The Salamander doesn't like the English and neither do I. You are here and, if your fellow countrymen observe their oath, you will be safe.' He flicked his fingers at Dimanche. 'I'll leave them to you.'

Athelstan sat down next to Edmonton, now lost in his own dark mood. Dimanche also made himself comfortable on a piece of rope matting which one of the crew provided.

'So, my friend . . .'

'I am not your friend,' Athelstan retorted. 'I never was and I never will be. So, tell me, what is your real name?'

'Roger de Montfort.'

'De Montfort?' Athelstan queried. 'They were once a great and noble family here in England.'

'My ancestor, Simon de Montfort, was Earl of Leicester, owning estates which stretched across the shires north of the Trent. You are correct they were once, indeed, a great and noble family.' Dimanche scratched his sun-weathered face, combing his moustache and hair with his fingers. 'Simon fought for the common people against the present King's ancestors, in particular Edward Longshanks, also called the "Hammer of the Scots". The conflict was bloody and savage. My ancestor, Earl Simon, was eventually trapped in battle and killed at Evesham some seventy years ago: his corpse was cut up and fed to the royal hounds. Simon's kin were hunted the length and breadth of Christendom. Edward despatched assassins, and these were relentless in their pursuit of anything or anyone to do with de Montfort. Eventually the surviving members of the family surrendered themselves to the King of France, who supplied us with estates and, of course, their protection. I was raised to give total allegiance to the Valois in Paris. I have and I will support them unstintingly. So, priest, now you know my origins and a little about the fire which burns within me.'

'One thing.' Athelstan steadied himself as the cog was caught by a powerful surge. He glanced at Edmonton, who now seemed more alert, staring at the crew now gathering along both taffrails.

'One thing?' Dimanche demanded.

'If I am going to die,' Athelstan replied, 'here, on this cog, I would love to know the reason for Master Thibault's outburst in the chapter house: that he knew what you were looking for?'

'Ah yes.' Dimanche now also seemed distracted by the crew congregating along the sides of the ship, staring back the way they'd come. 'I don't suppose,' Dimanche conceded, 'that what I tell you will do us any harm.' He paused. 'The Memorandum of Montreuil! Years ago,' he continued, 'after the death of his father, Edward the Black Prince, young Richard succeeded to the throne of England, a rather sickly boy, but still loved by prince and pauper.'

'True,' Athelstan replied, 'our young King has a charm all of his own. A sense of humour which stands him in good stead, especially with his precious uncle, John of Gaunt, self-styled regent of the kingdom.'

'We know,' Dimanche continued, 'that Gaunt is ambitious. He

would like to fly as high as he can. He dreams about his own dynasty becoming the royal family, and the only barrier to that, in Gaunt's eyes, is young Richard. Anyway, as I said, some years ago Gaunt met with the great lords of France – Burgundy, Orleans, and the rest. The meeting was secret and held in the small English enclave of Montreuil in Northern France. Fierce discussion took place about what would happen if young Richard died. Gaunt declared that if anything should happen to the young King,' Dimanche grinned, 'and you can make of that what you wish, the great lords of France would support, in every way possible, Gaunt's claim to the throne of England. In return, once King, Gaunt would make an eternal peace with France and the Valois. He would renounce his claim, England's claim, the Plantagenet claim, to the French Crown. As you know, that claim is quite potent, through Queen Isabella, daughter of Philip of France, wife of Edward II, no less a person than Gaunt's grandmother.'

'Sweet Lord!' Athelstan breathed. 'No wonder he sought the support of the French lords. The English earls would not be happy with such an agreement. Fortunes are made in France; the plunder pours into England like a river.'

'Now, according to what I know,' Dimanche continued, 'copies of that memorandum were drawn up, signed and sealed by each party, but never exchanged. My masters in Paris would love to get Gaunt's copy and publish it for the world to see. The divisions it would cause in England could last for decades. We searched, we probed, we reflected but, so far, nothing. Nevertheless,' Dimanche smirked, 'we will try and try again.'

'Of course you will.'

'Now . . .' Dimanche broke off as the master of *La Supreme* called his officers to a meeting at the foot of the mast. Dimanche rose and hurried to join them. Athelstan got up, Edmonton beside him, and stared over the taffrail.

'Sweet Lord,' Athelstan whispered, 'now I know why the master of *La Supreme* has called a meeting.' The friar stared, craning his neck to see what was happening. The two English war cogs had deliberately widened the gap between them and were now edging their way forward to stand off either side of *La Supreme*. In addition, the war barges which had followed Dimanche down the Thames were now massing between the two English cogs.

'Lord save us,' Edmonton hissed. 'They are going to attack. Brother Athelstan, Thibault swore a solemn oath.'

'Which means as much to him as a fly on the wall. See those barges, Edmonton, they followed us from King's Steps. I am sure they received brief but curt orders. They will attack. They've now begun their manoeuvres. It will be a fight to the death, and I pray that does not include ours.'

Athelstan fell silent as the master of *La Supreme* issued a spate of orders, despatching his officers to their posts. Somewhere a drum began to beat, a signal to prepare for attack. The cog's holds were opened, weapons passed up, including two small, wheeled catapults. Netting was hung between sail ropes; a defence against boarders. Braziers were fired. Buckets of tar and pitch were placed next to baskets of dust and sand, which would be used to smother any fire. Members of the crew hastily donned chainmail and ill-fitting helmets, warbelts were strapped on, crossbows primed and placed beneath the taffrails. The master of *La Supreme* ordered the great sail to be cut loose and lowered. He also despatched men up into the rigging, as well as the ship's boy as a lookout in the falcon nest at the top of the great mast.

'He hopes to outrun his pursuers,' Edmonton muttered. 'He has little chance.'

Athelstan glanced at the clerk, who now seemed calmer and more collected.

'What will happen to us, Brother? Can you swim?'

'Definitely not, and I would urge you not to even consider it. We are on the broadest reach of the river and its flow is fast and furious. All I can do is pray that God will have mercy on us, because Dimanche certainly will not.'

Athelstan paused at a shout from the falcon's nest. He glanced up as a ball of fire – rags and cloths dipped in tar and oil – smashed against the deck, shedding flames and sparks. Athelstan pulled Edmonton along the side of the ship to the small, dark enclosure beneath the quarterdeck. Both men squatted down. More fiery bundles hit the rigging and sails. Flames flitted like dancers across the deck. Orders were shouted. Buckets of sand and dust were hastily brought to douse the fire. Suddenly there was a crash. *La Supreme* shuddered, swayed, then righted itself.

Shouts, yells and war cries cut through the smoke, now turning thicker and darker.

'They have made a dreadful mistake,' Athelstan murmured. 'One of our cogs is almost alongside. *La Supreme* is finished. Pray God we are not.' He searched around for anything to use as a weapon.

'Athelstan!'

The friar turned. Dimanche emerged from the smoke, holding an arbalest raised and ready. Athelstan crossed himself then moved to protect Edmonton. Dimanche just stopped and stared, raised the arbalest as if in salute and disappeared back into the smoke. Eventually the noise of battle subsided; most of the fighting had raged at the far end of the ship around the prow. The smoke cleared, and Athelstan murmured a prayer of thanks as Cranston, his sword and dagger bloodied, emerged like Hector marching towards him.

'I could not come earlier,' the coroner declared. 'Most of the fighting was to prevent us getting aboard. Well, now we are. Come, my little friend.' He and Athelstan exchanged the kiss of peace. The coroner clasped hands with Edmonton, then grasped Athelstan by the arm. 'It is over,' he murmured. 'But you might be needed or, there again, I might be mistaken. Thibault is in a towering rage.'

They stood and watched as the smoke thinned and cleared. Thibault's mercenaries were now busy clearing the deck, which was strewn with dead and wounded. Athelstan knew that war at sea was bloody. He tried to remonstrate with the Master of Secrets, but Thibault, his chainmail jerkin soaked in blood, was obdurate. Those members of *La Supreme*'s crew who had survived had their hands and feet tied and were then tossed over the side, joined by their wounded and dead. Cries for mercy went unheeded as Evangelios supervised the hideous slaughter. Athelstan crossed to the taffrail, slipping and slithering on the blood. Once there, he drew in the icy breeze, fair remedy for the stench of battle. The friar quietly blessed those corpses now floating around the doomed ship. The executions ended and the mercenaries began to collect weapons and anything else of value, be it from the smouldering hold or stripped from the dead and those others hustled over the side. Cranston strode over to stand beside Athelstan, one gauntleted hand on his shoulder.

'*Pax et bonum*, little friar,' he murmured.

'Sir John, what happened to the captain?'

'Oh, he was killed as we boarded. A crossbow bolt straight to the head.'

They glanced up as Evangelios shouted that they should leave. The *Saint George* now stood off, in fear of fire from the crippled French cog. The war barges, however, were being brought forward to ferry the English wounded to the *Osprey*, which stood off the port side.

'You mention the captain of *La Supreme*,' Cranston declared. 'He deserved to die. He made a hideous mistake. He should have fled immediately when he took you and Edmonton on board. A vital hour was wasted, and thank God for that.'

'And what about Thibault's oath? Oh, I know he couldn't give a fig, but he still took that oath in a public place.'

'Oh, don't worry about him,' Cranston laughed. 'Master Thibault will be given an absolution from Holy Mother Church. You had probably not even reached the quayside before Thibault was issuing orders. Even then he was insisting on hoisting the red banner for attack, and the black standard to signify no prisoners would be taken: that was one order I did counter. It would have been foolish to give the enemy forewarning that it would be a fight to the death.' He paused as Thibault came across, calling his name. The Master of Secrets embraced Athelstan then Cranston.

'Well, well, well.' Thibault wiped bloodied spray from his face. 'This is over. Evangelios tells me that the flames are doused, but that was only as far as he could see. Let us leave. Let it burn. Sir John, Brother Athelstan, I thank you, and will do so again in a few days.'

Three days after the savage river battle and the total destruction of *La Supreme*, Master Vincent Edmonton turned into Snakes Lane and made his way down to his lodgings above the draper's shop. Edmonton was pleased, content, at peace with himself. Of course, he quietly cursed his stupidity in entertaining the likes of Dimanche in the first place. Edmonton had been truly astonished at Athelstan's revelations about the scavengers. Undoubtedly Edmonton had been duped, but so had Master Thibault and all his coterie. They had been tricked and betrayed, but that was now in the past. Dimanche and all his coven were dead, their corpses tangled in the undergrowth along the river bank, or floating down to oblivion in the estuary. All were dead and gone. Thank God no one could point a finger at him. Edmonton reached the shop and went up the outside staircase. He unlocked the doors and, with a sigh of relief, stepped into his comfortable chamber. He lit the candles and lanterns then paused as he heard a sound. A shadow emerged from the dark. Edmonton immediately recognized Dimanche; the man's face was cut and dirtied, his clothing stank sour, but the arbalest he pointed at Edmonton was dangerous enough. Dimanche forced a smile and went back to sitting in the chair placed in the shadows. He lowered the arbalest, grabbed the goblet from the table and swiftly gulped from it, his eyes never leaving Edmonton. He finished and gestured at Edmonton to sit on the quilted stool before him. The clerk did so, trying to control the panic rising within him.

'I thought you were dead, killed in the river battle. How did you . . .?'

'I slipped over the side of *La Supreme*. One body amongst many tumbling into the water. I swam to the bank. I collected what I could from some of the corpses, what the mercenaries had overlooked. I then crept away. I hid in the wild places, whether the countryside or here, deep in the dirt of London's underworld. But now I have the help and support of my good friend Edmonton.' He pointed at the clerk. 'I could have exposed you in the chapter house. I did not. I could have killed you on board *La Supreme*. I did not. Your debt to me is great, and now I want it repaid. Do you understand? I want to shave my hair and beard. I want to wash from head to toe. I need clean linen undergarments, stockings and stout sandals and the earth-brown robe of a Franciscan friar. I also want money and, above all, I want you to forge documents which will allow me, under my new name, Brother Philippe, the right to leave this kingdom for Boulogne or some other French port.'

'So, you are fleeing back to France. Of course, I will help. But why did you need me in the first place?'

'Oh, that is obvious. I truly wanted to learn the gossip among the clerks and I was proved correct. Our undoing, or at least the beginning of it, was the Ghostman. You mentioned how he wanted to speak to Norwic about the "Lords of the Air". Athelstan learnt the same and fastened on to it and then everything began to unravel. Athelstan posed simple questions. How and why were scraps of parchment, clearly from the House of Secrets, not found fluttering around the bailey? Those soaring walls should have kept them there. No, the scraps were found tangled in the vegetation well beyond the House of Secrets. How did they get there? Logic dictated that such scraps must have been taken beyond the walls. However, everyone is searched when leaving the House of Secrets. It would be far too dangerous to have documents found on you, hence Athelstan's conclusion that they were thrown over the walls, became loose, and the Ghostman's "Lords of the Air" did the rest.'

Dimanche shrugged. '*Fatalis casus*,' he whispered. 'A deadly accident which destroyed our plans. So, you see my friend, we deal in morsels of information; chatter and gossip which can be so dangerous and yet so important. But "*alea iacta est*", that's what you say in games of hazard, isn't it, Edmonton? *Alea iacta est* – the dice is thrown. The game is over, we have lost, but tomorrow and tomorrow and tomorrow comes. We shall return. I need your help to become Brother Philippe. You have the wherewithal, the silver, and the necessary items needed to forge a document. I should be gone within the week, and it is definitely in your interest that I do so safely and successfully.' Dimanche abruptly lunged forward, grasping Edmonton by the arm. 'And rest assured, my friend, I, Lord Roger de Montfort, will return.'

At the very hour Dimanche met Edmonton, Sir John Cranston and Brother Athelstan were sitting down to a most splendid banquet in the Abbot's Parlour in Westminster. Thibault was the host, and the coroner and the friar were his only guests. The parlour, luxurious all the time, had been made even more splendid, with fresh drapes, tapestries, and glittering ornaments studded with precious stones. The table had been laid for three. Thibault was sitting at the top, with Cranston and Athelstan to his left and right. Scented braziers sweetened the air, as did the perfumed logs, crackling fiercely in the mantled hearth. A host of silver spigots had been carefully placed around the parlour to provide pools of golden light which merged as they met. A bejewelled silver nef had been placed in the centre of the table, covered in thick white samite cloth. Precious plate was used, bowls and platters with pure glass goblets, specially imported from Venice, filled with the finest wines of France and Alsace. These included one wine specially bought by Thibault called Falernian. The wine – so the Master of Secrets asserted – that the emperors of Rome used to sip. He went on to explain how Falernian was also the wine Pilate drank as he questioned Jesus on that first Good Friday.

The rest of the banquet was sumptuous, the food delicious. Small dishes of considerable variety, be it meat or fish. Cranston, as usual, ate and drank as if he'd been fasting for days. Athelstan was more abstemious, keeping a sharp eye on Master Thibault, for whom he had some questions. At first, after the toasts were made, conversation became desultory, until Thibault tapped his ivory-handled knife against a goblet.

'My friends, thank you.' He lifted the goblet in toast. 'My Lord of Gaunt is, as I am, truly delighted at the return of the Redstone. Sir John, Brother Athelstan, we shall all render you just reward for your house, my Lord Coroner, and something equally precious for the chantry chapel in your church, Brother.'

Both Cranston and Athelstan murmured their thanks. Thibault grew more expansive, rejoicing in the total and utter annihilation of *La Supreme* and the *cohors damnosa*. He paused in his rejoicing to take a generous gulp of wine. He then stared at Athelstan.

'Brother, you seem troubled?'

'Not troubled, Master Thibault, more intrigued.'

'By what?'

'Dimanche, de Montfort, or whatever he wants to call himself, tried to kill me on at least three occasions but failed. On board *La Supreme*, he had me trapped. He carried an arbalest, already primed and ready. He could have loosed it and killed me in a matter of heartbeats.' Athelstan paused. Cranston lowered his glass. Thibault exclaimed in astonishment. 'I was,' Athelstan continued, 'the root cause of Dimanche's failure and the total destruction of his power. Dimanche was a killer to the very marrow, a true blood-drinker, so why show mercy to his sworn enemy?'

'And?' Cranston asked.

'At first, Sir John, I thought it was some chivalrous gesture in the heat of battle, then I recalled Edmonton standing beside me.

Dimanche raised his arbalest as if in salute, and I wonder if he was saluting Edmonton, not me. Moreover,' Athelstan held up his hand to still Thibault's questions, 'if Dimanche had killed me and spared Edmonton, and that was seen . . .'

'Edmonton could be viewed as Dimanche's secret ally.'

'Very much so.' Cranston breathed. 'Dimanche couldn't kill you without killing Edmonton. So, there must be a tie between that clerk and our bloodthirsty assassin.'

'If I were you, Master Thibault,' Athelstan declared, 'I would keep Vincent Edmonton under very close watch.'

'I certainly shall, Brother. You have more questions?'

'Yes, the oath you swore?'

'Oh, come Brother, forced out of me. *Peine forte et dure*, that is a legal term for forcing someone by pain, pressure or intimidation into agreeing to something he certainly would have preferred not to.'

'Master Thibault, I am fully aware of that. But let me move on. You and yours showed no mercy. You extended no quarter to either the crew of *La Supreme* or Les Mysterieux. Surely some of the prisoners such as Dimanche could have been taken alive? A valuable source of information about what happens in the Chambre Noir?'

'Oh,' Thibault smiled, 'we did take one prisoner.' He glanced over his shoulder and snapped his fingers at Evangelios, who was standing in the shadows just within the door. Thibault spoke swiftly in Spanish. Evangelios replied and left the parlour. He reappeared, pushing a short figure into the light.

'The Salamander!' Athelstan exclaimed.

'The same, Brother Athelstan, captured by Evangelios at my express command. He was seized as soon as we stormed *La Supreme*. It wasn't hard, the Salamander was eager to surrender, desperate to sell what he is and who he knows. I accepted. Salamander will prove to be a veritable treasure, a source of valuable information about the Chambre Noir, its members and all its doings. It might take months, if not years, before the Chambre Noir realizes the full truth of what happened on *La Supreme*. They probably believe all of its crew, together with the *cohort damnosa*, Les Mysterieux, perished that night. The Luciferi, who manage the Chambre Noir, will believe the Salamander also died. As you can see, he is very much alive and has promised to help me.' He turned to face the Salamander more squarely. 'We have reached an agreement, haven't we?'

Salamander, his thin face wreathed in a smile, nodded and whispered his agreement.

'You really have little choice, have you? I mean,' Thibault laughed, 'how can you return to France as the only survivor from that total disaster on the Thames. Oh no, Salamander, you are now mine. You will lodge comfortably, deep in my household, where Evangelios will look after you. So,' Thibault flicked his fingers, 'you may go now. Tomorrow we work.' The Salamander left and Thibault turned back to Athelstan. 'You have other questions?'

'No, Master Thibault, just an observation. You couldn't afford for any of Les Mysterieux to survive, could you? You could have taken prisoners, roped them together and led them in triumph through London to the Tower. You could then arraign them before the judges of King's Bench or the justiciars of Oyer et Terminer, or indeed any other court. You could be full of outrage at what they had perpetrated but, there again, your enemies in the Commons or elsewhere would start asking questions. Making allegations, and of course mocking you.'

'Mocking me?'

'Yes, Master Thibault mocking you. Here is the Master of Secrets recruiting French spies, albeit disguised, for the King of England's Secret Chancery.'

Thibault stared down at the table top. When he looked up his eyes were like black marbles. He glanced down again, and when he lifted his head the usual soft smile had returned.

'Continue, Brother Athelstan.'

The friar glanced across at Cranston. He had discussed this with the coroner before they left for Westminster. Athelstan was determined to show Thibault that other people could not be as easily duped as he thought.

'A great danger, Master Thibault. It would not have taken long for the likes of Dimanche, or indeed anyone else, to parade what they knew before the court and, of course, this would spread like fire across the city.'

'And what will you do with this?'

'Oh, Master Thibault, nothing. I fully believe in the old axiom, "let sleeping dogs lie". But I also recall another axiom, given in a lecture by an old Franciscan theologian. He was talking about the problem of evil. He claimed that God keeps wicked men close to his right hand to use for his own inestimable purposes.'

'In which case, Brother Athelstan, I must sit very, very close.'

'Oh, Master Thibault, you surely do.'

AUTHOR'S NOTE

Murder Most Treasonable is a work of historical fiction rather than historical fact. Nevertheless, I have incorporated many strands of English medieval history. For example, the teaching of John Wycliffe and the challenges posed by the Lollards. The Secret Chancery did exist, and was one of the many great offices of state based at Westminster, though sometimes it could also follow the King when he progressed through his realm. Of course, as with any office of state which deals in secret matters, it is hard to trace or delineate exactly what happened. Nevertheless, the Secret Chancery, together with the Office of the Privy Seal, were involved in important matters of state secrecy. Sometimes these can be traced. One of the best examples is the destruction of Edmund Earl of Kent in 1329, and the fall of Queen Isabella and her paramour Roger Mortimer in 1330. The young Edward III, alarmed by the destruction of his uncle Edmund, wished to break free from the influence of his mother and her paramour Mortimer. To achieve this, Edward needed the support of the wily Pope John XXII. The Pope, however, needed to know when he received a letter from the English King: was it really from Edward, or something dictated in his name by his mother and her lover? Edward sent a special envoy to Avignon to explain to the Pope that any letter which began with the words '*Pater Sancte*' – 'Beloved Father', came from him; anything else was the work of Mortimer. The Memorandum of Montreuil is of course fictitious, but it does reflect the bounding ambition of John of Gaunt. Gaunt remained faithful to his death, but Richard II was later deposed and probably murdered on the direct order of Henry of Lancaster, Gaunt's eldest son, who usurped the Crown. The Relics of Lucca were a wonder of the age, and I have incorporated only part of the real story. In the end, I hope my novel has transported you back to those hurling days during the 1380s when England was swept by the strong winds of change, be it in Church or State.